REEL OF FORTUNE

JANA DELEON

Copyright © 2018 by Jana DeLeon

All rights reserved.

No part of this book may be reproduced in any form or by any electronic or mechanical means, including information storage and retrieval systems, without written permission from the author, except for the use of brief quotations in a book review.

Design and derivative illustration by Janet Holmes using images from Shutterstock.

❀ Created with Vellum

CHAPTER ONE

I PARKED my Jeep in front of the General Store and prepared to go inside. It was a Thursday and midafternoon, so the store shouldn't be busy. The locals would be in the next day, stocking up for the weekend after work, but it would be mostly quiet until they started piling in. I'd planned my return to Sinful, and specifically my visit with Walter, that way on purpose. I stepped out of the Jeep and looked at it with a smile. Soon, it would officially be mine, as I was acquiring it along with the house.

In the weeks since the Ahmad takedown, so much had happened. First, I'd headed back to DC to wrap things up. I could have waited a week or two but the more I thought about it, the more it felt like something hanging over my head. So I decided the sooner I dealt with it the better and hopped a plane two days after the takedown and headed to my former home. The CIA paperwork didn't take long to handle, except for the human resources stuff, which seemed to be an extensive waste of time. But with the legal climate being what it was, it didn't surprise me.

I had a nice dinner with Harrison and finally met Cassidy,

his girlfriend, who was absolutely nothing like the model-looking airheads he'd usually gone with. And I could tell immediately that this one was going to take. Cassidy was a pediatrician who was as pretty as she was smart and had a relaxed way about her that made me feel comfortable from the get-go. It was clear that Harrison was over the moon about her and she appeared just as infatuated with him. I could see why he'd decided to quit the agency and couldn't have been happier for the both of them. He was considering several different job options, mostly involving the private security line of work—it was DC, after all—but wasn't rushing into anything.

The real Sandy-Sue had returned from her European vacation, and I'd finally met the woman I'd been portraying over lunch with Director Morrow. To say we were nothing alike and I'd pretty much gotten everything about her wrong was an understatement. Sandy-Sue was 100 percent USDA-certified girl and she loved every second of it. She was also one of those eternally perky women who smiled and greeted everyone she came in contact with. By the time we'd gotten from the foyer of the restaurant to the table, I was already exhausted. I could tell Morrow was amused.

But while the lunch was tiring, it was also productive. Sandy-Sue was more than happy to sell all of Marge's property to me for what Director Morrow and a Realtor called "a fair price." The estate attorney was drawing up the docs and my bank was on standby to wire money when everything was in writing and ready to sign. The entire thing was expected to wrap up sometime early next week.

I'd packed the stuff I wanted to ship to Sinful, which had taken all of two hours since I wasn't bringing most of it with me. Marge's house was already stocked with dishes and linens and all those other household-type things that I wasn't picky about, so I saw no reason to pay to ship a bunch more of the same stuff to Louisiana. Besides, Marge's stuff was nicer than mine. I shoved most of it into boxes and hauled it all down to a local charity, then boxed up some books and my clothes and shoes and carted it down to UPS. The CIA had agreed to fly my weapons in on the next military transport it had landing in NOLA.

Then in a temporary fit of insanity, I actually went to the hairstylist who'd put in my extensions and had them redone. I swear, I'd originally thought I'd just have them removed and see what was what, but when I looked at a photo of myself with two-and-a-half-inch hair, I didn't recognize that person anymore. And I liked looking in the mirror and seeing a glimpse of my mother. I figured it might take a while to grow it out so in the meantime, I was going to stick to fake. I had a small stroke over the cost—the CIA had paid for the first round—but I couldn't argue with the results.

The stylist assured me that in six to nine months or so, I'd have enough length to probably suit me, but I'd need the extensions redone several times before then. When I'd first come to Sinful, Ida Belle and Gertie had taken me to a stylist in New Orleans named Genesis, who'd fixed a torn extension, so I figured I had that part covered until nature fixed my previous hairstyle choice.

With the entire first twenty-eight years of my life wrapped up in five boxes on a truck to Sinful, I caught a flight back to Louisiana and had arrived home just an hour before. I'd given Ida Belle, Gertie, and Carter a call to let them know I was back—mostly because I knew they'd all been worried that I might change my mind—then I'd arranged to see them all later. But right now, I had business to attend to. Mainly the business of fessing up to the people who mattered a lot to me. People I'd lied to about who I was from the very beginning.

I was starting with Walter.

In a way, Walter was the cop-out route to confessing my true identity, because he already knew I wasn't Sandy-Sue and had probably guessed I was associated with law enforcement or the federal government in some capacity. He'd been clear when he'd told me he knew I wasn't Sandy-Sue that he didn't want any details, his assumption being we were both better off the fewer people who knew the truth. Along with Ida Belle and Gertie, Walter had been one of the people who'd had my back from the beginning and had shown a genuine interest in me. I just hoped his opinion didn't change when he found out what exactly my previous employment had entailed.

The store was empty except for Walter, who occupied his usual stool behind the counter in the back. The bells above the door jangled when I entered, and he looked up and smiled.

"I thought you were out of town," he said.

"Just got back a while ago," I said.

He put down his paper and raised an eyebrow. "So, I take it your situation has changed?"

"Why do you say that?"

"Well, you, Ida Belle, Gertie, and Carter disappear for a day, then come back, and you disappear for weeks. Despite the fact that you're gone, the other three are walking around smiling like they just won the lottery. And in a complete change of direction, the troublesome twosome are oddly quiet about everything. Let's just say I noticed a shift in the Force."

I laughed. "*Star Wars?*"

He nodded. "I see Gertie's got you watching more movies. So? Are you here to reveal your true identity? Or are you going to keep an old man waiting?"

"You've been waiting long enough. I really do go by Fortune, but the last name's Redding. Former CIA agent, Fortune Redding."

"Former? Hmmm. And the reason you were hiding out in Sinful? Is that handled?"

"A done deal."

His shoulders relaxed, and I could tell he was relieved. "I was really hoping that was what all the smiling was about. I won't ask for details, as I know you probably can't give them anyway. I'll just say I'm glad that you're safe, and that whoever was targeting you is no longer a threat."

"You and me both."

"So what are your plans now? Or have you had a chance to think that far?"

"I've thought about nothing else for weeks, and I have some of it figured out. I'm staying in Sinful, for one, and buying Marge's house. But I'd appreciate it if you keep that under wraps until the deal is finalized and money's exchanged hands. Should be all done next week."

He grinned. "I'll keep it quiet, but oh, I wish I could be a fly on the wall when Celia finds out you're staying. She's going to have a stroke."

"We should be so lucky. I'm hoping when rumor of my former employment makes the rounds, she'll be suitably impressed or scared stiff and back off. Mind you, I'm not counting on it though."

"Yeah, I wouldn't either. That one isn't right in the head, and she's fixated on you, Gertie, and Ida Belle. She'll keep making trouble as long as she's able, but I have no doubt you girls can handle it. So should we work on a regular weekly food and beverage order for you? That way you won't keep running out."

I tilted my head to the side. "You're really not going to ask me about the nature of my position with the agency?" Most people wanted to know everything, or at least, thought they did.

"I've overheard enough from the three of you and picked up on some of Carter's grumbling," he said. "And there's a couple situations this summer where the narrative didn't quite fit the outcome. When you put it all together, it adds up. Let's just say I wouldn't have a shooting match with you for money."

I smiled, relieved. I hadn't figured Walter would be awful to tell, but this had gone even easier than I'd imagined. Now I just had to hope that Ally wasn't completely pissed when I leveled with her. It was bad enough to find out the person you trusted wasn't even who they said they were. It added a whole different layer of shock value when you threw in CIA agent. And even though I wasn't passing out my résumé, I figured other people might put things together as Walter had. At least enough so that they decided to give me a wide berth.

"You're awesome, Walter. And I want to say thank you for supporting me from the moment I arrived. You've been a good friend, and I'm really glad we're going to stay that way. I'm lucky to have you."

Walter blushed at my compliment, and I could tell he was touched and pleased. "You've been quite a treat for an old man. This place needed a little shaking up and Lord knows you brought that in spades. And Carter needed someone who didn't bend over backward to kiss his butt. You're exactly the woman who fits with him, even though he didn't think so for a bit."

Now I blushed. "I think that goes both ways. I'm just glad he worked it out. We worked it out. Well, we're working on working it out."

Walter laughed. "You'll be fine. I don't think I've ever met two people more suited for each other and less suited for anyone else."

"I hope you're right." I looked down at the counter. "It's scary, you know?"

"Why?"

I looked back up at him and remembered that Walter didn't know anything about the real me. Nothing about my disinterested overachieving father, or my mother who died way too young. Nothing about my constant quest at the CIA to prove something to a dead man.

"You know," I said, "that's a long story. Basically, it's the story of my life. And I definitely want to share it with you, but I'd rather do it over burgers and beer and a batch of Ally's cookies, sitting in my backyard and looking out at the bayou."

Walter reached over and squeezed my hand. "That sounds perfect. Welcome home, Fortune Redding."

———

SINCE I WAS TEARING UP, I had to dash from the General Store before I made a public spectacle of myself. People were starting to mill around downtown, and it was hard to intimidate people if they'd seen you crying. And while I was looking forward to being an official member of the Sinful community, I preferred being one who was respected and somewhat feared. For some people, maybe a little more than somewhat.

I hopped in my Jeep and made the drive to Ally's house. I'd checked with the café and knew she worked the morning and lunch shift and should be home by now. That meant she'd either be on her back porch working on her recipe list or in the kitchen cooking up something incredible. Either way, she'd had plenty of time to shower, change, and de-stress from her shift at the café, so it was as good a time as any to come clean.

When she opened the front door and saw me standing there, she smiled as though she hadn't seen me in years. She launched forward and hugged me, then tugged me into her house, already laughing as I followed her to the kitchen.

"I'm so glad to see you!" she said. "Ida Belle and Gertie assured me you would be, but I could tell even they were afraid that maybe you weren't coming back. I mean, you've got a whole career and life up north and this was just a summer gig. I didn't figure you'd leave completely without saying goodbye, though. So what happened? Has your job not started yet?"

She tried to ask the question casually, but I could hear the strain in her voice and it made my heart clench. I'd never had people around me who cared like this. Who actually felt their lives would be lessened if I weren't around. It was a little overwhelming but also incredible, and I marveled again at just how lucky I was to have come to Sinful and had this life-changing experience.

So it was time to let the cat out of the bag and hope I didn't ruin things with one of the people who mattered most.

"Actually," I said, "I wanted to talk to you about some things. Serious things. Can we sit?"

"Of course. Do you want something to drink?"

I held up my bottled water. I'd bought one at the store before I left, figuring my mouth and throat would go dry as soon as I decided to start confessing. We took a seat at Ally's breakfast table, and I could tell she was nervous about what I might say. I'd rolled the scenario around my mind a million times, trying to figure out the best way to tell her about the real me, but I'd never hit on the one way I thought was perfect. Finally, I'd just given up trying to plan and figured I'd know what to say when I was there in front of her.

I was wrong.

"Fortune?" Ally asked. "Are you all right? You're not ill, are you?"

"No. Nothing like that. It's just that I have something to tell you that you might not like. I'm worried that once you hear it, you'll feel differently about me."

"I don't think that's possible. I mean, unless you're a serial killer or something."

It was dangerously close to the truth. Of course, my hits were government-sanctioned, but sometimes the average citizen didn't see it that way.

Seeing no better way than the blunt truth, I said, "I'm not Sandy-Sue Morrow."

I have no idea what Ally had been imagining I might say, but based on her shocked expression, I was certain that wasn't on her list.

"You're not... Then who are you?"

"I *do* go by Fortune, but my last name is Redding and until a couple days ago, I was a CIA agent."

Ally's eyes widened and her jaw dropped. She stared at me, as if waiting for the "just joking" claim, but when nothing was forthcoming, she took a drink of her soda and a deep breath.

"So why are you here?" she asked. "Why were you claiming to be Sandy-Sue? Did something happen to her? Is she in trouble?"

"Not at all. Sandy-Sue is the niece of my boss at the CIA. I was on a mission that went wrong, and a very dangerous man was looking for me. My boss sent me to Sinful posing as his niece to hide. The real Sandy-Sue is safe and sound and spent the summer on a European vacation."

"Oh my God! Are you still in danger?"

"No. That situation was handled a couple weeks ago, and I went back to Washington, DC, to wrap things up."

"You quit your job?"

"Yes. The truth is I didn't know what my life could be like until I came to Sinful. My parents are both dead. I don't have any other living relatives that I know of, and I never had close friends because given my job, it simply wasn't smart. Coming here was more foreign to me than some of the countries I've done missions in."

"You don't have any family?" Ally's eyes misted. "I'm so sorry. I know firsthand that they can be a blessing and a curse, but I can't imagine not having any."

"You know, what's funny is that I had no idea what I was missing until I came here and met Ida Belle, Gertie, you, Walter, and Carter. It was like I got adopted. I'm so sorry I lied to you. I know it sounds trite to say it was for your own good, but I swear, that's the truth. Well, and mine. But I never wanted to hurt anyone with my lies, and if you don't want to be friends anymore, then I understand completely."

Ally jumped up from her chair and threw her arms around me. "Are you crazy? You couldn't get rid of me if you tried."

I tried to maintain decorum, but it was too overwhelming. The tears that had been lurking during my talk with Walter finally spilled over. When Ally finally turned me loose and sat again, she grabbed napkins from the holder on the table for both of us.

"Lord, look at the two of us," she said. "We're a mess. So does this apology mean you're staying or are you just here to say goodbye?"

"I'm buying Marge's house from Sandy-Sue and staying in Sinful. For better or for worse."

Ally's grin stretched from one side of her face to the other. "I'm so happy for you, Fortune. And for all of us. And don't you ever let me hear you suggest again that we aren't friends. You've been nothing but a great friend to me. You let me live with you when my house caught fire. You protected me from the stalker."

She sucked in a breath. "All that jumping out of a dead sleep with your gun...what exactly did you do for the CIA?"

"I was a field agent. That's really all I can say."

She studied me for a moment. "Have you killed people?"

"Only the bad guys."

"Ha. Here I was worried that I was putting you in danger while I lived with you. Boy, I didn't know the half of it."

"No. But you weren't supposed to."

Her eyes widened. "Does Carter know? Never mind, of course he does. You wouldn't tell me before you told him. Wait, your breakup? Is that when you told him?"

"Sort of. Let's just say I did something that tipped him off to the fact that I wasn't really a librarian. It was a reflex and it gave me away. As you saw, he was a bit angrier than you are."

"Well, he's a man, and even though I like you a lot, our relationship isn't exactly the same. Ida Belle and Gertie?"

"They've known for a while. They both have military experience. The same thing happened with them that did with Carter. I stopped off and told Walter before I came here. That's my whole inner circle."

"So are you keeping it secret?"

"Not really. I can give my former job title, just not details about my work. That's all classified. And I have no problem with people knowing. In fact, I'm looking forward to that news making the rounds to a couple people. But I'm not going to advertise it in the church bulletin or anything."

Ally grinned. "Aunt Celia is going to have a cow."

"I really hope so. She deserves to have it come right back on her. Calling me a floozy at every opportunity. Not that I figure it will shut her up for long. She's too much of a nutbag for that to happen."

"Isn't that the truth? I mean, she's always been a handful, but I swear the older she gets the further away from normal she moves. So what are you doing now? Did you ship your stuff from DC? Do you need help unpacking? Redecorating?"

"I have a few boxes coming from my old place but honestly,

I like Marge's taste. It's solid, tasteful stuff and not frilly at all, so I doubt I'll change much."

Ally nodded. "Her place always fit you, right from the start. It's one of the things that surprised me because I was expecting a girlie-girl who would want to put a bunch of doilies everywhere."

"The real Sandy-Sue would. Trust me. She's nice enough, but it was all I could do to get through one meal with her."

"I can imagine. Well, then what do you need to help with? I feel like I need to be doing something."

"Do you have any cookies?"

"Unless I'm dead, I'll have cookies."

"What about champagne?"

"I always keep a bottle, just in case of an emergency celebration." She jumped up from the table. "And this is definitely cause for an emergency celebration. Oh, Fortune. This is going to be great. Just great."

I smiled. My life couldn't have done more of a 180 if I'd tried. But somehow, I knew she was right.

CHAPTER TWO

THE FOGHORN BLASTING through my house sent me launching straight out of bed, clutching my pistol. I looked across the bed and saw Carter standing on the other side, matching my stance.

"Rise and shine!" Gertie yelled from downstairs.

We lowered our arms and Carter shook his head. "One day, we're going to shoot each other."

"Well, not today, which means I have plenty of rounds for that foghorn."

He grinned. "You know, this is the first time in my life I can say that I don't mind having a gun pulled on me. You realize if we can't make this work, we're both going to die alone and clutching a nine-millimeter."

I laughed. He definitely had a point. It took a certain type of personality to handle the way we reacted to certain things. And that reaction time might slow as we aged, but I doubted it was ever going away. Unless we went deaf. Then maybe.

"I guess this is what I get for not going to see them last night," I said. "I better get down there before they come up here."

I'd intended to pay Ida Belle and Gertie a visit after talking to Ally, but once Ally broke out the champagne, she started asking questions about the real me and we talked for hours. I'd given them a call on the way to my house, letting them know that I'd broken the news to Walter and Ally and everyone was cool. Then I'd begged off from the promised visit because Carter was off work and on his way to my house when I called. They assured me that we'd have plenty of time later on. I suppose 7:00 a.m. the next morning fell into the "later on" category.

Carter glanced at his watch. "I need to head out myself. I've got two burglary cases to handle."

"Here in Sinful?"

He pulled his shirt over his head and gave me the don't-even-ask look. I put my hands in the air.

"I'm not trying to get in police business. Just wondered if we needed to be more careful about locking doors and such. Gertie is horribly lazy about it."

"Honestly, I think it's the same person—a teenager—and he's known to the victims. I think it falls under personal as well as covetous, so you're probably in the clear."

"Good. I am really hoping I can take some time off from the crazy."

He raised an eyebrow. "You want time off from crazy and you moved here?"

"Okay. I'd like time off from killing people. Is that better?"

"I'm seriously hoping you're retired completely from killing people. I've manufactured more bogus paperwork since I met you than I did in high school."

"Well, at least you don't have to do that anymore. If I kill someone now, you can put my real name on the record."

He gave me a slightly pained look. "How about we just avoid your name on police paperwork altogether?"

"I'll do my best."

He didn't look convinced. "So, what are your plans for the day?"

"Five minutes ago, I would have told you I didn't have any. But I guess I'll know once I get downstairs."

"Probably better if I don't know." He gave me a quick kiss. "I'll call you later."

He headed downstairs and I could hear Gertie catcalling.

"Hurry up, you floozy!" Ida Belle yelled. "We don't have all day."

I threw on yoga pants and a tank, shoved my pistol into my waistband, grabbed my tennis shoes, and headed downstairs. I had no idea what Ida Belle and Gertie had in mind for today, but no matter what, their plans usually required running shoes and a gun.

They were both standing at the bottom of the stairs, grinning like they'd won the lottery. I felt a rush of warmth pass through me when I realized that *I* was the lottery, at least as far as they were concerned. It was so totally cool but still somewhat foreign to me. I kept having to remind myself that this was real. That for the first time in my life, I was going to be a normal person with friends and a boyfriend.

Gertie tackled me as soon as I got to the bottom of the steps and squeezed me so tightly my ribs hurt. Ida Belle didn't show as much enthusiasm as Gertie, but I saw that her eyes were a little misty before she reached in for her hug.

"We would have come up with the horn," Gertie said, "but Ida Belle said you might not be decent. I told her that was the whole point, especially as Carter's truck was out front."

Ida Belle shook her head. "If you saw Carter in his skivvies, you'd probably turn into a pillar of salt."

Gertie sighed. "Boy, what a way to go, though."

"Anyway," Ida Belle said, "we're glad you're back."

"We worried the whole time you were gone that you'd change your mind," Gertie said. "That the CIA would tempt you with something so interesting you wouldn't be able to tell them no."

"You know, they didn't even try," I said. "I would like to say I'm disappointed, but Director Morrow was so surprised by my change in direction that he decided it must be true. My imagination simply isn't that good."

"I suppose it was a bit of a stretch from your previous life," Gertie said.

"Only because he has no idea what goes on down here," Ida Belle said.

"Isn't that the truth?" I said. "So I'm almost afraid to ask, but what's with the early-morning wake-up call?"

"Today is the fishing rodeo," Gertie said. "And you have to come with us."

I stared. I'd been an official resident for less than a day and I was already confused. "Does one ride the fish or is this a roping sort of thing?"

They both laughed.

"A fishing rodeo is a fishing tournament," Ida Belle said.

"Then why is it called a rodeo?" I asked.

They both shrugged.

"Come on," I said. "You mean there's no cool story like there was this one guy that was so drunk he thought he was riding a horse, but he jumped on a bull shark instead?"

"Junior Petrie did that last year," Gertie said, "but we were already calling it the fishing rodeo."

I grinned. That was one of the things I loved most about Sinful. When most people would be yelling "just joking" after a statement like that, I knew it was the God's honest truth.

"So no riding or roping fish," I said. "Then what's involved?"

"Basically," Ida Belle said, "you pay an entry fee, fish all day, and the person who catches the biggest fish—or has the best method of cheating—wins."

"Wins what, exactly?" I'd been in Sinful long enough to know some things you didn't leave open-ended.

"First prize is an offshore fishing trip," Ida Belle said. "Second prize is a new rod and reel. Third prize is a case of beer."

"We're gunning for third place," Gertie said.

"I approve of this plan," I said. "What do I need to bring?"

I wasn't much of a fisherman but worst case, I could work on my tan and finish up the Tom Clancy book I'd started in DC.

"You don't need to bring anything," Gertie said. "Ida Belle and I already stopped to pay the entry fees, and Francine's Café furnishes lunches. We've got three bags of yummy goodness that Ally put together. I've got a cooler of drinks in Ida Belle's SUV and my tackle. But we were sort of hoping we could use your boat."

I wrinkled my nose. "You want to use our aquatic getaway vehicle for stinky fish?"

"I promise I'll scrub every inch of it," Gertie said. "You'll never know there was a fish in it when I'm done."

It really was the best option. Gertie managed to keep both her and Ida Belle's boats broken, usually by a spectacular accident that I always wished I'd captured on film. On the other hand, since we were taking my boat this time, maybe I should be careful what I wished for.

"Okay, but I'm holding you to the cleaning thing," I said. "What do I wear?"

"What you have on is fine," Ida Belle said. "You'll want to grab a hat and some sunglasses, though. It's pretty hot."

"Okay, but we have to eat breakfast first," I said. "I'll starve to death before lunch."

Gertie pointed to a box on my coffee table. "Raspberry Danish. I figured those and some protein shakes would cover all the essentials."

"And coffee," Ida Belle said. "I put coffee on when we got here."

"Then why are we standing in my living room?" I asked.

I grabbed the box of heavenly sugar and headed for the kitchen. I snagged protein shakes out of the fridge, Ida Belle poured coffee, and Gertie pulled out paper plates and served up the Danish. When I sat down at the table with the two of them, I couldn't help smiling. This was it. This was my life. Today, tomorrow, the next day.

"You look like the cat who swallowed the canary," Ida Belle said.

"I was just thinking how cool it is that today, I'm sitting here as me. The real me. And I don't ever have to leave."

Gertie shook her head. "You have to leave in about a half hour if you're going with us. But I get what you're saying." She grinned at me.

"I think it's still all sinking in," I said.

Ida Belle nodded. "I imagine it's going to take a while before this seems normal. You were in hiding for several months and it was never a permanent thing. When Gertie and I came back from Vietnam, it was a culture shock, and this was our hometown. But the lives we'd been living in the service were so vastly different. I can't imagine what your mind is trying to assimilate."

"It's definitely a big leap," I said. "But a good one. I think I'm going to be happy here."

Gertie winked at me. "Looked like Carter is going to be happy here as well."

"Carter was already happy here," I said.

"He thought he was," Gertie said. "But then he met you and realized everything he'd been missing."

"Oh, he's been missing things all right," Ida Belle told her. "Murder, explosions, arms dealers, lying on official paperwork...he's really been living the good life this summer. And I haven't even gotten into the list of trouble you've caused."

"If you started on Celia, you'd be here for all of eternity," Gertie said. "I'm just saying I don't think Carter knew that his life was lacking until he met Fortune."

Ida Belle smiled. "I don't think any of us knew that. Now let's get the boat loaded and win us some beer!"

I grabbed sunglasses and a ball cap and fetched the cooler of drinks from Ida Belle's SUV. Ida Belle hauled the cooler for fish and Gertie carried the fishing tackle—one small box and rod for Ida Belle and a suspiciously large duffel bag and three rods for Gertie—then we tossed in the sack lunches and we were ready to roll. As usual, Ida Belle was piloting the boat. I'd taken some flak about never driving my own boat from Walter, but when I pointed out that Ida Belle knew the bayous like her own backyard and sometimes there was gunfire exchange and I was the best call on that one, he'd relented. He'd looked slightly frightened, especially when I got to the gunfire exchange part, but he couldn't argue with my logic.

Gertie positioned her specially made cushion in the bottom of the boat in front of the bench, I climbed into the passenger's seat and grabbed the armrests as if my life depended on it—and it might—and we were off.

I figured Ida Belle and Gertie had already discussed the best place to land the big one, so I just concentrated on my death grip and enjoyed the ride. The boat shot up the bayou from behind my house and as soon as we hit the lake, Ida Belle made a hard right turn and set off at breakneck speed close to the bank. I glanced down to see Gertie with her legs braced against the ice chest and both hands clutching the handles I'd installed on the front of the bench. But the memory foam cushion was doing its job. She was still upright and not rolling around the bottom of the boat, cursing at Ida Belle.

When we were halfway down the side of the lake, Ida Belle cut the throttle and it was all I could do to keep from pitching forward onto Gertie. I kept threatening to get a racing harness, and despite the fact that I'd be mocked for all eternity, I was getting more and more serious about it. Being mocked and in one piece was better than being mocked in a hospital bed.

"You're not there yet," Gertie said.

"I know," Ida Belle said. "I figured I better cut the speed and slowly cruise up to the spot we picked."

"You're sneaking up on the fish?" I asked. "Is that a thing?"

"Not so much sneaking as not announcing our presence," Ida Belle said.

"I'm pretty sure that turn you made at the end of the bayou announced our presence all the way to Florida," I said.

Gertie waved a hand in dismissal. "The fish only care about other fish. This place is usually packed with algae that the little fish eat, so the big fish come here for a buffet. The boat engine will only make them leave for a second, then they'll be right back."

"Cool," I said. "Hey, I probably should have asked this before I got in the boat, but do you guys expect me to fish?"

They both laughed and Ida Belle shook her head.

"I only paid the entry fee for you so I could get you a lunch," Ida Belle said.

It was really nice to hang out with practical people. Ida Belle cut the engine entirely and motioned for me to throw out the anchor. I got the boat secured and Gertie and Ida

Belle baited up their lines. Then I dug my book out of my backpack and got back on my perch to read.

"Don't even bother to get into that book," Gertie said, and she cast her line. "At least, not until you've told us how your homecoming is going."

"Agreed," Ida Belle said. "Inquiring minds and all."

"And I meant all of your homecomings—not just Walter and Ally," Gertie said, and winked.

Ida Belle shook her head and sighed. "You need to read a romance novel or something. Stop pestering the woman to tell you all the X-rated parts of her life."

"Why?" Gertie asked. "She hasn't signed an NDA for those, as far as I know. Not like her CIA work."

"Maybe you and Carter should draw one up," Ida Belle said. "Might get her to pipe down."

I grinned. "Carter and I are good. That's all I'm saying, and you are welcome to invent whatever your heart desires. We haven't had any big discussions since the takedown, and I don't anticipate any soon. We're just trying to feel our way around regular living without all the secrets hanging over our heads."

"Not to mention the terrorist hell-bent on killing you," Gertie said.

"Yes," I agreed. "That was a bit of a buzzkill. Anyway, I saw Walter yesterday afternoon at the store. I figured I'd start with him since he already knew I wasn't Sandy-Sue and had probably already formed a good opinion of what I really did, so I took the easy way out for my first confession."

"And I assume he took it in stride," Gertie said, "because it's not like he hasn't had a lifetime of dealing with Ida Belle as experience."

"I'm sure that didn't hurt my case," I said, "but yes, he was all calm about it, and really happy that I'm going to be staying." I smiled. "I really like Walter. I mean really, really like him."

Gertie nodded. "He's a good man. Ida Belle is a fool. But that discussion hasn't gone anywhere the last fifty years and isn't going anywhere today."

"I never said he wasn't a good man," Ida Belle objected. "Walter is one of the best ever made, which is exactly why I'm not burdening him with my nonsense."

"That's probably the one thing you've said about him that makes sense," Gertie said.

"I decided I preferred burdening you," Ida Belle said to Gertie.

Gertie shrugged. "That's a two-way street."

"Some days it sure doesn't feel like it," Ida Belle grumbled. "Feels more like I'm standing in a one-way trucking lane and the convoy is bearing down on me."

The description was so accurate, I had to laugh. Gertie was an awesome woman and a great friend, but she should come with safety warnings. And her purse should be banned from the planet.

"So what about Ally?" Gertie asked. "You were over there a long time. We couldn't decide if that was good or bad. Since we never heard sirens, we were leaning toward good."

"It went well," I said. "She was surprised, of course. Of all the people I'd gotten close to, she was the only one who had no idea at all. But she took it all well and didn't even bat an eyelash at all my lies. She was more worried about my safety."

"Ally is a class act," Ida Belle said.

Gertie nodded. "And one of the nicest people I've ever known."

"Definitely," I agreed. "I'm lucky to have her as a friend, and I'm really glad she doesn't hold grudges. It was kinda interesting watching things click with her after I told her the truth."

"What things?" Ida Belle asked.

"Jumping out of a dead sleep with my pistol at ready," I said. "Insisting she stay with me when she had a stalker. We spent the whole evening going over the events of the past two months, with her speculating what we were really up to and my role in it, and with me neither confirming nor denying. She has a good imagination. She made us all sound like superheroes."

"Hell, we are superheroes," Gertie said.

"Do *not* give her a good reason to buy us capes," Ida Belle said. "She's been harping on it the entire time you were gone."

"You wear capes with tights," I said. "I'm totally out of that one."

"So is Gertie," Ida Belle said. "For *all* our sakes."

"I'm totally going as Wonder Woman for Halloween," Gertie said.

"Really? Guess Fortune and I will be 'going' as vacationers then," Ida Belle said. "Complete with remote location."

"You're going *where* as Wonder Woman?" I asked. I had picked up on a lot of oddities attributed solely to Sinful during my summer stay, but I had a feeling that was only the tip of the iceberg.

"There's a huge costume party in the park, complete with a terror-filled maze made of hay bales," Gertie said. "The streets surrounding the park are completely closed off. There's food trucks and a band and a costume contest. It's a wild party."

"How wild can it be in a town that's dry?" I asked.

"The Sinful Ladies have a cough syrup booth," Ida Belle said. "And pretty much everyone brings their own flask."

I had a feeling that most of the residents had a flask on them every day, not just Halloween. I was positive they were all armed. It didn't sound like the safest event I'd ever attended, but the "wild" part was probably accurate.

"Look," Gertie said, pointing to a boat anchoring about fifty yards away.

I looked over to see a stout woman with a braid of black hair hanging halfway down her back. She hefted the anchor like she was throwing a Kleenex, then proceeded to pull out five rods and position them in holders all over the boat.

Midforties. Five foot ten. Two hundred forty pounds and a lot of it muscle. Probably hell in a close-quarters fight. Outside, I'd outrun her.

"Uh-oh." Gertie pointed to a boat approaching the woman. "That's Hooch."

I looked over.

Fifties. Five foot eleven. Two hundred fifty pounds. Mostly flab. No danger at all to the woman he was approaching.

"What's a Hooch?" I asked.

"Second place," Ida Belle said.

"Who's the woman?" I asked.

"First place," Gertie said.

I clapped my hands. "Ooooooh, fish fight!"

"My money's on Dixie," Ida Belle said.

Before I could even get out a question about the Southern naming convention, Gertie jumped up and shoved her binoculars at me as Hooch pulled up alongside Dixie's boat. "You can read lips. Tell us what they're saying."

"They're angled from us," I said, "but I'll give it a whirl."

"Fill in anything you miss," Gertie said. "Trust me, this is not going to be an advanced conversation."

"Okay, here we go," I said. "Starting with Dixie."

"Go away. This is my spot."

"You know damned good and well I always fish here."

"Not today. Today it's mine."

"I don't see your name on it."

"*Wouldn't matter if it was since you can't read.*"

"*You uppity cow. Why don't you get out of that boat and bake a cake or something? You and that gun-toting old crow are ruining everything in this town.*"

I glanced over at Ida Belle, who raised her hand. I kinda figured.

"Dixie again," I said.

"*It's not our problem you can't win a contest.*"

"*If this town was run right, you wouldn't even be allowed to enter.*"

"*You checked a calendar lately? Women had rights before you were born.*"

"*Not in Sinful they didn't.*"

"*Well they do now. Adapt or move. You can start with your boat.*"

"*You gonna make me?*"

Dixie reached into her jeans and pulled out a .44 Magnum. Holy crap!

CHAPTER THREE

I COULDN'T MAKE out anything after that. Hooch turned fifty shades of red, then threw his hands in the air and shook his fist at Dixie. A couple seconds later, he started his boat and drove away, giving her the finger as he went. I could see plastic wrappers flying out of the back of his boat.

"He's totally littering," I said.

"He doesn't care much about the environment," Ida Belle said. "Hooch doesn't care about much of anything except his next drink."

"And beating you and Dixie?" Gertie said.

I looked down at Gertie. "Is Dixie related to you?"

"Not that I'm aware of," Gertie said. "Why?"

"You have similar taste in weapons," I said.

"You mean gross overcompensation?" Ida Belle asked.

"I am not overcompensating for anything," Gertie said. "I merely like large, long things that pack a punch." She started giggling hysterically.

Ida Belle rolled her eyes. "Well, I guess the show is over. Looks like Dixie is moving as well."

Gertie frowned. "You think she decided the fish aren't biting here?"

"Maybe. Or maybe she noticed us and wants more privacy."

"Privacy for what?" I asked, wondering if Dixie had some trade secret on how to attract the winning fish. If so, I hoped it didn't involve nudity. The last thing we needed was Gertie getting ideas. None of us needed a free case of beer that badly.

"So she can cheat," Ida Belle said.

"She cheats?" I asked.

"There are only two types of fishermen," Gertie said. "Dead and cheaters."

Since Gertie was always fishing, I was intrigued. "Exactly how does one cheat—bring a fish from a market?"

"Not anymore," Gertie said. "They check the temperature. Even if you thaw it out, it's easy to tell that it was frozen and has been dead a while. But there's all sorts of other ways. Like putting lead in the fish so that it weighs in heavier. Or buying from a fish farm and keeping them in a live trap until the day of the tournament."

"Seriously?" I asked. "For a trophy and a rod and reel?"

"For a trophy *and* bragging rights," Ida Belle said. "Granted, the big tournaments pay out big cash—some of them tens of thousands and more—but fishermen would cheat simply for the right to say they won."

"Last big tournament, Hooch got caught trimming the tail on a fish," Gertie said. "He got tossed out and Dixie won."

"Why on earth would you trim the tail?"

"If there's lots of categories, it puts the fish in a different slot," Ida Belle said. "The fish appears to be in a smaller length category but weighs more than other fish that are really that length. This is a small tournament so the type of fish is limited and the biggest one wins."

I shook my head. "All of this for a trophy and bragging rights? I've seen less dedication on CIA missions."

"Fishing is serious business in southern Louisiana," Gertie said.

"I'm not required to do it, right?" I asked. "I mean, there's not some law that says once I own property here, I have to become a fishing cowboy or I'll do jail time."

"That hasn't been a law like that since Brody Hawkins," Gertie said.

"I'm almost afraid to ask. Who is Brody Hawkins and why were the laws changed because of him?"

"Brody was the best cheater in Sinful," Ida Belle said. "He moved here from Florida where he used to run a fishing charter. He was determined to retire and never look at a fish again. Then he spent a weekend in jail for not fishing in the tournament, so he decided to put it back on the town."

Gertie nodded. "Brody proceeded to enter every fishing tournament within a day's driving distance, and he won them all. I mean, hands down, biggest fish, and not a single person could figure out how he did it. He's been dead for over a decade, and we still don't know. He took that one to the grave."

"Anyway," Ida Belle said, "since Brody was upsetting half the state, they changed the law about fishing so all the other cheaters had a fair chance."

Only in Sinful could that sentence make sense. I was just about to ask how Gertie planned on cheating when a giant boom carried across the lake, making the water vibrate.

I immediately dropped out of my seat and into the bottom of the boat, pulling out my pistol as I went, then popped up to peer over the side, gun perched on the edge of the boat. I looked over at Ida Belle and Gertie, who hadn't moved so much as an inch and were watching me with slightly amused expressions.

"Sorry," I said, and rose back up. "Sometimes I forget I'm not in Iraq. But that was an explosion. Someone's still?" A lot of Sinful locals weren't interested in making a drive to pick up their alcohol, so they resorted to the old-fashioned way of moonshining. Not everyone was competent at it, and explosions were a semi-regular event.

Gertie shook her head. "Fishermen."

"Good God!" I stared at her. "Isn't that taking things too far? I mean, I know people want to win but they're not blowing up the competition to do it, are they?"

"No," Ida Belle said. "They're blowing up the fish. Drop a charge into the water, it kills a bunch of fish, and they float to the top. Then you pick up the big ones that don't have blast damage and it saves you hours of actually fishing."

I narrowed my eyes at Gertie. "You don't have any dynamite in your purse, do you?"

"I always have dynamite in my purse," Gertie said. "But I only brought my duffel today."

I was mollified for a second, then I remembered who I was dealing with. "Do you have dynamite in your duffel?"

Gertie sighed. "Only two sticks."

"So there are only two completely illegal explosives on my boat?" I asked.

"Technically, three," Gertie said. "I have a grenade."

"Hand them over," I said, and stuck out my hand. "You'll have to find another way to cheat. I am not going to jail on my first official full day as a Sinful citizen."

"It's going to happen sooner or later," Gertie said. "You should consider getting it out of the way."

"No," I said. "It's not going to happen sooner or later."

Ida Belle raised an eyebrow. "Because you intend to be a law-abiding citizen?"

"Because I don't intend to get caught."

"That's my girl."

Gertie grumbled but dug the dynamite and grenade out of the duffel and handed them to me. I secured them in the bench storage and locked the padlock that only I knew the code to.

"You think we should move?" Ida Belle asked.

Gertie looked over to where Dixie had been anchored and frowned. "Maybe. If Dixie picked the spot, then it must have something going on. She's only been wrong once—last year—but that was the day she had a heart attack so we all gave her a pass."

"That so nice of you," I said, briefly wondering what had happened to give a woman in her forties a heart attack. Then I remembered it was Sinful and the options were unlimited.

Gertie picked up the binoculars and scanned the lake. "I don't see Dixie anywhere. Let's go ahead and move."

Gertie and Ida Belle reeled in their lines, I pulled up the anchor, and Ida Belle moved us forward until we reached the spot where Dixie had been. I waited for the nod from Gertie, then tossed out the anchor again.

Gertie leaned over the side of the boat and studied the water. "It's clearer here. What's the depth?"

Ida Belle checked the depth finder. "Eight feet."

"I see minnows all over," Gertie said. "I bet she baited the water to bring them in."

Ida Belle nodded. "Hard to find a spot this clear, too. That Dixie sure knows her coastline."

"I'm surprised anyone knows it better than you," I said.

"I know it better for hunting," Ida Belle said. "Fishing is

more Gertie's thing than mine. And it's pretty much what Dixie lives for."

"I guess we all need something to live for," I said. Even if it was smelly fish. "So are you going to cast a line or just gaze into the water?"

"You know," Gertie said. "Given how clear the water is here, I think I might switch things up." She opened up her duffel bag and started digging around. I hoped to God she didn't have any other explosives that I should have confiscated.

It was worse.

She rose up grinning from ear to ear and holding a speargun.

"I've been wanting to test this baby out ever since I bought it on eBay," Gertie said. "These conditions are perfect."

Ida Belle stared at her in dismay. "That does it. I'm taking your computer away."

"You are not going into the water with that thing," I said.

"Why not?" Gertie asked as she put the gun down and reached into her bag of tricks again. "I have a mask and a small tank. The water is hot as heck, so I don't need a wet suit, and I'm wearing my Playboy Bunny bathing suit under my clothes."

"Let me shoot her with that gun and save us all the horror," Ida Belle said. "You know that's where this is going."

"You are not parading around my boat in a Playboy Bunny bathing suit," I said.

"You two are horrible prudes," Gertie said.

"No," Ida Belle said. "We're just looking forward to lunch and don't want anything interfering with our enjoyment of it."

Gertie waved a hand in dismissal. "Whatever. I'll wear a T-shirt over it. Satisfied?"

"I'm not," I said. "I don't care if you're wearing a tuxedo. I still don't think you with a speargun is a good plan."

"Why not?" Gertie asked. "Look how long that thing is. It's not like I can shoot myself with it."

"If there's a way," Ida Belle said, "you'll find it."

"And you can shoot someone else," I said.

"You two will be in the boat," Gertie said. "You're perfectly safe."

I looked over at Ida Belle, who shook her head. We both knew the only way we were assured of safety was if we pulled up anchor and left once she was in the water.

"She's going to do it regardless of our opinion," I said. "Did you bring a medical kit?"

"Always," Ida Belle said. "I've also been taking some EMT courses online."

The fact that her statement not only made sense but actually made me feel better was scary. Especially since I was no longer a CIA agent on a mission. This was a fishing tournament, for goodness' sake. Only Gertie could make it an event requiring emergency medical care.

Gertie pulled off her pants and blouse and sure enough, she had on a black bathing suit with the Playboy Bunny emblem cut out in the middle of the chest. The back came complete with a poufy tail. Ida Belle winced and Gertie gave her the finger before pulling a white T-shirt out of her duffel and pulling it on.

"This is just going to weigh me down, you know," Gertie said.

"If that T-shirt is the difference between you staying afloat and drowning, then we've got way bigger problems," Ida Belle said.

Gertie pulled on the tank and put her mask and regulator in place, testing the airflow. Then she sat on the side of the boat, gave us a thumbs-up, and flipped backward over the side.

She surfaced a couple seconds later and pulled out the regulator.

"I forgot the speargun," she said.

"This is going well," Ida Belle said as I handed her the gun. "You want to take bets on how long before she shoots the boat?"

"Will that thing pierce the hull?" I asked.

"I don't think so, but just in case, we should probably put our cell phones in waterproof cases and haul out some life jackets."

"This day took a sharp turn from my planned Clancy reading."

"Things with Gertie often do."

I heard a thump against the side of the boat and we both peered over but couldn't see anything. A couple seconds later, Gertie surfaced about twenty feet from the boat, clutching a piling that was part of an old pier. She yanked off the regulator and started coughing.

"Are you all right?" I asked.

"I dropped the damn gun," Gertie said. "I had a big one in my sights and then something big bumped into me and I dropped it."

I felt the start of a small panic. Something large enough to make her drop the gun was not a random lake fish. "Get out of there, now," I said.

"I've got to find my gun," Gertie said.

"That gun won't do you any good if a gator eats you," Ida Belle said. "You better hustle that bunny butt into this boat."

Gertie's eyes widened a bit as she finally clued in to our worry, and she put the regulator back in her mouth. As she let go of the piling, I heard a faint whistling sound coming from the water. Gertie put her arm out for the first stroke and then appeared to flop backward, disappearing under the water.

"What the hell?" Ida Belle leaped off her seat and leaned over the side of the boat next to me.

I was just about to jump in when Gertie surfaced next to the piling again.

"What are you doing?" Ida Belle asked. "Get out of there."

"I can't," Gertie said. "The gun went off and shot a spear through my T-shirt. I'm pinned to the piling."

"Unbelievable," I said. "She managed to shoot herself."

"If you two hadn't made me wear a T-shirt, this wouldn't have happened," Gertie said.

"Well, tear it," Ida Belle said. "Just get moving."

The water near the boat rippled and I peered into it. "Holy crap! Move now! There's something huge down there and it's coming straight toward you."

I pulled out my pistol and fired into the water where I'd seen the shadow. Nothing happened so I fired again, but I couldn't see any movement anymore. In the meantime, Gertie was yanking on the shirt, trying to tear it away from the piling. Ida Belle had thrown the anchor in the boat and was climbing back into the driver's seat to move us closer.

"Did you hit something?" Ida Belle asked as she started the boat.

"I don't think so," I said. "I don't see it anymore."

Ida Belle scanned the water, then pointed to a place just past the piling. "There! Bubbles! Something's surfacing. It's an alligator! Get out of that shirt! Just take it off."

CHAPTER FOUR

WE REACHED Gertie and I leaned over and grabbed her shirt, trying to pull it off the spear, but it was wedged tight. I popped the release on her air tank and snagged the strap. "Go under and duck out of that shirt."

Gertie threw her arms in the air and went under, wriggling out of the shirt. I seized the tank when her arms were clear of the harness and threw it in the bottom of the boat. The alligator went under and I fired off another two rounds at the ripples. Gertie sprang up and clutched the side of the boat, and I dropped my gun and pulled her over the edge, depositing her in a lump in the bottom.

The alligator surfaced in the spot where Gertie had just been, and she peered over the side.

"It's Godzilla!" she said. "I hope you didn't hit him."

"I ought to shoot him right now," I said. "I know you think you have some sort of connection with that animal but you're wrong. He's not a house cat. He's a killing and eating machine."

"He just recognized me and wanted food," Gertie said.

"Maybe you should just shoot her and fix it all right now," Ida Belle said.

Gertie gave her a dirty look. "He's just hungry. I brought a casserole just in case. I haven't seen him in weeks. I was worried poachers had gotten him."

She dug into her duffel bag and brought out a casserole wrapped in tinfoil. I made a silent vow to check Gertie's bags before going anywhere with her again. From this point on, I was the TSA of Sinful. At least when it came to Gertie and things with zippers. At least then my only concern would be what she could fit into her bra.

Ida Belle climbed into the driver's seat. "Throw that food to the monster and sit down. If there were any fish around, they're gone now and they're not coming back with him hanging around."

Gertie flipped the casserole over the side and into the waiting mouth of the gator. "Oh! There's fish. Grab that piling, Fortune, and move us around to the other side."

I leaned over the edge of the boat, careful not to fall onto Godzilla, who was happily munching down on his snack, and pulled the boat around the piling. Gertie glanced over at Godzilla, then leaned over the other side of the boat and reached into the water. A second later, she popped up with a thick fishing line.

"There's several of these attached to a piling under the water," she said. "Two of them still have fish on them."

"That's why Hooch wanted to fish here," Ida Belle said. "That's his regular cheat."

"They're alive?" I asked. "Where did he get them?"

"He fishes for several days before the tournament," Ida Belle said, "then hangs some fish on a line early that morning before daylight."

I frowned. "That plan is so full of holes I could drive my

boat through it. What if something ate the fish—like Godzilla, the alligator always looking for an easy meal?"

"My guess is that's why some of the lines are empty," Gertie said.

"Okay," I said, "but what's to stop anyone who lives on the water from just keeping fish in a live trap for a couple days, then swinging by their house and pulling them up? Or to make things even easier, why not just collect the fish before you leave for the tournament and put them in your ice chest? It's not like anyone came to inspect ours."

"Walter is running the rodeo," Ida Belle said. "That's the only reason we weren't asked to drive by for a boat inspection. He knows we don't pull any of those shenanigans, and you don't know about them, so..."

Gertie nodded. "But everyone else's boat is checked, and he sends volunteers to the houses on the bayous to look at live traps. It's not foolproof, but it cuts down on the laziest of cheaters."

I shook my head and climbed into my chair, completely done with the entire mess. "Then steal those fish, or whatever you had planned, and let's get out of here before someone sees you and you get eliminated."

"That's a really good specimen," Ida Belle said of one of the fish Gertie had hauled in on the line. "It would be a shame for it to go to waste."

"An even bigger shame would be if Hooch collected all these and won," Gertie said, and tossed the fish in the ice chest.

"Like that's going to happen," I said. "You've got the world's laziest alligator just feet away from a meal that can't escape. Those fish wouldn't have lasted another ten minutes."

Ida Belle hauled in another big fish. "I'd rather grill these up myself than give that gator another free meal. I don't suppose we have any way to haul Godzilla in, do we?"

"No," I said. "And he's never allowed in my boat. Not even if he's sedated and in a straitjacket. That animal does not like me."

"That's because you startled him the first time you met him," Gertie said.

"He was in your bathtub," I said. "*I'm* the one who was startled."

Gertie waved a hand in dismissal. "He was just cooling off."

They hauled in four more large fish and then declared that was it. Gertie emptied a package of potato chips into the bayou and we headed across the lake and down one of the bayous, hoping that if we moved far enough away, Godzilla wouldn't try to follow. Given what he'd just consumed, my guess was he would crawl up the nearest bank and take a nap, but either way, no one was going in the water again. The speargun might have been lost, but there was no telling what else Gertie had in her bag of tricks.

"You guys are going to be the death of me," I said. "This was supposed to be a quiet day on the water. I was in less danger with the CIA."

"Wait until hunting season," Gertie said.

———

AFTER THE GREAT SPEARGUN DEBACLE, I searched Gertie's bag and confiscated a flare gun, two more sticks of dynamite that she swore she didn't know were in there, and a set of Chinese throwing stars. I didn't have any idea how she'd intended to use throwing stars in a fishing rodeo, but there was no way I was going to find out.

With the tricks in the bag of horror safely locked away, the rest of the day was reasonably uneventful. Of course, Gertie managed to fall in twice and one time, got caught on the bow of an old shrimp boat that was partially sunk. It took both Ida Belle and me to lift her off of it. An alligator that had been hiding in the marsh grass on the bank slid into the water as we worked to get her off the bow, but he apparently decided a silver-haired woman hanging off a piece of rusty metal didn't look all that appetizing. He surfaced once and paused, studying her, then turned around and headed the other direction.

True to form, Gertie was offended.

It was a long, hot day, but lunch was great, and I finally managed to finish my book. I also talked PI shop with Gertie and Ida Belle, talked about when we'd take that vacation we kept mentioning, and talked about everyone in Sinful finding out the truth about me, especially Celia. Basically, we drank water, ate a fantastic roast beef sandwich and homemade cookies, got sunburned, ran our mouths, and caught some fish. Well, Gertie and Ida Belle caught fish. One was bigger than Hooch's stash, and Gertie was sure it would get her the coveted title and case of beer. When I pointed out that she hadn't even cheated to do it, she told me not to get used to that.

The official weigh-in was happening at the dock behind the General Store, so we headed back thirty minutes prior to quitting time just in case we ran into any problems on the way. Gertie had informed me that "problems" could include anything from engine trouble to sabotage. I kept a watch out for any troublemakers along the way, but honestly, unless they were equipped to hit a target moving as fast as lightning, I'm pretty sure Ida Belle outdrove any shenanigans someone might have planned.

We drove the airboat up on the bank next to a glowering

man in overalls and a Dale Earnhardt hat. Since his glare was mostly directed at Gertie, I assumed he was another fisherman used to finishing outside the top three. Ida Belle and I grabbed the ice chest and headed for the dock, where Walter was manning the scale and tape measure. Everyone leaned in as we set the ice chest next to Walter, and Gertie reached inside. When she came up with the big fish, the grumbling began.

Walter took the fish and inspected it up and down on both sides—I assume looking for blast damage or bullet holes or whatever other insane way people cheated. Satisfied that the fish was good, he then inserted a thermometer and checked its temperature, which he recorded on a notebook. Then he took out a tape measure and measured the fish from front to back, calling out the length as he recorded it next to the temperature.

More grumbling ensued.

Finally, he placed the fish on the scale and everyone stared as the needle moved up. When it stopped rocking, the grumbling turned to cursing.

"Second place," Walter said. "We've still got one more fisherman to weigh in."

"Second?" I looked at Gertie and Ida Belle.

"Who's missing?" Ida Belle asked.

"Hooch," Walter said.

"There's your second place," I said.

"If he don't get here in time, it don't count," a man in the crowd yelled.

I assumed he was currently sitting in third and already trying to figure out exactly how many cans of beer were in a case.

"He's got six more minutes," Walter said, "so everyone just chill out. I've never known Hooch to miss a weigh-in."

Everyone shuffled around, glancing at their watches and mostly grumbling. "Is this normal?" I asked.

"At least one person always shows up at the last minute," Gertie said, her voice low. "They don't catch something they think will place and stay out as long as possible. And since Hooch wasn't able to snag his stash, he's probably pushing the limit, trying to land a legit catch."

Ida Belle nodded. "I am a little surprised, though. Hooch isn't overly ambitious. With his cheating cut short, I figured he'd give it a couple hours, then head back in for air-conditioning and a nap. He rarely stays out past lunch."

"Maybe he passed out drunk in his boat," I said.

"Anything is possible," Gertie said. "Except him not showing up at all."

But as the minutes ticked by and there was no sound of an approaching boat, I began to wonder if this was going to be the first time for something.

"Ten seconds," Walter called out.

The crowd started counting down and I looked over at Ida Belle, who was frowning. "What's wrong?" I asked.

"Maybe nothing," she said. "But something doesn't feel right."

The crowd got to one and started cheering.

Gertie sighed. "Like I need another rod and reel."

"You didn't *need* beer," I said.

"Everyone needs beer," Gertie said.

I laughed. "What I need is a shower and some AC. I scammed cream puffs from Ally yesterday. Wardrobe change, then meet at my place for dessert? I have beer."

"You had me at cream puffs," Gertie said. "But the beer is always a nice touch."

Gertie collected her rod and reel and a trophy that looked like a bass and we headed for my boat. We were just climbing in when I saw Carter pull up to the sheriff's department's dock, and he didn't look happy.

"I wonder why Carter was out in the boat," Gertie said.

"I figured he'd be policing the fishermen, no?" I asked.

Ida Belle shook her head. "Law enforcement has a long-standing tradition of staying out of the middle of fishing rodeos. It's just easier all the way around."

"Even when they use dynamite?" I asked. I could see turning a blind eye to drunken boating and trespassing as long as no one got injured, but I figured no way would Carter ignore the use of explosives. Especially considering a lot of the fishermen were probably both trespassing and drunk.

"He would investigate any reports of explosives," Ida Belle said, "but we only heard the one and that was first thing this morning. He wouldn't have been out all day over that one blast."

I watched as he stalked to the building, not even glancing over at us. He had his cell phone pressed to his head and his expression was grim. "Something's going on," I said. "Look at his face."

"Maybe it's Hooch," Gertie said. "Maybe he fell in and drowned."

"I told you something didn't feel right," Ida Belle said.

Carter entered the sheriff's department, slamming the door behind him without so much as a backward glance. A minute later, Deputy Breaux hustled out the back door and hurried over to the boat Carter had just exited. He quickly started it up and took off down the bayou.

The rest of the fishing tournament crowd had dispersed, and none of them seemed to notice the interesting actions of the local law enforcement. Except for Walter. He was still standing on the dock and staring at Deputy Breaux as he passed in the boat.

"You hear anything?" Ida Belle called out.

He looked over at us and shook his head, but I could tell he had the same bad feeling Ida Belle did. I had a strange suspicion that a second-place opening in local fishing rodeos might be coming available. And I was pretty sure I wasn't the only one who felt that way.

"Let me know if you get something," Ida Belle said.

Walter nodded. "I should be telling you that. Those womenfolk of yours will have the scoop before my nephew opens his mouth about police business. But I'll be watching. If I get a whiff of something, I'll let you know."

I climbed into the boat and took my seat. "What do you think is going on?" I asked.

Gertie shook her head. "An accident of some kind, maybe."

"If it was just an accident, Carter wouldn't look that worried," I said.

"She's right," Ida Belle said. "Hooch doesn't have any family he's responsible for, so there's no one depending on a paycheck come Friday. If it was an accident, Carter would have looked a bit sad and gone about his paperwork. Worried is a whole different animal."

Gertie looked up at me. "You think he'll tell you?"

"Please," I said. "We'd hear about a conviction on the evening news before Carter shared anything about an investigation with me."

Gertie shook her head. "In the movies, having the inside connection always gives a person the scoop."

"That's why they're fiction," Ida Belle said. "I wouldn't count on Fortune getting us anything unless Carter talks in his sleep."

Gertie gave me a hopeful look.

I shook my head. "He doesn't even snore."

"Well," Gertie said, "I suppose that's a plus, at least."

"Might as well get going," Ida Belle said. "We'll know soon enough."

I clutched the armrests as Ida Belle took off, but this time, her driving was more subdued. I had no doubt that by the time we'd showered and reconvened, Ida Belle would have heard from one of the Sinful Ladies. One was a dispatcher at the sheriff's department and even though Carter had threatened her with firing if he found out she was feeding information to Ida Belle, it wasn't going to stop her.

Added to that, the Sinful Ladies had nephews and nieces in almost every arena of employment—the phone company, hospital, paramedics, fire department, and coroner's office covered most bases. One of them was bound to know something. Ida Belle wouldn't even have to put the word out. As soon as one of them got wind of anything outside the Sinful norm, the first call they made would be to her.

Then I remembered Hooch's fight with Dixie. I'd seen her collect her trophy and certificate from Walter, but she'd had her back to me, so I couldn't see her face. I didn't recall seeing her afterward.

But I wondered.

CHAPTER FIVE

"GET YOUR SKINNY BUTT DOWN HERE!" Ida Belle yelled from downstairs in my living room.

I'd just gotten dressed after a very long shower but was still surprised that Ida Belle had made it back so quickly. She must have heard something. I shoved my pistol in my waistband, grabbed my tennis shoes, and headed downstairs to find Ida Belle and Gertie standing in my living room.

Ida Belle's hair was styled in her usual short cut and she wore jeans and a button-up. Clearly, she'd finished getting ready before she'd dashed out the door. Gertie hadn't been as lucky. Her hair was still wet, and it hung in ringlets down her face, dripping onto her blue Batman T-shirt. The green sweatpants she wore didn't even remotely match the shirt and she had two different sandals on her feet. One with a heel. One a flat. She wiped her face with a towel and was glaring at Ida Belle as if she wanted to strangle her with it.

"Okay, woman," Gertie said, "out with it. You burst in and dragged me right out of the shower, barely letting me get decent enough to travel."

I frowned. The jury was out on decent, but at least she was only traveling to my house. I had different standards than pretty much the whole rest of the world.

"It's just Fortune," Ida Belle said. "And she's seen you in way worse. And far less."

"I assume the gossip train made a trip to your cell phone?" I said.

Ida Belle nodded. "Hooch is dead."

Gertie stopped blotting her hair and stared. "Dead? I figured he was sleeping off a drunk or didn't catch anything and went home. And was sleeping off a drunk. Worst I could imagine was some sort of accident, but I never really believed he'd died, even though I suggested it."

"I don't think it's as simple as death, either, is it?" I asked. Ida Belle had felt something was wrong the minute Hooch hadn't shown, and I'd felt the same when I'd seen the look on Carter's face. "Let's move this to the kitchen."

"Definitely," Gertie said. "You owe me cream puffs and I'm eating two, maybe three."

We headed back and Gertie started in on the dessert while I grabbed us drinks and then sat.

"They would have done an autopsy anyway, given it was an unattended death and there was no obvious cause," Ida Belle said. "A local running his crab pots found Hooch slumped over in his boat. He checked for a pulse but said he was already gone. He called Carter and waited. He said Carter took one look at the body and called the ME, then secured Hooch's boat as a crime scene."

"How reliable is that account?" I asked. Sometimes information filtered through several sources before Ida Belle got it. The more sources, the more chance for things being overly dramatized or simply incorrect.

"Highly reliable," Ida Belle said. "The guy who found him is Myrtle's cousin, Kenny Bertrand. He's widowed, isn't a big drinker, and has never been one for making a fuss. Once Carter released him, Kenny went straight to Myrtle's house. She said he was still freaked out."

Myrtle was a dispatcher at the sheriff's department and a main source for Ida Belle's law enforcement information. If she thought her cousin was telling it straight, then I was happy to believe her.

"What else did he see?" I asked. "No visible wound?

Ida Belle shook her head. "Hooch was slumped over, so Kenny couldn't see his face. He just felt for a pulse but said the body was already stiff. When he realized Hooch was dead, he jumped right back into his boat and called Carter. Myrtle pushed him for more information, but he was vague. I'm guessing he didn't stomach it all too well and didn't want to get into it in detail."

Gertie sighed. "Kenny always was a bit of a pansy. He probably spent the rest of the time looking the other direction. I really wish people would man up in these situations. It's way harder to get information when Carter and the ME are the only ones with the details."

"Yes," Ida Belle said. "All these regular citizens refusing to inspect dead bodies and disrupt crime scenes are definitely the problem."

"I'm just saying," Gertie said.

"Regardless of the strength of everyone's stomach," I said, "the biggest takeaway here is that it doesn't sound like Carter thinks it was natural causes, which I find interesting."

"Why?" Gertie said.

"Because it means that something about Hooch tipped Carter off," I said. "And since there wasn't something obvious, like a giant pool of blood, or a bullet hole through his back, or a hungry alligator snacking on a limb next to the boat, then we have to assume that it was something Carter has seen before, which is why he zeroed in on it to begin with."

Ida Belle nodded. "So the real question is who wanted to kill Hooch."

I shrugged. "This is where I have to defer to you guys. I'd never heard of him until today. Does he have any enemies? What does he do for a living? Is Hooch his real name? Any competition who would like to see him go away? Ex-wife? Girl-friend? Boyfriend? Kids that will inherit?"

Gertie frowned. "Given name is Boone Carre. He's single. There's an ex-wife, but she left town over a decade ago. One son. He left town with the ex-wife and I haven't seen him since. No girlfriend that I'm aware of. My guess is that Hooch attracts the kind of women who get paid for their time."

"Probably a good guess," Ida Belle said. "He's a Swamp Bar regular, last I heard."

"What does he do for work?" I asked.

"He's a contractor," Gertie said. "Sort of."

"How is one 'sort of' a contractor?" I asked.

"When you don't show up half the time for the jobs you've scheduled," Ida Belle said, "then you get the 'sort of' designa-tion. I think he only works enough to get by and if he still has money in his pocket, then he just doesn't show for any jobs he's bid on until he runs out again."

"Has he left anyone hanging in a bad way?" I asked.

"It's definitely possible," Gertie said. "Contractors usually take some money up front for materials. If he took money, then didn't show, there's probably some unhappy people walking around."

"But unhappy enough to kill him?" I asked. "And if people

know he has a reputation for doing this, would they give him a bunch of money up front?"

"My guess is no one is handing him over a large amount," Ida Belle said. "I know a few who got him to make up a list of materials and they ordered them themselves. At least that way, if Hooch flaked, they could hire someone else but weren't out anything."

"Is it really so hard to find a contractor that people are willing to go through all that trouble?" I asked.

"Yes!"

They both answered at once and their expressions were a combination of aggravation and resignation. I made a mental note to learn construction and pray that nothing broke at my soon-to-be-acquired home that I couldn't fix myself. Clearly, hiring a contractor in Sinful was an adventure I didn't want to go on.

"Okay," I said. "I get it, but are they all as bad as Hooch? I mean, if there's someone more reliable, why does he get work at all?"

"Because there's too much work for the more reliable people and sometimes things can't wait," Gertie said. "And then there's still some folk that hire him because they feel sorry for him."

"Why would they feel sorry for him?" I asked. "He didn't seem all that pleasant today when he confronted Dixie."

"Rumor has it his wife ran off with another man," Ida Belle said. "His son was just a boy and went with his mother. I don't think he stayed in touch with Hooch at all. People asked about him for a while, but Hooch always evaded the question. Finally, people stopped asking, figuring it was rude to keep pushing a sensitive issue."

"That's unfortunate," I said, "but not a good enough reason for me to put up with his crap."

"Me either," Ida Belle said. "But neither of us would qualify for any Sympathetic Human Being awards."

"If by sympathetic, you mean enabling bad behavior, then no." I shook my head. "I guess the good news is, this one doesn't have anything to do with us."

"You don't think—" Gertie started.

"No," I said. "I don't think there's any rational reason for us to involve ourselves in a murder investigation, especially when we don't even have confirmation yet. I'm sure Carter has been wrong before, and he's likely to be wrong again. Today might be one of those days. But we don't have a stake in this, and neither does anyone close to us."

"Carter does," Gertie said.

"That's not a stake," I said. "That's his job."

Ida Belle nodded. "I have to agree. At least for the moment, there's no reason for us to go poking our nose in. No use winding Carter up and getting Fortune on the outs with him over nothing. She just got back. She has plenty of time to piss him off later on."

Gertie gave Ida Belle an aggravated look. "You dragged me out of the shower for marginal gossip and to tell me we're not doing anything about it? You could have waited for me to dry my hair, at least."

"You're right," Ida Belle said. "I don't know what got into me. Come on. I'll take you home before you throw a hip out walking uneven in those shoes. I don't expect it, but let us know if you get anything out of Carter."

"I will."

They headed out of the house and I watched as they climbed into Ida Belle's Blazer. Something was still off. Ida Belle didn't usually jump the gun on things, but the information she had was marginal, at best. Dragging Gertie over here, still dripping and half-ass dressed, wasn't like her usual approach of logic and planning. I could only think of one reason for the rational woman I knew to do anything even remotely irrational.

Intuition.

Something was telling Ida Belle that this situation was all wrong and that things were going to go south somehow. If it was bothering her that much, then I had no doubt that our reason for poking into police business would surface sooner rather than later. I knew a little something about intuition. And when people like Ida Belle had a feeling this strong about something, it was usually right.

I just hoped the fallout wasn't on someone I cared about.

———

CARTER and I had a loosely agreed upon dinner planned at my house, which tonight meant frozen pizza and beer. Neither of us was fond of my cooking. Carter was the king of the grill, but all of the really great meals we'd shared together had been prepared by other people. I used to toy with the idea of learning to cook, but the one time I'd tried to get Gertie to show me something I'd fallen asleep on the counter before she got to the third step.

The bottom line was I was far more inclined to be the person bagging the dinner with a rifle rather than the person serving it on a platter. I wasn't either person if it involved fishing. I still couldn't get into it no matter how many times someone thrust a rod into my hands. But I might give hunting a whirl the next time something was in season.

Given the situation with Hooch, I figured Carter would end up working later than his scheduled quitting time, so I went about my normal nightly business of folding towels and cleaning my gun and had a snack to tide me over until he could get away. At nine o'clock, I finally got a text.

Eat without me. I'll call you tomorrow. Lots going on. Sorry.

I frowned.

It wasn't unusual for Carter to send me a text like this, but it was under these circumstances. We hadn't spoken since this morning and I was positive he knew that news of Hooch's death had already swept through Sinful. Which meant only one thing—he was avoiding me.

And that was very interesting. It was also troubling.

Carter was aware that Hooch was no one in particular to me. He probably figured, correctly, that I hadn't even known of him before today. And Carter would also be aware that Hooch wasn't a friend of Ida Belle and Gertie and had no family they'd need to concern themselves with if he died. So why avoid me?

I knew absolutely that Carter didn't want me involved in police business, but he must have had a reason for thinking I'd butt in. Otherwise, he'd have shown up for late dinner and simply refused to answer my questions. The fact that he was ensuring that he didn't see me or even speak to me was telling.

Something was up.

But what?

I sighed. I could have sat here all night and never come up with a solid reason. I was completely in the dark on this one. I couldn't see any way that Hooch's death, even if it was indeed murder, had an effect on me or Ida Belle or Gertie. Not beyond the general scope of having someone you knew murdered, at least. But I didn't like it. Between Ida Belle's intuition and Carter's disappearing act, I had a feeling Hooch's death was about to explode in our faces.

I was just about to call Ida Belle when my phone rang. It

was a local number but one I didn't recognize. I answered the call and a hysterical-sounding woman started yelling.

"Something's happening!" the woman yelled. "She said to call you. Hurry!"

"What's happening? Where? Who said to call? Who is this?"

"It's Bernice Parker. Carter's done lost his mind. He's arresting Ally!"

CHAPTER SIX

I RAN FOR THE KITCHEN, slowing only long enough to grab
the keys to my Jeep before running into the garage. The door
had barely made it completely up before I tore out of there in
reverse. I didn't even bother pausing to put it back down. In
my haste, I completely miscalculated the curve at the bottom
of my drive and ran right through part of my front lawn. But
that didn't even get so much as a blink out of me.

I floored the Jeep and took off down the road, tires squeal-
ing. I passed a couple cars on the way and thought I saw one
driver give me the bird, but I didn't care. All I could think of
was Ally. Surely Bernice was wrong. But even as I thought it, I
knew it wasn't the case. Bernice lived across the street from
Ally, and she was a lot of things, but hysterical and inaccurate
weren't two of them. She'd been panicked when she called me,
and there was no way she'd even have my phone number if Ally
hadn't given it to her.

When I turned onto Ally's street, my heart plummeted
when I saw Carter's truck in front of her house. Carter was at
the curb, assisting Ally to his truck. Relief swept through me
when I saw she wasn't handcuffed, but it was clear from the

look on her face that she didn't have a choice about going with him. I slammed on my brakes, barely stopping before I hit his bumper, threw the Jeep into Park, and jumped out without even turning off the engine.

Carter glanced over at me and immediately looked away, but I could see how unhappy he was with my presence. He shot a dirty look at Bernice, who was standing on the sidewalk in front of her house, clutching her cell phone. Bernice put her hands on her hips and stared back at him, clearly not having any of it.

"What the hell is going on here?" I asked as I hurried over.

"He said he has to question me," Ally said. Her eyes were wide and I could see that any minute, she was going to start crying. "He thinks I killed Hooch."

"I did not say that," Carter said. "I just need to ask you some questions, on the record."

"At the sheriff's department?" I asked. "At 9:15 p.m.?"

Carter opened the passenger door to his truck. "Get in," he said to Ally.

I grabbed her arm before she could move forward. "Do not say a word. I will get you an attorney."

Ally glanced at Carter, whose jaw was clenched, then looked back at me. "He'll put me in jail if I don't talk."

"I've been there before," I said. "It's not that bad and you'll be out by tomorrow."

"But I didn't do anything," Ally wailed. "Why do I have to go to jail?"

I could tell she was on the verge of hysterics and once she launched, it would be all over but high blood pressure and crying. So I did the only thing I could do.

I kicked the mirror off Carter's truck.

They both stared at me as if I'd lost my mind, and I wasn't

quite sure I hadn't. Only Bernice seemed unfazed as she yelled "Go girl!" from across the street.

"What the hell?" Carter exploded.

"That's vandalism to an on-duty officer's vehicle," I said. "You can't press charges tonight, so I guess you'll have to lock me up with her."

Ally threw her arms around me. "Oh my God, I can't believe you did that."

"Everything will be okay," I said, carefully avoiding looking at Carter, who I'm sure was ready to kill me. "Just get in the truck and we'll get it all sorted out later."

I looked across the street at Bernice "Turn off my Jeep and call Ida Belle and tell her what happened."

Carter groaned softly.

"You bet your butt I will," Bernice said, and lifted her phone to dial. She shot one last dirty look at Carter, then stomped over to my Jeep.

"Let's do this," I said to Ally.

As I climbed in the truck, the only thing I could think about was that I hadn't even had dinner.

––––––––

CARTER WAS COMPLETELY silent as he ushered us into the sheriff's department. Myrtle was on shift and gave us a startled look as we walked in. Clearly, she'd clued in that this wasn't a social call. Ally stood in front of Myrtle's desk, biting her lower lip. Carter looked at the two of us.

"Are you going to answer my questions?" he asked Ally.

Ally glanced at me and I shook my head.

"No," she said quietly.

Carter sighed. "Myrtle, please escort Ms. Lemarque to cell number one."

Myrtle rose from the desk and stared at Carter as only an older Southern woman could manage. "Carter LeBlanc, have you lost your mind? Do I need to call the paramedics or should I just call your mother?"

"You're going to be calling the unemployment office if you don't put Ms. Lemarque in that cell. She made her choice. I don't have one."

"That's the biggest bunch of crap I've heard in this office," Myrtle said. "And I've heard more than my share. I just never figured the smelliest of it would come from you."

Admitting defeat, Carter chose to ignore her completely and turned to me. "I don't suppose there's any way I can convince you to go quietly home."

"If you try to get out of arresting me, the next thing I kick won't be inanimate," I said.

"Fine. Take them both, Myrtle. They can share a cell."

"Don't we get a phone call?" Ally asked.

"Don't worry," I said. "Bernice called Ida Belle. That's all the backup we need."

Carter closed his eyes for a moment and I'm pretty sure he was praying.

"I'll call for some blankets," Myrtle said. "There's a draft in those cells. Have you eaten tonight?"

"I haven't," I said. "I was waiting on my date." I shot a look at Carter, who sighed and shook his head.

"Since the deputy has lost all sense of how to treat people decently, I'll get you something to eat as well," Myrtle said. She yanked a set of keys off the wall and motioned to Ally and me to follow her. She shot one last angry glance at Carter before huffing off down the hall.

"I swear to God, I don't know what is wrong with that man," Myrtle said as we walked. "I can't imagine what you two did that would prompt this. Short of killing someone, anyway."

"He thinks I killed Hooch," Ally said quietly.

Myrtle stopped dead in her tracks and turned around to stare at Ally. "You've got to be kidding me. And that's not the first words that came to mind. He's lost the plot. I'm definitely calling his mother."

"While I, for one, would love to see Carter dealing with Emmaline on this one," I said, "let's not get ahead of ourselves. Carter wants to question Ally concerning Hooch's death. I told her not to talk without an attorney present because that's what everyone being questioned as a suspect in a murder investigation should do. Since we can't make an attorney materialize at this time of night, that means Carter has to hold her overnight."

"Why?" Myrtle asked. "It's not like she's a flight risk."

"Of course not!" Ally said.

"We all know that," I said, "and Carter does too, but my guess is he's doing this by the book to protect everyone. If he's accused of favoritism, it could affect his ability to control the investigation. And no one wants the state police to take over. They might insist on holding Ally in New Orleans if they come up with a good enough reason to."

Myrtle seemed a tiny bit mollified, but I was betting that Emmaline would get an earful as soon as Carter left the building. "Then why are you here?" she asked me.

"Oh, I couldn't let Ally sit here alone all night, so I kicked the mirror off Carter's truck."

Myrtle's lips quivered and finally the smile broke through. "I would have paid to see that. Well, best get you two criminals locked up before Carter sends me to that unemployment line."

———

ALLY AND I sat in silence for several minutes. I figured Ally was silent because she'd never been in jail and was scared to be there now, especially given that we had no idea what Carter knew or why he'd zeroed in on her in the first place. I was silent because I was hungry and honestly, had no idea what to say except that. As it didn't sound very comforting to blurt out, 'I'd kill for a ham sandwich about now,' I figured I'd just wait for Ally to take the lead on the whole conversation thing.

"I don't understand what's happening," Ally said. "How could Carter think I killed someone?"

"I'm sure he doesn't, but there must be some evidence pointing to you as a suspect. Can you think of any reason why someone would assume you have a grudge against Hooch?"

Ally's eyes widened. "Oh my God."

"That doesn't sound promising. Better tell me what's up."

"I hired Hooch to rebuild my tool shed in the backyard. I knew he was unreliable, but he approached me about it and needed the work, so I decided to forgo the contractor I was going to use and hire him instead."

"Did you give him any money up front?"

Ally bit her lower lip. "Yes. I know, it was stupid, especially given his reputation, but it wasn't an emergency sort of situation, so I figured even if he slacked off, the work would eventually get done."

"I take it that it didn't?"

"No. He started by removing the old roof to shore up the framing and covered it with a tarp to keep the contents from ruining if it rained. It was only supposed to be for a couple days. That was three weeks ago. I've been outside nailing that tarp back down a million times since then and finally, it just tore completely in two in the middle of a storm. It took me two days to go through all my contents and try to salvage what I could, but some things are a lost cause. Probably a couple thousand dollars, but it's not worth filing on my homeowner's insurance."

"How much money did you give Hooch to start the job?"

"Two thousand."

"So you're into him for four to five thousand?"

"That sounds about right."

I held in a sigh. I knew Ally would never kill someone over any amount of money, and I was certain Carter did as well. But I could see how someone might make more of her situation with Hooch if they knew about it. Which led to my next question.

"Did anyone else know about your problems with Hooch?"

Ally blushed. "Probably everyone who was in the café last week. Hooch came in and when I asked him about the shed, he got belligerent and I might have said a few things I probably shouldn't have. I was really embarrassed afterward and apologized to Francine, but she just said he deserved it and called him a choice name or two."

"He did deserve it. And I'm sure you were a lot nicer than I would have been."

"So do you think that's why Carter brought me here? Because of the shed and what I said at the café?"

"I think it's probably part of the reason, but it's not enough. My understanding is that Hooch was known for that sort of behavior. I'm sure you're not the only one in Sinful who's taken a loss hiring Hooch. But you're the only one here tonight. Carter knows something else. He's just not sharing it."

"But what could he possibly know?"

I shook my head. "I'm not sure. But we need to find out what killed Hooch. Based on some other gossip, I'd already figured Carter didn't think his death was from natural causes, but no one has gotten the scoop on the cause. That is information we need."

"You think there's something linking me to the cause of his death? But what could that possibly be? I was working a shift at the café from early morning until midafternoon. It's not like I could sneak off from my tables and jet down the bayou to kill someone without my customers noticing my absence. So unless he was killed after 3:00 p.m., then I don't see how I could be a suspect for anything."

"It does seem a bit odd. And I'm sure Carter checked your work schedule." I sighed. "Unfortunately, I think we're going to have to wait until we have more information. Whatever Carter knows, he'll have to divulge to your attorney."

Ally's eyes filled with tears. "But I don't have an attorney. I don't even know one to call. I mean, I've been talking to one about setting up my bakery business but I'm pretty sure he doesn't handle murder charges."

"Don't worry about that part. I have an idea."

She looked a tiny bit hopeful but I could tell she wasn't convinced. I wasn't convinced, either, given that I had no idea what Carter knew. But I was certain of one thing—it wasn't good, and it tied Ally directly to Hooch in some way because Carter would never go this route otherwise.

I had to find out what Carter knew.

No way was he going to put it in writing anywhere Myrtle might access it, which meant no computer logs and no file kept at the sheriff's department. And no way was he going to put it in writing anywhere I might access it, which meant no file at his house, either. But he had to keep the records somewhere. That was one angle.

The other was the medical examiner. Surely Ida Belle had someone in her network who could ferret out a cause of death for us. That would give us a starting place in figuring out what happened, and God forbid, building a defense, if it came to that. I glanced at my watch. We'd been here for fifteen minutes. I figured Ida Belle would show up any minute.

Not a second later, I heard arguing coming from the front of the sheriff's department. I looked over at Ally and grinned.

The cavalry had arrived.

————

THERE WAS several seconds of shouting, then I heard some stomping and the door to the cells swung open. Carter stepped inside and waved for Ida Belle to enter. She strode past, refusing to even look at him, Gertie right behind. Gertie gave him the finger as she walked by. Then I was surprised to see Francine behind Gertie.

"You've got five minutes," Carter said. "And I'm going to be standing here for all of them."

Francine gave Carter a disgusted look and stepped forward. "Myrtle said you were hungry. I can't imagine what is wrong with our illustrious deputy, locking up people who haven't had a proper dinner."

Gertie nodded. "Especially when one of the people locked up was waiting on the illustrious deputy to eat. Bad manners all around."

Carter closed his eyes and leaned back against the wall.

"Anyway," Francine said. "I threw together some vegetable soup from today, roast beef sandwiches, chips, and apple pie. It's not gourmet, but I wasn't exactly given notice. I'll be back with a much better spread tomorrow morning."

She looked over at Carter and motioned to the door. "I'm no physicist, but I don't think this basket is going to fit through those bars."

Carter pushed himself off the wall and opened the door to our cell. Francine passed me the basket, shot one last dirty look at Carter, then whirled around and left the jail. I placed the basket on the cot behind me and looked at Ida Belle, wondering how we were going to have a conversation with Carter standing right there.

"I know an attorney I can call," Ida Belle said. "But it will have to wait until morning, of course."

"I already have something in mind in that regard," I said. "Of course, it would help if we knew what to tell the attorney." I looked over at Carter, who studied the ceiling tiles.

"Is there anything else we can get you?" Gertie said.

"No," I said, "but if one of you could drive my Jeep home, that would be great. Bernice has the keys."

Gertie nodded. "I brought a couple of blankets. I know from experience there's a draft in here at night. I told someone to get it looked at, but you know how things run around here."

She shoved the blankets through the bars and Ally took them and placed them on the cot next to the basket of food.

"I'm sure we'll be fine," I said. "Maybe a little bored since we had to give up our cell phones, but I suppose we could just sleep it off."

Ida Belle pulled a deck of cards out of her pocket and handed them to me. "This might help if you're not able to sleep."

"Thanks," I said. As I took the cards, I saw a certain look in Ida Belle's eyes. A look that told me there was more to their visit than just checking on our welfare.

"Be sure you eat," Gertie said. "I know you're stressed, but it won't do either of you any good if you get weak and sick."

"You don't have to worry about me," I said. "I'm starving. And I'll make sure Ally eats something."

Ida Belle looked at Ally. "Everything is going to be fine. I promise you. Don't worry about this. We've been in some precarious positions with the law ourselves. There's just some things to work out and all of this will blow over."

"Thank you," Ally said, and I could tell Ida Belle's words and the strength of her conviction as she spoke them had helped calm Ally a bit.

"Okay, time's up," Carter said.

"We'll be back tomorrow," Ida Belle said, and she and Gertie strolled out of the jail, not giving Carter so much as a backward glance.

He'd been expecting an argument, and I could tell he was somewhat surprised that they'd left without one. He looked over at Ally and me.

"Do you need anything before I go?" he asked.

"We're good," I said.

"Well, if anything comes up, ring the bell. Myrtle will check on you periodically." He hesitated and I could tell he wanted to say something more, but ultimately, his sworn duty must have won out and he closed the door behind him.

I felt a tiny bit sorry for him, but far sorrier for Ally. Despite the repugnant nature of his job at the moment, Carter was equipped to deal with it. Ally, on the other hand, did not belong in a jail, or deserve being questioned for murder. In fact, I couldn't think of a less likely person to commit such an act than Ally. It defied all logic.

Which led me right back to needing more information because clearly, there was something I didn't know. Something big.

I glanced at the door, making sure it was shut, and sat on the cot to open the deck of cards.

"You want to play cards now?" Ally asked.

"No. I think Ida Belle slipped something in here with the cards." I pulled them out and sure enough, found a piece of folded paper in the stack. I unfolded it and saw Ida Belle's handwriting. I read the words and felt my back tighten.

"What does it say?" Ally asked. "What's wrong? I can tell something's wrong."

I could have lied to her, but what was the point? It wasn't like either of us was going to get a decent night's sleep.

"It says Hooch died from ingesting cyanide. That's why Carter knew it was murder. He probably saw it during his service time and recognized the symptoms and the smell."

Ally paled. "Oh my God. I packed all of the lunches for the rodeo. That's why Carter wants to question me. I packed the lunch and Hooch cost me a lot of money. Fortune, what am I going to do?"

Her voice shifted to a higher octave and I could tell her stress level was about to shoot through the roof.

"Let's not get excited," I said. "This is good news."

"How in the world can this be good news?"

"Because you're not the only one with access to the food. You're just the one that Carter knows for sure had opportunity and motive, so he's talking to you first. It's all circumstantial. He can't prove anything from this, and the DA will tell him just that."

"Then he'll be questioning everyone at the café, right?"

"Yes, and don't forget all the random people who stroll in the back door."

Ida Belle, Gertie, and I had recently investigated food theft from the café and had run into a bit of trouble nailing down the perpetrator due to the lax policy of the unlocked back door and the propensity for locals to waltz into the kitchen whenever convenient. There was no telling how many people other than staff had moved through the kitchen while the lunches were being prepared and packed.

"Oh, that's right," Ally said. "That's encouraging."

I nodded. "And given Hooch's reputation for falling down on the job, I can't imagine you're the only person in Sinful he's in the hole with."

"I'm sure I'm not. But it's a big stretch from being hacked at someone over money to killing them. Surely someone didn't poison Hooch over a construction job."

"I doubt a loss on a construction job is what's behind this, but that doesn't matter as far as you're concerned. All we need for reasonable doubt is for someone else to have had access to the food and been screwed by Hooch, and I'm just betting the odds are really good on that. A DA won't touch a case that has multiple potential perps. And honestly, given your appearance and reputation, they'd darn near need video of you stabbing someone to death before a jury would believe it."

"Oh." Ally was silent for a couple seconds and I could see she was processing what I'd said. "That actually makes sense. Not that I want other people going through this or anything, but I guess he can't put everyone with a motive in jail, right?"

"Not for very long. Not without pressing charges."

"So do I really need a lawyer, or should I just talk to Carter and clear this all up?"

"You need a lawyer. Carter is not the issue here. I'm certain he knows you didn't kill Hooch, but he has to follow the investigation wherever it leads, and right now, it's pointing to you."

Ally's shoulders slumped a bit. "I don't want Carter to get in trouble, and I definitely don't want the state police taking over the investigation."

"Exactly. It's no big deal. We'll spend a night on these uncomfortable cots and then tomorrow, we can put it all behind us."

Ally gave me a small smile. "What about you? You damaged Carter's vehicle and then threatened to damage him. You think he's going to let you off?"

"I think he'll do anything to avoid the hassle of booking me. I'll pay to fix his mirror."

Ally tilted her head to the side and studied me for a minute. "Out of curiosity, would you really have hit him?"

"Of course. What are friends for?"

Now her smile was real. "I'm so glad you're staying. I can't imagine going through this without you." She reached for the food basket and opened the top. "Friends are also good for providing tasty snacks. You hungry?"

"Starved!"

Ally handed me a sandwich wrapped in paper and I frowned. The side felt a little hard. I unwrapped the sandwich and found a cell phone inside. It was pink and covered with diamonds.

"That's Francine's," Ally said. "Now we have a way to call out."

"Probably not," I said. "Francine wouldn't know it, but Carter put cell phone blockers down here. That's probably why he didn't bother to search the basket. It wouldn't matter if a cell phone got in. We still wouldn't be able to use it."

Ally frowned and pressed a number into the phone. "You're right. It doesn't connect." She tossed the phone back into the basket. "Well, hell."

She looked over at the blankets. "Do you think Gertie snuck something in for us?" she asked.

"Probably. It's Gertie. I'm just not about to hazard a guess as to what."

Ally reached for the blankets and started to unfold the one on top. Her eyes widened and she held up the contraband. "Is this dynamite?"

I grinned.

Best. Friends. Ever.

CHAPTER SEVEN

It was a long night on a thin, saggy cot. Ally and I played cards for a while and chatted a bit about her plans to open a bakery and my plans for living in Sinful full time. I hadn't told her about the PI business yet because I wanted Carter to know before other people did, but I thought about it while we talked. The funny thing was, things weren't changing a whole heck of a lot for me from the way things were before. I was leaving Marge's house, soon to be my house, as is. I didn't see a need to change furniture or decor. I was going to get a license that guaranteed my existence would officially hack off law enforcement. And I was going to pursue that hacking off with my two partners in crime fighting.

So pretty much the same.

Myrtle had checked in on us a couple times, always apologizing that she couldn't let us out to sit up front or in the break room. Apparently, Carter had figured that's exactly what she would do and had decided to take up residence in his office for the night. She'd insisted on letting us use the staff bathroom, but Carter had been wisely out of sight the two times we'd traipsed down the hall for a visit.

When the conversation slowed and Ally started yawning, I suggested she try to get some sleep. I didn't have any doubt that come tomorrow night she'd be sleeping in her own bed again, but getting through the interview process with a lawyer was going to be stressful. It was always stressful for innocent people. Only criminals seemed utterly confident and patently bored by the entire thing.

Ally tossed and turned for a while, but finally, her breathing slowed and I could tell she'd drifted off. It took me a lot longer to force my mind to slow down enough to fall asleep. The last time I'd checked Francine's phone, it was 4:00 a.m.

It seemed like I'd only been asleep for minutes when I heard Ally moving around. I opened my eyes and saw her rummaging through the food basket Francine had provided. She looked over at me and froze.

"I'm sorry," she said. "I was trying to be quiet so I wouldn't wake you."

"No worries," I said as I sat up. "It's not like sleeping here is all that restful. Besides, since I am gainfully unemployed, I have time to catch up on it later."

"I was going to have pie for breakfast since we didn't eat them last night. You interested?"

"You have to ask?"

Ally grinned and passed me a foam container with a huge slice of apple pie and a plastic spoon.

"What time is it, anyway?" I asked. I'd stopped wearing a watch and without my phone or the ability to see the sun, I was pretty much ignorant of time, especially when my sleeping had been anything but regular.

"It's a little after seven."

"Really?" I said, a bit surprised I'd managed three hours of sleep on that lump passing for a bed.

"I know. I can't believe I slept that long. I figured I'd be awake all night."

"Exhaustion kicks in sooner or later."

"I guess. Thank you for getting arrested with me. I would never have been able to sleep if I were here alone."

"Myrtle probably would have locked the front door and moved in here with the cordless phone."

Ally laughed. "I'm sure she would have wanted to. She's a nice lady. But we both know Carter wouldn't have let her. So I really appreciate what you did. My mind would have conjured up the worst-case scenarios for everything if I had been here alone."

"Hey, you would have done the same for me."

"Well, I wouldn't have kicked off Carter's mirror. I couldn't have kicked that high or that accurately, and I'd probably have broken my foot in the process. But I carry a .22. I could have shot out a taillight."

"Promise me, next time I'm arrested, you'll do that just so I can see the look on Carter's face."

"What do you mean, 'next time you're arrested?'"

"Come on. You know this isn't my last time to visit these four walls. Following the rules isn't in my DNA. How do you think I got a price on my head in the first place?"

Ally grinned. "It's going to be so much fun having you here. Just as soon as I'm not a murder suspect."

"That's the first order of business for the day."

I heard a rattle of keys and looked up to see Myrtle enter the jail carrying a pot of coffee and some foam cups.

"I figured you would be awake by now and could use some morning refreshment," Myrtle said.

She opened the jail cell and passed me the pot and cups.

"I thought you'd be gone already," I said.

"Oh, I've been clocked out, but Carter's not about to try to make me go home. He's still afraid I'm going to call his mother."

"Are you?" I asked.

"Of course! She should be up now. I just needed to get this coffee in here and then I'm off to ruin Carter's morning. Do you want a restroom trip?"

"I can wait until after coffee," I said, and looked over at Ally, who nodded.

"Great," Myrtle said. "I'll be back in a few to let you have a ladies' visit."

She gave us a nod and headed out of the jail, shoulders back and jaw set. I wished I could overhear the conversation between her and Emmaline. I was certain it would be epic.

"What do you think Emmaline is going to do?" Ally asked.

I shrugged and poured us each a cup of coffee. "I have no idea, but I'll bet it's going to be interesting."

"Don't you feel just a tiny bit guilty about Myrtle calling Emmaline?"

"Not even remotely. I learned quickly that Southern mothers trump everything, including law enforcement. No way am I getting in the path of that train."

"You have a point."

We polished off our pie and were each on our second cup of coffee when Myrtle came back into the jail to get us for our potty break. Technically, she was supposed to cuff us if we were leaving the cell before being officially released, but I'd heard her tell Carter that if he wanted us cuffed he'd have to do it himself. Since he hadn't made an appearance, I figured he'd wisely opted out of that path.

We each took our turn in the restroom and were heading back down to the front of the building when we heard the front door alarm sound. A couple seconds later, Emmaline LeBlanc stormed into the hallway wearing pink pajamas with cats on them and a pissed-off look so severe I actually stopped in my tracks. She gave us all a nod but didn't say a word as she pushed past and barreled right into Carter's office.

"Have you lost your mind?" Emmaline's voice carried through the door and down the hall.

"Let's just wait here a minute," Myrtle said and grinned.

"Did Myrtle call you?" Carter asked.

"Doesn't matter who called me," Emmaline said. "What matters is that I raised an idiot and a bully."

"How am I either?"

"You're a bully for putting Ally in jail. You know good and well that girl wouldn't harm a fly. She'd probably have had a nervous breakdown if Fortune hadn't gotten thrown in the clink with her. And you're an idiot for arresting your own girlfriend."

"She wanted to be arrested."

"No. She didn't want Ally to spend the night in jail alone. You're telling me you couldn't have waited until this morning to question Ally? It absolutely had to be last night?"

"Yes. That's exactly what I'm telling you, because that's what the ADA told me. There are people I have to answer to."

"I know. I'm one of them."

Myrtle did a fist pump and Ally covered her mouth with her hand. Emmaline was on a roll.

"You have done some foolish things in your life," Emmaline said, "but this one ranks right at the top. Even higher than when you tied my bras onto a bedsheet and jumped off the roof of the house thinking you were going to parachute and broke your arm."

I choked back a laugh. As soon as I had time and wasn't incarcerated, I needed to spend an evening with Emmaline and a bottle of wine.

"Now you go and throw your girlfriend in jail," Emmaline

continued. "The first woman who's managed to put up with your bull and still want to be around you, and you lock her up like some common criminal. I swear to God, you got all your looks from me, but you got your brains from your father. He could pull some crap, but even he wouldn't have pushed the envelope this far."

"Look," Carter said. "I understand you're upset, and I'm not happy about it either, but I didn't have a choice. This is my job. And if you want me to keep control of this investigation, which is decidedly in Ally's best interest, then I can't go against the ADA's recommendation. If he thinks I'm not up to the job, he can request the state police come in on this. Then it becomes much harder on everyone."

There was silence for a moment and I knew Emmaline was running the possibilities through her mind. She wasn't going to like them, but she was a sharp lady and would understand that while not ideal, what Carter had done was the best option given the situation. Still, I'd enjoyed her telling him off. I figured every hot man needed to be taken down a notch now and then. And in the South, no one did that better than mothers.

Their voices got too low to hear and Myrtle motioned to us to move. We hurried back to the cells before Carter caught us listening in the hallway. Even though he probably figured Myrtle had heard it all. She locked us up and rushed out in the nick of time. Not a minute later, Carter came into the jail, looking exhausted and harried.

"Would either or both of you like to make a phone call?" he asked.

"I would," I said.

Ally shook her head.

Carter opened the cell and waved me out. I followed him in silence to Deputy Breaux's office. He waited as I picked up the phone and dialed, then walked away. I was sorta counting on that. There was no real legal requirement or limit on the whole phone call situation, but I needed to make at least two.

The first one was to Director Morrow, who wasn't even remotely surprised to learn that I'd been thrown in jail my first full day back in Sinful. Or that the man I was in a relationship with was responsible. But he had a good chuckle over my kicking the mirror. He gave me the number I wanted, told me to call if he could do anything else, and then advised me to take it easy on the general population as they weren't accustomed to dealing with someone with my particular skill set.

I thanked him and made the second phone call. I'd never met him or spoken to him directly, but I'd provided evidence for many of his cases. He was retired now, but I had a feeling that if I asked for a favor, he wouldn't hesitate. The fact that he was living in New Orleans also factored in. All it was likely to cost him was a couple hours' driving time.

He answered on the first ring and sounded happy to hear from me. I gave him a brief rundown of the situation, and he told me to tell Ally he was on his way and let Carter know that she had representation. I hung up the phone and headed out of the office, still smiling.

Carter was at the front desk, talking to Myrtle, when I entered the reception area.

"All done?" he asked.

"Yep. Ally's attorney is on his way. He's coming from New Orleans so it shouldn't be long."

He gave me a nod and motioned to Myrtle, who rolled her eyes and headed back with me to the jail.

"I thought you were off the clock," I said.

"He made me clock back in until Deputy Breaux gets here," Myrtle said. "The new guy had a pipe burst in his bathroom and he's waiting on the plumber."

"Carter doesn't look happy," I said.

"He's fit to be tied," Myrtle said. "Been bitching at me for calling Emmaline ever since he closed you up in that office. Threatened to fire me even, until I told him to show me the law that says a sheriff's department employee can't call a deputy's mother when she's off the clock and tell her that her son is a butthead."

I smiled. "I almost feel sorry for him. Almost."

Myrtle waved a hand. "Don't waste your time. Carter's fine and this is just part of the job. If Sheriff Lee ever retires, it's only going to get worse for him, not better, so he might as well figure out how to navigate the locals, the politics, his mother, and you sooner rather than later."

"You forgot Ida Belle and Gertie."

Myrtle laughed. "Oh, there's no navigating that brick wall."

"They might be easier to navigate than me."

Myrtle stopped walking and gave me a hard stare. "I don't doubt that for a minute. One of these days, you and I need to have a chat. I've heard some talk, mostly gossip, but I figure somewhere in there is a grain of truth. I'm betting you're not exactly what people think you are."

"I'm not anything that people think I am."

She smiled. "I predict Sinful is going to lose its collective mind when they find out the truth. If I were a betting woman, I'd put my money on Xena, warrior princess."

"Have I told you how much I like you?"

"Ha! That's the side I plan on staying on."

IT ONLY TOOK Alexander Framingham III an hour and a half to make it to the sheriff's department. Carter opened the jail, looking rather dazed, and motioned to us.

"Your attorney is here," Carter said. "He'd like to speak to both of you at the same time. If that's all right with Ally."

"Of course," Ally said, and I could tell she was relieved that I would be with her.

"Cool!" I said. "Let's get this show on and off the road. I need a shower and a nap in my own bed."

We followed Carter out of the jail and down to the interview room. Alexander was a trim, distinguished fifty-five and looked ten years younger. He wore a custom gray suit and a two-hundred-dollar haircut and looked every bit the old-money, hyperintelligent, hard-nosed federal prosecutor he'd been for ten years. He smiled when he saw me and moved forward to shake my hand.

"It's a real pleasure to finally meet you in person," he said. "I can't tell you how many stories I've told about you at the bar after court. You're a household name in some circles."

"Retired household name these days," I said. "Thank you so much for doing this."

"Are you kidding?" he asked. "I should probably be funding you a beach house somewhere. This isn't even dipping a toe into the debt of gratitude I owe you. I have no idea what kind of nonsense is going on here, but let's get to clearing it up so you can get back to enjoying your retirement. You've certainly earned it."

He shot a disparaging look at Carter as he made the "nonsense" part of his statement. Carter shook his head and headed for the door.

"I'll leave you to it," Carter said as he shut the door behind him.

I turned to Ally. "Ally, this is former federal prosecutor Alexander Framingham III, otherwise known as the Grim Reaper."

Alexander grinned. "I did have a lot of fun with my job." He extended his hand to Ally.

Ally stared at him, eyes wide, and shook his hand. "Federal prosecutor? For real? Do I need that kind of representation?"

"I'm sure you don't," I said, "but why drag it out with a local when I can get the best here and have this all wrapped up this morning? Alexander, this is my good friend Ally Lemarque. As you can see, she's clearly both a threat to the local population and a flight risk."

Alexander nodded. "You know, when you kill someone in these parts, you're supposed to dump the body in the bayou. Less chance of recovery that way. And it's hard to make a case without a body, especially in Louisiana. Lots of reasons to go missing on the water down here and most don't have anything to do with murder."

"I'm going to guess most have to do with stupidity," I said.

"Well, there's that." Alexander motioned to the chairs. "Take a seat and let's go over everything. I know there's not much, and that's a good thing. I'll get up to speed, we'll have a brief chat with the deputy, and you can be on your way."

He looked over at me. "You didn't say why you were in here. Are you a suspect as well?"

"No. I kicked the mirror off the deputy's truck so Ally wouldn't have to spend the night in here alone."

"I like it!" he said. "We can probably get you out of here with Ally as long as you agree to pay for the damage. Do you anticipate any pushback from the deputy?"

"Not if he likes the benefits of his current situation," I said. "We're sorta in a relationship."

Alexander stared at me for a moment, then began to chuckle. "You are everything I hoped for and more. Now let's get this dangerous woman out of here."

Alexander flipped open a pad of paper that already

contained some notes from my phone call, asked some more questions, then proclaimed himself ready to speak with Carter. I volunteered to go get him, as I wouldn't be able to sit in on the official interview, and left Alexander prepping Ally for the chat.

CHAPTER EIGHT

CARTER WAS SITTING in his office, staring out the window, and looking slightly miserable. I rapped lightly on the door. "They're ready for the interview if you are," I said.

Carter looked over at me and shook his head. "You called in a favor to a federal prosecutor. And not just any Fed. The Grim Reaper." He looked slightly peeved but mostly impressed.

"You know Alexander?"

"Everyone who's provided evidence for a federal trial knows Alexander. His reputation kinda precedes him."

"Yeah. He was definitely the best. And I wouldn't have anything less for Ally."

"You know that isn't necessary, right?"

"I know she didn't kill anyone, and I'm certain you do as well. But evidence is evidence, and I don't want someone here making a stink about favoritism and getting you kicked off the job. I also don't want an ADA with a ladder-climbing agenda thinking he can get a quick conviction and push himself up a rung. You following procedure to the letter of the law keeps the first from happening. Alexander is insurance against the second."

He didn't like it. Heck, neither did I. The entire mess stank to high heaven. But he couldn't argue with my logic. My way was the only way to cover all our bases. Even if it pissed off a lot of people.

"Okay," he finally agreed. "But did Myrtle have to call my mother?"

"You'll have to take that up with Myrtle. I don't have any dog in the whole Southern-mother hunt. It's a world I know nothing about and looks more dangerous than Iraq."

His lips quivered just a bit. "That's true. I guess I better get this over with. I assume your attorney is here to address your situation as well?"

"Of course."

"You know, you didn't have to damage my truck."

"Sure I did. It was the only way to be tossed into the clink with legit paperwork. But you don't have to press charges."

He tilted his head to one side. "And what if I decide I want to? You haven't exactly spent the summer making my job easy."

I pulled the stick of dynamite and matches out of my pants and placed them on his desk. "I could have made your job a lot worse last night."

He grabbed the dynamite and stared at it for a couple seconds. "Gertie?"

"Who else? But when she asks, you better tell her you found and confiscated it because that's what I plan on doing. She probably sat up half the night waiting for an explosion."

"I'm sure it's safer in here than in her house."

"Her purse. She usually carries some in her purse. It's why Ida Belle and I don't allow her around anything likely to create a spark."

He gave me a pained look. "Maybe we should just make a pact that when it comes to Ida Belle and Gertie, I don't ask things that might lead to answers I need to do something about in a law enforcement capacity. And you don't offer me any information in that regard."

"And when you're too nosy to skip the questioning?"

"Lie."

I stared. "You're telling me to lie to you."

"I'm begging you to, actually. It might be the only way this relationship has a chance."

I shrugged. "It's a little hard to take you seriously on that one, so I'm just going to chalk it up to lack of sleep talking."

He sighed. "Does that mean you're not going to lie?"

"Who, me?" I smiled.

He rose from his desk and was still shaking his head when he left the office. Figuring I had some time to kill, I headed into the break room and brewed a pot of coffee. I was just having my first cup when I heard Gertie raising hell at the front desk. I walked down the hall and saw Deputy Breaux looking extremely uncomfortable as he attempted to explain why Gertie and Ida Belle could not "just visit" me in jail.

"It's cool," I said, and Deputy Breaux whipped around, eyes wide. I had a moment of panic when he made a move for his gun, but then he changed his mind and went for the handcuffs.

"Relax," I said. "Carter let us out. Our attorney is here. He's taking care of Ally's interview first, then we'll settle up after."

Deputy Breaux didn't look convinced. "If I let you get away, Carter will kill me."

"First off, I'm not going anywhere. Second, trust me, Carter would not hold you responsible if I got away. He'd be far more surprised if you managed to keep me somewhere I didn't want to be. We're going to move this party to the break room and wait for Carter to finish up with Ally. If you need us, we'll be just down the hall."

I motioned to Ida Belle and Gertie and we headed off, leaving Deputy Breaux standing there staring after us. At least he knew when he'd been completely and utterly defeated. And he didn't even know about the whole CIA thing yet. Wait until he found that out. He'd probably cross the street when he saw me coming.

"For a minute," Ida Belle said, "I thought he was going to shoot you."

"He could have tried," I said as Ida Belle and I sat at the break room table.

Gertie laughed and poured her and Ida Belle a cup of coffee before taking a seat. "Would have been funny to see, but probably not a great outcome for our young deputy."

"I'm really trying to start off on the right foot here," I said. "I've already assaulted a vehicle being used in the commission of police business. I'd prefer not to assault an actual law enforcement officer."

Gertie grinned. "Not according to Myrtle. She said you threatened to kick something pertinent if Carter didn't lock you up with Ally."

"Yeah, well, that was different. It was Ally."

Ida Belle gave me an approving nod. "Some people bring out the mama bear in us. Who's the attorney you brought in?"

"A former federal prosecutor," I said. "Retired now, but happy to do me a favor. I've provided, uh, evidence for him a time or two."

"Is he any good?" Gertie asked.

"His nickname was the Grim Reaper."

"Nice," Gertie said. "At least that technicality is covered. You'll both be released."

"But not off the hook," Ida Belle said.

Gertie waved a hand in dismissal. "No one believes Ally killed Hooch."

"You might be surprised," Ida Belle said. "And even if there's not enough evidence to pursue a case against Ally, until the killer is caught, she has that black cloud following her around. Look how people treated Marie all those years."

Marie was one of Ida Belle and Gertie's closest friends and had long been suspected of killing her missing husband. My first day in Sinful, the dog Sandy-Sue had inherited uncovered one of his bones in my backyard, which was how I'd gotten involved with Ida Belle and Gertie.

"And Ally's trying to start her own business," I said. "She can't afford to have a 'might be a killer' tag following her around. Especially when it was poisoned food that killed him."

Gertie frowned. "When you put it that way, I can see where it might be a problem."

"No might about it," Ida Belle said. "If the real killer isn't caught and convicted, Ally will have to leave Sinful if she ever has a hope of opening a business."

I felt my back tighten at Ida Belle's words. I'd only been in Sinful a couple months when I was faced with the possibility of leaving, maybe forever. It had made me sick to my stomach. I couldn't imagine what it would do to Ally, who'd lived here practically her entire life.

"We're not going to let that happen," I said.

Gertie clapped her hands. "A new case!"

———

ALEXANDER WRAPPED up things with Carter quickly and an hour later, Ally and I were on our way out the door, ready for a hot shower and a soft bed. Unfortunately, a welcoming committee awaited us outside at Ida Belle's SUV with Public Enemy Number One, Celia Arceneaux, leading the charge.

She stood, hands on hips, in front of her pack of foolish followers, wearing a yellow dress with bright blue horizontal stripes and the most ridiculous floppy yellow hat I'd ever seen. It was the size of a sombrero and had pink daisies glued around it. The entire outfit was capped off with black-and-white tennis shoes. Fashion certainly wasn't my thing, but I had to wonder if Celia even owned a mirror.

Deputy Breaux had escorted us out of the sheriff's department, but he took one look at Celia and her mob of angry Catholic women and dashed back inside, probably to yell for Carter. I couldn't really blame him. If Celia didn't force me to interact with her, I'd pawn her off on someone else too.

I stepped in front of the angry mob. "What now?"

Celia stiffened and glared at me. "Like you don't know. Ever since you came to town, there's been nothing but trouble here."

"Not on my accord," I said. "You people managed to build this Peyton Place long before I showed up."

A blush swept up Celia's face. "Well, my niece wasn't part of any nonsense until she took pity on you and became your friend. I hope you're back here to sign off on a sale of that house. This town has put up with your Yankee crap for far too long."

Ally stepped forward and I could tell she was exhausted but ready to tear into her aunt. Given how she'd spent the last twelve hours, my money was on Ally. But despite the fact that Celia was a huge bitch, she was still Ally's aunt, and I didn't need her causing a fray with family over me. Especially over me. I was more than qualified to stand up for myself.

So I placed a hand on her shoulder and shook my head. She

must have understood what I was about to do, because she simply smiled and waved a hand as if directing me to proceed.

"Wait a minute!" Gertie shouted. "I want to record this."

"Good," Celia said. "Then I can use it as evidence if this hussy puts her hands on me."

"If Fortune put her hands on you for real," Ida Belle said, "you wouldn't be alive to subpoena that video."

Celia shot Ida Belle a look that said, 'try me.' Ida Belle gave me a thumbs-up. I will admit that I had a split second of temptation, but it passed. I wasn't really into fights that weren't a challenge, and Celia would be even less of a challenge than Carter's truck mirror.

"As it happens," I said, "I don't have to put my hands on you to do harm. Talking will be enough. You're absolutely right that I'm back in town to sign off on the sale of the house. But I'm the buyer, not the seller. You see, I'm not Sandy-Sue Morrow. The real Sandy-Sue is back in Yankee land, handing out books to kids, and she was more than happy to sell me all of Marge's property."

A hush fell over the crowd as they stared at me, their looks a mixture of confusion and disbelief. Except for Celia. She wore a look of triumphant self-righteousness.

"I knew you were a fraud!" Celia shouted. "Does Sandy-Sue know you impersonated her and smeared her good name? Is she aware of all the trouble you've caused and the harm you've done to her family's reputation?"

"Sandy-Sue knew about me from the beginning and spent a lovely all-expenses-paid summer in Europe in exchange for letting me take her place here."

"Why would she do that?" asked Dorothy, Celia's cousin and number-one yes-woman.

I glanced over at Ida Belle and Gertie, who were both grinning. This was the moment they'd been waiting for. I looked at Ally, who mouthed "do it."

I turned back to Celia and Dorothy. "She did it as a favor to her uncle, who was also my boss. I needed a place to lie low and he thought Sinful would be perfect."

"I knew it," Celia said, looking smug. "You're a criminal. Only criminals need to hide."

"Not just criminals," I said. "My name is Fortune Redding. Former CIA agent, Fortune Redding."

CHAPTER NINE

CELIA STARED at me for a couple seconds, then let out a single guffaw. "Like anyone would believe that. I don't know what you're trying to pull now, but you're not going to get away with it."

"Oh, for Christ's sake," Ally said, "she's not trying to pull anything. She's telling you the truth. A bad guy was after her, she was hiding here, that's all over and now she's resigned from the CIA and plans to live in Sinful. Are we all caught up?"

Celia gave Ally a disapproving look. "I promised your mother I'd look after you, but it's impossible to keep you on the straight and narrow."

"Unlike your own daughter, right?" Ally asked.

Celia gasped. Her daughter Pansy had been a first-class blackmailer and an even bigger floozy and had ended up murdered over her chosen profession. After her murder, all sorts of sordid information about Pansy had surfaced, much to Celia's dismay. I had to give Ally credit—she'd hit Celia low and hard.

But instead of Celia striking back at Ally, she turned her ire to me, which I kinda expected.

"This is all your fault," Celia said. "You've corrupted my niece and ruined this town with your lies, and I won't stand for it another minute." She took a step closer to me and poked me in the chest with her finger. "You need to leave now. I don't know who you are or what kind of scam you're running, but it's over. This is my last warning."

Somehow I knew it was going to come to this—my having to offer up evidence before some believed what I was saying. But since I'd run out of my house without my ID and then been arrested, I didn't have anything to prove who I was and where I was once employed. So I did the next best thing.

I took one step back, then leaped straight up in the air and executed a perfect flare kick, knocking Celia's ridiculous hat right off her head. I caught the hat on my way down, then landed with my right hand less than an inch from Celia's temple.

Everyone surrounding Celia took a step back, and I heard a gasp from behind me as Deputy Breaux ran forward. Celia's face paled and her hands shook as I handed her the hat.

"Any other questions?" I asked.

"This woman assaulted me," Celia told Deputy Breaux. "I want her arrested."

Deputy Breaux had been staring at me in disbelief ever since he'd slid to a stop next to me. He looked back and forth between Celia and me, and it was clear Celia was about to come out on the losing end of the deputy's threat assessment.

"I saw you touch her first," Deputy Breaux said to Celia. He turned to me. "Would you like to press charges against Ms. Arceneaux?"

"Not unless it's a crime to wear that hat," I said.

"Only on Labor Day," Gertie said.

"No one is going to be arrested." Carter's voice sounded behind me. "I would have preferred this information circulate through church and texts, like regular gossip, but since Ms. Redding has seen fit to make a public announcement, I'm going to vouch for her words and her credentials. If anyone would like to verify her status, you can contact CIA Director Morrow. Given the unusual circumstances created by Fortune's stay here and her decision to remain after resigning from her position with the CIA, he's expecting phone calls. I have a number available for Director Morrow for anyone who thinks I'm also a liar."

The crowd's looks of surprise shifted into shock with a hint of fear. Good. I had them right where I wanted them.

"Anyone else got a hat they'd like me to kick?" I asked. "I can do this all day."

"I don't think that will be necessary," Carter said. "Now, unless you all want to be arrested for causing a public disturbance, I suggest you go about your business and let our newest resident go about hers." He looked at Celia. "You might as well start getting used to the idea, because reality is not going to change."

"We'll just see about that," Celia said, then whirled around and stomped away. Dorothy gave me one last lingering look, then hurried after Celia.

"Show's over!" Carter yelled.

The crowd of women all gave me one last suspicious look, and Deputy Breaux took a step back when I turned around.

"I could have handled it," I said.

"Yeah," Carter said. "I see how you were handling it. I didn't want to have to bother the paramedics."

I shrugged. "Some people need more than words."

"Ha!" Gertie said. "Celia needs therapy."

"Celia needs an exorcism," Ida Belle corrected.

I looked at Carter. "Would you like to arrest me for assaulting her hat?"

Carter sighed. "Just go home. And try not to offend anyone between here and there."

"Impossible," I said. "My presence alone offends some of the good citizens of Sinful."

"Fine, then don't touch any of them or their hats on the way home." Carter turned around and headed back into the sheriff's department.

Deputy Breaux looked at me as if he wanted to say something but was slightly afraid. Finally, curiosity won out. "Was that the truth?" he asked. "You were really a CIA agent?"

I nodded and his eyes widened.

"Like James Bond and stuff?" he asked, showing a bit of excitement.

"Well, that's a different country, but it's the same idea."

"That's so awesome. I mean, you're like a superhero or something."

"Or something," I agreed. I was sorta liking all the superhero references.

He nodded. "Do you think you could teach me some stuff? I mean, that kick you did with the hat was just like Bruce Lee. If I knew a move like that, it would help me with my job."

"You gonna use that move on some poachers?" Gertie asked. "Or just unruly old women with funny hats?"

Deputy Breaux frowned. "No. I would never kick a lady, not even in her hat."

"Celia is not a lady," Gertie said.

"But she's a woman," Deputy Breaux said.

"Or a demon," Gertie grumbled.

"Anyway," Deputy Breaux said, "I was thinking more about the drunks at the Swamp Bar. We mostly stay out of things down there, but if we get a call, we can't ignore it. And the crowd there is a bit unruly."

"The crowd there is a bunch of redneck thugs," Ida Belle

said. "But I think kicking off their hats might set you up for bigger problems."

"I don't mean kicking hats, specifically," Deputy Breaux explained. "I just meant if Fortune taught me some of those martial arts moves, it might help me when I'm trying to get someone drunk under control."

Given that I'd seen the deputy dancing at a local celebration, I had serious doubts about his balance and coordination, and he'd been completely sober at the time. But I could appreciate his desire to improve himself in order to do a better job, so I did something I never would have done before now. I took pity on him.

"It takes a really long time to get good enough to do things like what you just saw," I said. "I've been training since I was three years old. But if you're serious about learning, I could work with you a couple hours a week."

"Really?" Deputy Breaux's voice went up several octaves. "You'll do it?"

"Yes, but I don't make any promises. I'll show you the basics, but you have to practice—a lot—or I can't ever show you anything advanced."

He nodded, his head bouncing up and down like a five-year-old who'd just promised to clean his room for a trip to Disney. "I'll practice every day. And every night. I'll be just like that American dude who kicks butt."

"Jack Reacher?" Gertie asked.

Deputy Breaux frowned. "No. Chuck Norris. Who's Jack Reacher?"

Gertie sighed and shook her head. "No one. Chuck Norris is probably a better fit for Sinful anyway."

"Sure he is," Deputy Breaux said. "I've seen every movie and television show he's ever been in. He's the baddest of the bad. I mean, except John Wayne, but since he's dead, then

Chuck Norris is the man."

I was pretty sure I could take Chuck Norris one-handed and wearing a dress, but I let it slide. "Great. Let me know when your next day off is and we'll get started. We'll need to do this outside. Given that I don't like to do intense workouts in the morning and it's hot as heck, that means late evening. We can work in my backyard under the big oak tree. I can hose us down periodically so we don't pass out."

"That sounds awesome!" Deputy Breaux said. "I can't wait. This is going to be so cool. Thank you!"

He hurried off, practically skipping, and we stared after him, Ida Belle shaking her head.

"That man is going to hurt himself with the training alone," she said.

"Probably," I said.

"Maybe you could give me lessons too," Gertie said.

"Ha!" Ida Belle said. "She's not crazy enough to take you on. Besides, if her insurance company found out she was teaching martial arts to women who walked the earth before the wheel was invented, they'd cancel her homeowner's policy."

Ally laughed, then sobered. "I'm sorry about Aunt Celia. God, I feel like I should just have that printed on cards and carry them around with me."

"You are not responsible for what your aunt does," Ida Belle said, "although I can appreciate the horror of being related to her. It's one of the many reasons I'm thrilled I was an only child and my parents never associated with extended family. I don't have to suffer fools simply because we share a bloodline."

I shook my head. "I can't see you suffering fools even if they gave birth to you."

"I suppose that's true enough," Ida Belle agreed.

"Still," Ally said. "She's not going to give up, even if she can be convinced that you're telling the truth. She's fixated on you in a way I've never seen before."

"It's because of everything that got exposed this summer," Gertie said. "Celia can't handle knowing she married a louse and raised a floozy criminal. She needs someone to blame in order to live with herself."

Ally nodded. "And that someone is you, Fortune. I don't think she can manage to do something to cause real trouble for you, but I have no doubt she'll keep trying."

"Maybe we should start a GoFundMe to get her to leave Sinful," Gertie said. "I bet we'd raise a pile of money."

"There's actually some merit to that idea," Ida Belle said.

"I thought shooting her would be easier," I said.

They all looked at me for a moment, and I could tell Ally wasn't completely convinced I was joking. Even more troubling, she looked slightly hopeful.

"The woman isn't worth wasting a bullet on," Gertie said, "much less the death penalty."

"There is that," I agreed. "Well, hopefully the drama will be over long enough for Ally and me to get a hot shower and a nap."

Ida Belle looked over at me and gave me a slight nod. She knew I wanted to get Ally safely in her own home before we tackled the problem ourselves. The hot shower wouldn't wait, but the nap was going to have to.

We piled into Ida Belle's SUV and dropped Ally off at her house. She gave me a hug before getting out, thanking me again for everything I'd done. She promised to try to get some sleep before returning Francine's phone. Then we headed to my house, where Gertie volunteered to whip up some leftovers she'd brought for lunch while I jumped in the shower.

The entire time I was showering and dressing, I couldn't

stop thinking about what might have happened. But the problem was I knew next to nothing about Hooch, so all my theories were the complete and utter fictional kind. Of course, this was Sinful, so a couple of them might not be completely off the mark. Except maybe the UFO one, although I had to confess that of all the things I'd come up with, that was the one I'd like to see the most. If it was going to happen anywhere, I was betting it would be here.

By the time I got back downstairs, Gertie had sandwiches, chips, and beer on the table and we were ready to eat and hash out this whole fiasco. I took a bite of my sandwich, thanked Gertie for her ability to put together an excellent meal in a short amount of time and with little to work with, then looked at them both.

"Tell me what you know," I said. "Your phones had to be buzzing all night with rumor and speculation. I assume you've separated what people know from what they think they know?"

Ida Belle glanced at Gertie, then back at me, and nodded. "We've had a lot of calls and we've discussed the offerings at length, but I'm afraid we are in agreement that no one knows anything."

"How is that possible?" I asked. "This is Sinful and you are the hub of all information. You have earlier and better access than the local newspaper and the sheriff's department."

"I know," Ida Belle said. "That's why it's so troubling. Usually a theory emerges that takes hold and is more workable than anything else, but in this case, all the theories are the same and none of them point to any individual over another."

I sighed. "So everyone is on the 'he screwed someone over' bandwagon, and that list is long."

Gertie nodded. "Longer than we thought. We took down twelve names that we have on good authority lost a minimum of a couple thousand to Hooch over shoddy or incomplete work. But it's hard to imagine anyone going this far over that amount of money."

"It's hard for her to imagine," Ida Belle said. "People have killed over less in the past and will continue to in the future."

"But this isn't some street robbery in New Orleans," Gertie argued. "This is Sinful, and this murder was carefully planned. We know everyone on this list. If you can show me even one of them who you think was that angry and that clever, then go for it."

Ida Belle shook her head. "Unfortunately, she has a point on that one. I know we never really know someone, but I'm having trouble casting anyone on that list as the bad guy."

"Okay," I said. "So cover them all with me. I probably don't know some of them and those I do, not very well, so I come into this with few preconceived notions about the suspects."

Ida Belle pulled out her phone and accessed her notes. "Gertie and I did a quick-and-dirty check this morning and I think we can eliminate six of the people on the list. One is confined to a wheelchair, two work petroleum and are offshore, and two are a husband and wife who are on vacation."

"That's five," I said.

"Ally is on the list," Ida Belle said. "I wanted to be accurate."

"Of course," I said. "Okay, that's good. Cuts it in half anyway."

"Assuming it's even someone on that list," Gertie said.

"We have to start somewhere," I said. "What's the worst that can happen? We eliminate six more Sinful residents from the pool?"

Gertie nodded. "I guess that's true. This detective work seems sorta slow though."

"We can't always run around blowing up things and getting shot at," Ida Belle said.

"I guess not," Gertie said wistfully.

Ida Belle looked at me and shook her head. "Anyway, first up on the list is interesting, but unfortunately, I don't think she's our perp. It's Celia."

I perked up. "Celia? I guess it's not surprising that she would get taken by Hooch given her awful taste in men. But I have to agree with you that she's an unlikely candidate for first-degree murder."

"Unless she plotted to hold those big panties of hers over your face," Gertie said.

Ida Belle grinned. "I'm pretty sure Myrtle's cousin would have noticed a big pair of panties over Hooch's head. And as much as I'd love to cast Celia as the bad guy, I don't see it. I know she's a complete horror but even if I bought her being able to plot and carry out a murder, I still don't think she's awful enough to do it in a way that would put Ally in the hot seat."

Gertie nodded. "She's probably trying to salvage what's left of her family's reputation. A lost cause, if you ask me. Ally is the only one who was ever worth a hoot."

"So one more eliminated," I said. "Who are the rest?"

"Pastor Don, Francine, Dixie, Ricky Marks, and your buddy Ronald."

I clasped my hands together and looked upward. "Please, God, let it be Ronald."

Ronald Franklin was my next-door neighbor and all-around kook. We had a love-hate relationship—he loved to hate me. Most recently we'd had a run-in over Godzilla, who chased Ronald up a tree in my backyard and caused him to ruin his shoes. His red high-heeled pumps. A Confederate soldier's uniform had completed his outfit.

"I definitely don't put Ronald in the clever enough category," Gertie said.

"True," I said, "but a girl can still dream. Okay, so Pastor Don is probably not a good fit. I think he's clever enough and hey, I'm not foolish enough to discount someone as a murderer simply because he's a religious leader, but I just don't see it."

"I don't either," Ida Belle said. "But until we have an alibi, he remains on the list of possibilities. I think we should approach this the same way the police do. So essentially, everyone is a suspect until eliminated. But I agree we shouldn't waste much time looking into him."

"Or Francine," I said. "I know, opportunity and all, and as soon as Carter hears she got shafted by Hooch, I have no doubt she'll be in the hot seat for questioning just like Ally. But I'm still not putting her up for this, even with motive and opportunity."

"But the ADA might," Gertie said.

"If it comes down to that, I'll get my lawyer friend on the job," I said. "At least we know the legal end of things is covered."

Ida Belle nodded. "It's really good that you have someone like that on your side. Given our past exploits and future plans, he might come in handy."

I was hoping not, but I was also a realist. "Who is Ricky Marks?" I asked. "I don't think I've ever heard that name before."

"No one knows much about him," Ida Belle said. "He's a roughneck and fairly new to town. Rents an old farmhouse some ways out in the sticks. Walter probably sees him more than anyone. He comes in every week or two to stock up on groceries."

"Why is he on the list?" I asked.

"Because one of the Sinful Ladies tried to pump him for

information in town one day," Ida Belle said. "She claimed he refused to look her in the eye and seemed ready to bolt over the most basic of inquiry."

"Basically," Gertie said, "she thinks he's hiding something. And let's face it, he probably is. But that doesn't mean it's anything about Hooch."

"He's an unknown subject," I said, "so we'll look into it. We should talk to Walter and see what else he can tell us. But I don't see him being much of a suspect given that he's new and renting. He wouldn't have hired Hooch for anything."

"I wouldn't think so," Ida Belle agreed. "But Hooch likes to gamble. Locals know better than to play with him. He cheats."

"Naturally," I said.

"But a new guy in town might have gotten taken over a card game or something," Ida Belle said. "It's a long shot, I know, but we don't have many suspects so I figured might as well keep him on the list."

"Overall, this collection of names isn't all that promising," I said. "But we'll alibi them anyway. More importantly, I think we need to expand our search. Did Hooch own anything of value? And if so, who gets it?"

Ida Belle nodded. "Money is a prime motivator but in Hooch's case, I'm not sure that angle works. He sold his house in town after his wife left and moved to his camp. I figure he's already drunk away the money from the sale of the house. The camp is not any more impressive than any other camp you've been in, so I can't fathom it being worth killing over. But then, I've been surprised and dismayed by people before and probably will be again."

"And who inherits?" I asked.

Ida Belle shrugged. "Unless Hooch left a will, which I would find surprising, I assume his son."

"Anyone seen the son or ex-wife recently?" I asked.

"I haven't seen either since they left town," Gertie said. "I'm not sure anyone has. At least, not in Sinful. It wasn't exactly an amicable parting."

"Given what I know about Hooch," I said, "I can't imagine it was an amicable coupling."

"That's true enough," Gertie said. "Most people never understood why Margarita took up with Hooch. But if you paid attention, it wasn't that hard to figure out."

I stared. "Margarita?"

Gertie nodded. "Her mother's favorite drink. Her father leaned more toward straight whiskey or rotgut moonshine. I don't think it was an easy household to live in, even though her parents kept their drinking problems pretty much on the down-low. But a teacher notices things, and long sleeves in the summer in Louisiana isn't a common thing."

"You think her father beat them," I said.

"That's the general consensus of the observant," Ida Belle said.

"So why didn't anyone do anything about it?" I asked.

"Didn't have time to," Gertie said. "Margarita's family moved to the area her senior year of high school. She turned eighteen during the school year and before any signs of the abuse came out. I contacted social services once I suspected what was happening, but they wouldn't send a case worker for an adult unless they were incapacitated physically or mentally."

"She hooked up with Hooch during her senior year and married him right after graduation," Ida Belle said. "Her father worked oil field construction, and they moved that summer when the job moved again."

"So Margarita jumped on the first opportunity to get out of her parents' house," I said.

Ida Belle nodded. "She was a shy girl and average-looking. Choices of males in Sinful are limited to begin with but if you're not a cheerleader, you're unlikely to snag the best of the lot. Hooch was older by a couple years and worked a regular job at the time. His parents had retired early and moved to Mexico. They transferred their house over to him and he had a small note on it."

"So from Margarita's standpoint, Hooch looked like a catch." I shook my head. "That is a depressing commentary on the state of dating in Sinful."

"Tell me about it," Gertie said. "You and Ida Belle have the only decent available men locked up."

"Technically," I said, "Carter had me locked up."

They both laughed.

"Touché," Gertie said.

"I don't have anyone locked up," Ida Belle protested.

Gertie waved a hand in dismissal. "Please. Walter will go to the grave pining after you. No matter how many times you turn him down."

"That's his choice," Ida Belle said, "and none of my doing."

"All talk of eligible bachelors aside," I said, "does anyone know how to get in touch with Hooch's son?"

Gertie looked at Ida Belle and they both shook their heads. "Not that I know of," Ida Belle said. "I can ask my ladies, but I think if anyone knew they would have already mentioned it."

"Won't Carter have to do that?" Gertie asked.

"Of course," I said, "but Carter won't give us any information on Hooch's ex or his son. And I think we should do some checking around, just in case they're in dire need of the paltry funds an old camp would bring. Or in case Hooch is one of those crazy millionaires with money in his mattress. But we need something to go on—a city of residence for starters."

Gertie waved her hand at my laptop. "You're good with the Google thing. Maybe you can find them online."

"I'll definitely try," I said. "Give me the names."

"Margarita Livingston was her maiden name," Gertie said. "Never knew of a middle name. Their son is Boone Carre Jr."

"Is it safe to assume Hooch is Boone Sr.?" I asked.

"It's probably never safe to assume much in Sinful," Ida Belle said, "but in this case that is correct."

I nodded. "Then I'll do some digging and see what I can come up with. You guys check your sources and see if anyone knows what Margarita and Junior have been up to since they left town."

"Sounds like a plan," Gertie said. "But we don't have to start on it right away, do we? I mean, Ally's out of jail and Carter's not likely to put her back in, and as long as you don't go kicking his truck then you're in the clear..."

Ida Belle narrowed her eyes. "What are you up to, old woman?"

"I'm not old," Gertie said. "I'm just in my third act."

"You're in the twentieth release of a bad horror franchise."

I laughed, then began to worry that maybe Ida Belle was onto something. "What *are* you up to?" I asked Gertie.

"I'm not up to anything," Gertie said. "I just might have booked us for some fun this afternoon—before I knew we were going to have a murder and overnight jail stays and all."

Ida Belle shot me a look and I could tell she was as nervous as I was. Gertie's definition of fun could be anything from pedicures to a raft trip down the Amazon.

"What kind of fun?" I asked.

Gertie squirmed a bit in her chair. "Skydiving."

CHAPTER TEN

"HAVE YOU LOST YOUR MIND?" Ida Belle threw her hands in the air. "It's official. You have a death wish."

"I don't want to die skydiving," Gertie said. "Hurtling toward the ground at breakneck speed is still far too long to reflect on all the things I didn't get to do. When I go, I want to get struck by lightning. Something really fast and with no time to work in regrets."

"'Breakneck' is the operative word here," Ida Belle said.

Gertie rolled her eyes. "It's not like we've never done it before."

"That was in Vietnam, and there wasn't much choice as we couldn't exactly land in enemy territory and offer them coffee. That was also so long ago our parachutes were probably made from dinosaur hides. You are not twenty years old anymore, regardless of what those silly affirmation quotes you read tell you."

I'd listened to the entire exchange in silence, mostly because Ida Belle had made all the same points I would have, except for the not-diving-since-Vietnam part. I hadn't known they'd partaken in that sort of thing back then. It was yet another interesting fact about two women I knew better than anyone else on the planet, but also proved that I hadn't scratched the surface in getting to know them and all their escapades. One of these nights, when we didn't have a murder to solve, we were going to have to break out a twelve-pack and trade war stories.

"Speaking for myself," I said, "I'm not interested in making a jump. I've done it a million times already, so the thrill's not really there, especially given that it's unlikely anyone will be shooting at us while we drop."

"It *is* Sinful," Gertie said. "There's always the possibility that someone will make it more interesting. All this heat and a round of beer can make for peculiar behavior."

"You mean like naked boating?" I asked.

One of the locals was known for her lack of boating attire. Unfortunately, she didn't have the kind of build that people wanted to see naked, assuming you wanted to see someone naked and boating in the first place.

Ida Belle gave her an alarmed look. "You weren't planning on skydiving in the buff, were you?"

"Of course not!" Gertie said.

Ida Belle narrowed her eyes. "So what exactly were you planning on wearing?"

"Clothes, just like any normal person," Gertie said, but I noticed she didn't meet Ida Belle's gaze when she said it.

We had the option, of course, to let Gertie set off on her falling-to-the-earth mission on her own, but that just wasn't the way we rolled. And I knew, without a doubt, that nothing was going to keep her from doing what she'd set out to do. So we could either be there to mitigate damages on the spot or we could clean it up later. Either way, it was bound to get messy and I would ultimately be involved.

"What time do we leave?" I asked.

Ida Belle shot me a look of dismay but I could tell she'd come to the same conclusion I had. Gertie clapped her hands and bounced up and down in her chair, entirely too excited about doing something that could result in serious injury or even death.

"So help me God," Ida Belle said, "if you have a heart attack on the way down, I'm going to let Celia sing at your funeral."

"Celia's not allowed in the Baptist church," Gertie said smugly.

I looked at the two of them. "Should I even ask?"

"There was this issue a couple years ago with her running over Pastor Don with her car," Ida Belle said. "She claims that she was looking for something in her purse and didn't see him, but it was the day after he'd taken his turn at a revival that most everyone in Sinful had attended, and everyone knew Celia had taken issue with the content of his sermon."

"Pride? Hate? Having a daughter who was a blackmailing slut?" I asked.

Gertie grinned. "Worse. Gluttony."

"Well, good grief, everyone who's eaten a meal at Francine's is guilty of gluttony," I said. "I have no idea how people live in this state and aren't guilty of gluttony. Before I had to go get arrested last night, I ordered a treadmill because it's too darned hot to run and my pants are getting tight."

"A little tightness isn't a big deal," Gertie said.

"My *yoga* pants," I said.

It was one thing for a pair of jeans to get a little snug. It was completely another when your elastic-waist cotton pants started to dig a little. No way was I going to become that agent who retired and ballooned up, but the food around here was nothing to scoff at. It was a natural enemy of the fit and those wanting to avoid clogged arteries.

"Anyway," Ida Belle continued, "Pastor Don convinced a judge that it was intentional based on Celia's ranting at the revival the day before—all of which was caught on phone video—and the judge agreed and issued a restraining order."

"So Celia can't go in the Baptist church," Gertie said. "Not for another year, anyway."

"Which means if you die sometime after the next year," Ida Belle said, "you run the risk of having Celia sing at your funeral, assuming you die from something stupid."

"Everything people die from is stupid," Gertie argued.

"Yes, but not necessarily of their own making," Ida Belle pointed out.

I put my hand up. "Stop. No one is dying. Not on my watch. It's sort of a general rule of mine, and if I managed to pull it off in the Middle East, then I'm pretty sure I can manage one little skydive in Sinful, Louisiana."

I didn't say I was certain.

I was pretty sure Ida Belle noticed.

———

THE ADVENTURE GERTIE had booked consisted of a private airstrip and a prop plane that was built before I was born. The Cajun running the Bayou Bombers show greeted us chewing on a toothpick when we pulled up.

Midforties. Six foot even. Two hundred twenty pounds. Bad knees. Too many jumps or bad parachute packing.

I asked to review the maintenance logs and the liability insurance before I would even consider boarding. Then I insisted that Bomber Bruce, as he'd asked to be called, pack a parachute for me so that I could ensure he was doing it properly. When I requested the logs, I saw the shift in Bruce's expression and figured he was about to tell me to take a jump, just not from his plane. So I flashed my CIA credentials, and he narrowed his eyes.

"You're that broad who attacked Celia Arceneaux with her hat," he said.

I sighed. If that was what the locals were calling an attack, I was in trouble. "Guilty," I said.

He grinned. "I can't stand that hypocritical bitch. Heck, you guys can jump for free. Any time you want. Just give me a holler."

Gertie hooted and bounced up and down. Ida Belle gave him a look that should have disintegrated him into dust on the spot. Once I pronounced everything aboveboard, we were ready to get on with the jump. Ida Belle seemed willing to go along with my judgment on the matter. Or she'd stopped caring if anyone died on the way down, including herself. Jury was still out.

Bruce loaded the packs into the plane, then took out some spare ones and began the teaching part of the course. "Have any of you jumped before?" he asked.

We all nodded.

"Where did you do your jumps?" he asked. "I want to make sure you didn't pick up any bad habits from my competition."

I started to point out that any habits picked up from the competition couldn't be too bad or we wouldn't be standing here, but irony wasn't overly popular in Sinful. Or easily recognized. Sarcasm often missed the mark as well.

"I did my jumping with the CIA, mostly into the Middle East," I said.

He raised his eyebrows. "That's hard-core. I was a Navy pilot, but we didn't see too much drop time unless your plane went down. You could probably teach me a thing or two."

"Well, I've only jumped from one plane going down, so

that probably works both ways. Hopefully it won't be something we need to tap into today."

Ida Belle shot me a what-the-heck look. Bruce just laughed. "My insurance company frowns on me crashing planes, especially with customers in them," he said.

"There you go," I said to Ida Belle and Gertie. "He has to bring us back alive or there's a problem with his insurance."

"Got that right," he said, and turned to Ida Belle and Gertie. "What about you ladies? You been jumping with that outfit over in Mudbug?"

"No," Ida Belle said. "We did our jumping with the military in Vietnam."

His eyes widened. "No shit? Well, hell, I got a whole lot of professionals here today. This is going to be a piece of cake. The gear probably looks a little different from when you two did your jumping, but the concept is still the same."

He covered how to deploy the chute and access the reserve in case things went sideways. Then he showed the toggles and explained how to use them to direct the chute as needed.

"Where will we be landing?" I asked. The size and terrain of the landing spot was a much larger component of an easy landing than knowing how to direct the chute.

"Right out there in the field. Got ten mowed acres, all flat. Worse thing that could happen out there is you roll in some fire ants, but I got a water hose here and some lotion that fixes that right up."

I looked out at the expanse of field and nodded. Unless those ants could open fire, this was probably going to be the easiest jump I'd ever made.

And that scared me. A lot.

This was Sinful. I'd attempted to cover all my bases. Everything appeared to be sound and all potential issues minimalized. But I couldn't stop thinking that I'd missed something. And in Sinful, there was always something.

"So, you ready to fly?" he asked. "I take you on a bit of a tour around the area first...to get your money's worth and all. And people seem to like seeing the area from the sky. Things look different up here. Prettier, actually."

I nodded. That was one thing Bruce and I agreed on. Even the ugliest of areas could look interesting from the air. We all climbed in the plane and Bruce pointed at the benches we'd be sitting on.

"When we get to the drop point," he said. "I'll call back and let you know to stage. Gertie, you'll go first, then Ida Belle, then Fortune. Just leave a second or two between you. The air will do the rest. Watch your altitude and pull your chute when you reach 2,500 feet. There's some occasional gusts of wind, but nothing that should set you outside the field."

I looked at the wind sock at the edge of the hangar. It was currently flopped down without so much as a ruffle. I hoped it stayed that way. At least until we got on the ground, then a breeze might be a pleasant change in this heat.

"Go ahead and suit up," Bruce said, "and I'll get the plane fired up and ready to go. When you get your chute on, just take your seat. Gertie next to the drop door. Fortune across from her. Ida Belle, next to Gertie. That will put two of us per side which will keep the weight balanced out."

I had a moment of pause when he got to the part about Gertie being nearest the door, but there was a half wall there and a rail running from the half wall to the top of the plane. No way could she accidentally fall out. And if she got tossed out of her seat, around the barrier and out the door, then we had way bigger problems, and being out of the plane was probably safer than being in it.

Bruce moved to the cockpit and started up the engines. Ida Belle and I reached for our packs and started putting them on. She turned around to hand Gertie her pack and groaned. I looked over and saw Gertie standing there, hands on hips and grinning like an idiot. But that wasn't what had made Ida Belle groan. Her reaction was all about Gertie's outfit, which was not the pair of slacks and pink blouse she'd been wearing when we boarded the plane.

No. The perfectly good outfit had been shed and Gertie stood before us now decked out in a Wonder Woman costume.

"How do I look?" Gertie asked.

I opened my mouth to respond but had no words. Fortunately, Ida Belle had enough for both of us.

"You look like a two-hundred-year-old woman wearing a kid's pajamas," Ida Belle said. "Cover yourself up before you make our eyes bleed."

Gertie gave her a dirty look. "I should have known you wouldn't like it. You've been wearing the same jeans and button-up shirts since the '70s. It's like one day you just hopped off the fashion train."

"*This* is not the fashion train," Ida Belle said, waving her hands up and down at Gertie's costume. "This is a travesty of fabric."

"If that's the fashion train," I said, finally finding some words, "I'm getting off now. Like right now and before that stop."

Gertie shot me a look of dismay. "You too? I figured of all people you would get it."

"Get what?" I asked. "I'm sorry, but I'm really not seeing the point."

"It's a superhero costume," Gertie said, "and not just any superhero but the best female superhero. Since we met you and have been fighting crime, I feel a tiny bit like one of those superheroes. And since the best ones can fly, I wanted to wear this costume for my flight."

"Wonder Woman didn't fly," I said. I mean, I thought it was kinda BS that she didn't, but I didn't write the character.

I looked over at Ida Belle and could tell by her expression that she was softening a bit. It was hard not to. Gertie was definitely a hero, and if wearing a Wonder Woman costume and jumping from a plane made her day, then who was it really hurting? It wasn't as though anyone was going to see us but Bruce, and I had a feeling he'd seen his share of crazy. Probably a lot of it in the mirror.

"Okay, but you put your other clothes back on before we drive home," I said.

"I suppose that's fair enough," Gertie said.

Bruce looked back at us and did a double take when he saw Gertie. "You best land on your feet," he said. "If you have to roll, that field grass is going to eat up your heinie. I'm ready to head out, if you guys will stop yapping and get geared up."

We all pulled on our chutes, then checked one another's straps and took our seats. I yelled at Bruce and he gave us a thumbs-up and started the plane down the path to the runway. Gertie sat across from me, grinning like a five-year-old at her birthday party. Ida Belle gave her a sideways glance and shook her head. We made a turn onto the runway and the airplane increased speed.

"Here we go!" Gertie said as the plane lifted off the ground.

I had to give Bruce props. His takeoff was textbook. I wondered how he was on landings but since I was going to be handling that part myself, I wouldn't be able to find out. We circled around the area, Ida Belle and Gertie pointing out landmarks as we went. But not the usual sort of thing, like a famous house or museum or statue. This was the Sinful version.

"There's the pond where the senior class went skinny-dipping and all got that flesh-eating bacteria on their privates."

"There's Shorty's old place. Looks like he still hasn't rebuilt since that stampede of wild hogs tore it down."

"Look. That's old Farm Road 882. We used have a still at the end until that s'mores accident in '72."

I studied the topography as we flew, mainly because the perspective from the air was completely different, and I spent a lot of time being turned around on the water. Ida Belle knew the bayous and channels like the back of her hand. I hoped that one day, I knew a tenth of what she knew. As it stood now, I only took my airboat up and down the bayou in front of my house if I was alone. Maybe into the lake, but never into the other channels. It was a surefire way for me to have to send up smoke signals, and the last thing I wanted Carter to have on me was that he had to rescue me from my own stupidity.

When we circled back toward downtown, Billy turned around and yelled. "Going to get rough!"

"What?" Gertie yelled back. "You're up?"

She jumped up from her seat and hopped in front of the exit. I leaped up to stop her but at that exact moment, we hit the patch of clouds that Billy had seen coming. The plane dropped, then bumped from right to left, pitching Gertie out the exit. I didn't even hesitate before diving out after her.

CHAPTER ELEVEN

THE CLOUDS BLOCKED my vision for a couple seconds, then I fell out of them and spotted Gertie below me. She appeared to be in good shape so far, her arms out and her body in good position. The question was where she was going to land. I looked down and spotted downtown Sinful just a bit to our west. Winds were out of the east, so it was likely she was going to land somewhere near downtown. That could be good or bad, depending on her exact landing spot. Landing in a back-yard versus the middle of an alligator-infested bayou with limited access would be good. Landing on power lines or in someone's lit barbecue pit would be very bad.

Given my body positioning, I was closing the gap between us, which was the point of my jumping headfirst. Essentially, it allowed me to drop at a greater rate of speed than Gertie. I wasn't trying to catch her in the air—this wasn't the movies—but I did want to be as close as I could while still being safe myself when she landed. That way if there was any issue with the landing site, I'd be right behind her to help.

The ground was rushing toward me and I checked my altitude. Any second now, Gertie would deploy her chute. We were still east of downtown a bit and the winds had remained mild, but once she pulled the chute, it wouldn't take much wind to move her considerably beyond the downtown area. All I could do now was pray for no wind and hope she landed in a clear patch.

Gertie's chute deployed and she instantly righted and slowed. I waited another couple seconds, getting as close as I safely could, then deployed my chute. I looked down and saw we were still drifting slightly toward downtown. So far, no gusts. I hoped Gertie had realized she was far away from the landing zone and was prepared to direct the chute, but given her questionable vision and refusal to upgrade her glasses, that was a big if. For all I knew, everything looked like a big brown and green blob to her. But even Gertie's crap vision wouldn't fail to miss buildings once they started rushing toward her.

We were about a hundred yards from the ground when the first gust hit. It pushed us both over the middle of the bayou that ran parallel to downtown. Given the local wildlife, that wasn't optimum. But the real danger was that the current would grab the chute and pull her under before she could release herself from the harness. I had to be ready for a water recovery and hoped someone with a boat readily available was watching and could help out.

We were only seconds away from landing when the next gust hit, lifting us both up a little and pushing us into downtown. The bayou disappeared, and the steeple of the Catholic church rose in front of me like a giant skydiver-catching rod. I saw Gertie grab for the toggles to change the direction of the parachute and held my breath as she narrowly missed catching herself on the structure. I cleared the building and scanned the grounds behind the church for a clear landing path.

Unfortunately, the grounds weren't empty, as normal. In fact, they were full. People, tables with food and drinks, chairs, tents, and one of those bouncy houses. It was some sort of party and it was a big one, with at least fifty adults and children occupying a relatively small space.

And we were only seconds from plowing into all of them.

Someone on the ground yelled and pointed at us and people began to scatter. Unfortunately, no one knew which way to run, so they tumbled over one another and didn't manage to get out of the way. Gertie was coming in too fast to make a calculated landing and I could tell by the way she was yanking on the toggles that she was having trouble controlling the direction of the chute.

Even worse, there were power lines behind the church grounds. One good gust would put her right into them. There was no way I was going to catch her dangling in the air, so I did what any former CIA would do. I yelled a warning for those below, then released myself from my chute and dropped into the bouncy castle.

Fortunately, kids were just starting to enter the castle when I dropped, so I didn't take any of them out with my fall. But as my weight connected with the giant pocket of air, the castle bowed and sent two of them tumbling backward out the entrance. I bounced once and did a roll, then sprang up and leaped over the fallen kids and ran after Gertie.

She was only fifteen feet or so above the ground and coming in hard. A table with a banner that read *First Communion* and held a giant cake and two punch bowls was directly in her path. I ran as fast as I could but before I could reach her, she collided with the cake and wrapped her arms around it. It was the body's natural response to falling to attempt to grab on to something to stabilize you, but the cake was no match for a grown adult hurtling from the sky.

The entire cake came off the table along with Gertie and hit Celia Arceneaux right in the face, knocking her to the ground. Gertie released the cake on impact and reached for the next solid object in sight.

A nun.

She grasped the shoulders of the woman's habit, and I figured she'd take them both down. But at that moment, a big gust of air caught her parachute and launched her upward...still clutching the nun's habit.

I leaped onto the table that had held the cake and jumped as high and as far as I could, trying to grab hold of Gertie's feet before she could do any more damage. But I was short about two inches. I hit the ground and rolled, then bounced back up in time to see the habit slide over the nun and lift off with Gertie.

I shut my eyes for a second, not wanting to see a nun in her delicates, or even worse, commando. Then I stared in surprise when the habit revealed bike shorts and a Van Halen T-shirt. The one with the toddler angel smoking a cigarette. The nun screamed bloody murder, and I yanked the tablecloth from the table behind me and tossed it to her before sprinting off after Gertie. I had to catch her before she hit the power lines.

Fortunately, the gust that had taken her skyward disappeared and she started to drop again. As long as another gust didn't materialize, she was going to miss the power lines, but not by much. She'd dropped the habit and was back to trying to direct the chute, but I don't think it was doing any good anymore as she was close to the ground.

Cemetery ground.

I turned up my speed to the final notch, trying to get close enough to help break her fall or prevent her from crashing into one of the mausoleums, but I couldn't reach her in time. She hit the side of one of the large cement structures face-first, and the parachute looped over the cross on the top, leaving her dangling on the side like a sack of potatoes.

Gertie groaned as I rushed up and helped her turn around so she was facing out.

"Are you hurt?" I asked, scanning her up and down. "Is anything broken?"

"I don't think so," she said. "But the day's not over yet."

"What the heck are you talking about?" I asked as I worked on the straps to free her from the harness. "We're going straight home and you're going to sit in a recliner for the next forty years, even if I have to handcuff you to it."

"There's a problem with the mausoleum," Gertie said.

"No way you damaged this thing," I said. "It's concrete and has been here for at least a hundred years."

"A hundred and fifty-two years. It's Celia's family crypt."

I stared at her in dismay.

She grinned, then started to laugh. "She's going to kill me. Oh my God. What are the odds? I stripped a nun and desecrated Celia's family crypt all in one swoop. That's got to be a record, even for me."

"You didn't desecrate it. You couldn't even put a scratch on this thing."

"I'm hanging on her family's tomb in what Celia would consider my underwear."

I paused. "Point taken. Let's get you out of here before she shows up."

"Too late."

I turned around and saw a blob of white, silver, blue, and pink icing barreling toward me. Her face was completely covered, only her eyes and mouth showing, but there was no doubt it was Celia. Even before she opened her mouth.

"You have taken your hatred of me and this town to a whole new low," Celia said. "I expect you to treat me with disrespect as you don't seem capable of anything else, but to ruin a children's party is too much, even for you."

"Well, they are Catholic children," I said, but my joke was completely lost on the raging Celia.

I looked behind her and saw a weary-looking Carter headed our way. Celia pointed at us and yelled at Carter. "I want them both arrested for assault and destruction of private property. This is the last time Gertie and her whore bring ruin down on this town."

Carter stepped up to the mausoleum and lifted Gertie up so I could release her from the harness, then set her on the ground.

"Will someone please tell me what the hell is going on here?" he asked.

There was an intake of breath and all the women gathered behind Celia made the sign of the cross. Carter didn't look the least bit contrite.

"We were skydiving," I said, "and there was a miscalculation with the drop."

"Bomber Bruce?" Carter asked.

I nodded.

Carter shook his head. "You missed his place by a good five miles. That's not a miscalculation. That's a screwup of the first order."

"It was my fault," Gertie said. "I thought he told me to go, but apparently I was wrong."

"Didn't you look out the plane before jumping and think for one moment, 'Maybe this isn't right'?" Carter asked.

I pointed to my eyes and inclined my head toward Gertie.

"I can see just fine," Gertie protested.

"You jumped over downtown," I said.

"Dressed in her underwear," Celia said. "She should be arrested at once for public indecency."

"This is a costume," Gertie said. "Not underwear. And it's perfectly legal to wear it in public. Perhaps not the best choice for a religious celebration, but I didn't know I'd be crashing your party. Literally."

Carter closed his eyes, and I could see his lips moving. Either he was praying or trying to talk himself out of arresting us or just shooting us on the spot. Finally he looked up. "I have a murder to investigate. I do not have the time or inclination to deal with the fallout from your absurd choice of activities and the mistakes that ensue from there. Will you please both, for the love of God, go home and stay there?"

"For how long?" Gertie asked.

"Until I retire," Carter said.

"You're not going to arrest them?" Celia asked, her outrage clear.

"Accidents, even stupid ones, are not criminal," Carter said. "The DA would laugh me out of the sheriff's department if I even suggested he bring charges against them for crashing a party and ruining a cake."

Celia pointed at me, her hand shaking. "She assaulted children."

"I did not touch a single child when I landed," I said. "They just bounced a little."

"Was anyone hurt?" Carter asked.

"That's not the point," Celia said. "For Christ's sake, they defrocked a nun!"

Carter stared at Celia for a moment, probably trying to figure out the inherent meaning of her comment since the literal one probably wasn't computing. Then he looked over at me. I shrugged.

"Did you undress a nun?" Carter asked.

"Not me," I said, and pointed to Gertie.

"I didn't do it on purpose," Gertie said. "I was just trying to grab on to something to keep me from flying off again and the habit just kinda went up when I did."

Carter stared at her silently for a couple seconds. "Was the nun, um, underneath..."

"She had on clothes," I said.

"Thank God," Carter said, and looked over at Celia. "Would the nun like to press charges?"

"Sister Mary Catherine left the event in disgrace."

"Probably that Van Halen T-shirt she was wearing," I said.

Carter's bottom lip quivered. "The one with the baby angel smoking?"

"That's the one."

"Look," Gertie said. "I'm sorry I crashed into the party. It wasn't my intent. I will pay for everything I damaged and will furnish another cake and whatever else is needed to redo the entire shindig."

"That's good enough for me," Carter said. "Celia, send the bills to Gertie and she'll be happy to promptly pay them."

"And what about the buffoon that allowed them to jump out of his plane?" Celia asked. "Surely he has some responsibility here."

"Do you want me to have him pay for the damage instead of Gertie?" Carter asked.

"No! I want them both to pay and the whore and that witch Ida Belle. I know she's in on this too."

"I was not *in* anything, except the bayou." Ida Belle's voice sounded behind Carter, and I peered around to see her walking up, soaking wet.

I figured she would drop after me but when she hadn't appeared in the cemetery, I thought either she'd decided against it or hadn't been taken by the wind like Gertie and me. Apparently, it was the latter and Ida Belle had landed in the bayou.

"Well, I'm not making all of them buy you cake," Carter

said. "So pick one and let's get on with this. I have serious work to do. I'm not wasting any more time on this nonsense."

Celia whirled around to face him and glared. "You consider the taxpaying citizens of Sinful a waste of your time?"

"Not at all," Carter said. "But since one of those citizens is lying on a slab in the morgue, that takes priority over your fallen cake." He looked over at Gertie. "I'm going to make a guess that skydiving was your idea, so you can foot the bill. I want all three of you to go home and I swear to God if I see you outside even checking your mail, I'll arrest you on principle."

He turned around and strode off, but I could tell by the set of his jaw when he left that his frustration with all of the ridiculous things that happen in Sinful—many prompted by Gertie—had reached a boiling point. It was probably time for the three of us to lie low.

Just as soon as we got Ally's name cleared.

CHAPTER TWELVE

Unfortunately, it hadn't occurred to Carter, or he hadn't cared, that since we'd jumped out of an airplane, we didn't exactly have transportation home. I had no problem with the walk, physically, but I was less than thrilled about having Wonder Woman along for the stroll. I'd been stared at enough today. So we did what any trio of women who'd botched skydiving, ruined a children's party, and defrocked a nun did. We went to the General Store to hit up Walter for help.

He was already laughing when we walked in the door, so the Sinful gossip train was clearly on the job. He took one look at Gertie and doubled over. Not the most polite of responses to a woman's choice of wardrobe, but I couldn't really blame him. When he finally came up for air, he leaned across the counter and drew in a big breath.

"Did you really undress a nun?" he asked.

"It was an accident," Gertie said.

His eyes widened for a moment, then he started off on another round of laughter. I figured I had a couple minutes of shopping time while he pulled himself together, so I grabbed some snack stuff and a loaf of bread and hauled it all back to the counter. Walter was wiping his eyes with a rag, his face still red.

"Oh my God," he said when he got another breath. "I thought I'd heard some stuff, and I have to admit, when this story came around, I didn't believe it. Not all of it, anyway. But this has to be one of the top five Gertie mishaps in the history of Gertie mishaps."

I looked over at Ida Belle, who shook her head.

"It's probably top five of publicly known mishaps," I said.

Walter pointed at me. "That's valid. I imagine if I knew the details of the things you guys got up to when no one was around to report them, it would make all those ridiculous videos on YouTube look tame."

"Or fit right in," Ida Belle said. "While I can appreciate your desire to have a good laugh at our expense, and don't blame you one bit, we're here because we need some help."

Walter reached under the counter and pulled out his truck keys. "I'll have Scooter drop me off after work at Fortune's to pick it up."

I smiled. "I appreciate a man who assesses a situation and comes up with a solution before being asked."

"Well, it was either that or sell you a tarp for the walk home," he said. "But the laugh alone was worth the price of the truck borrow."

"I don't know," I said. "You got a whole lot of laughing in for one truck borrow. We may need some credit in our account." I pointed to my items. "Ring me up and we'll get out of here."

Walter shook his head, put the items in a bag, and handed it to me. "On the house for ruining Celia's day."

"If I'd known you were giving away groceries," I said, "I would have picked up steaks."

"Freezer's on the way out," he said. "Might as well grab

some for your grill. Your backyard might be the only place outside of your house that you're allowed to go. I'll be by this evening for the truck. If for some reason you decide to completely ignore Carter's order and you're not going to be home, just leave the key to the truck in the visor."

"Thanks, Walter," I said. "You're the best."

He smiled. "I keep saying that."

I could hear him laughing again as we left the store.

We climbed into Walter's truck and I looked over at the other two. "Did anyone leave anything at Bruce's place? Wallet? Purse? Stick of dynamite?"

Ida Belle shook her head. "I know better than to bring things with me to a drop." She looked over at Gertie.

"What?" Gertie asked. "Did you see my giant purse anywhere? Oh, well, technically I left my other clothes in the plane."

"Hazard of jumping as Wonder Woman," Ida Belle said. "I'm not going to risk sitting in jail overnight in order for you to retrieve a pair of slacks and blouse that you've probably had for longer than Fortune's been alive. I'll get my SUV tomorrow."

"If it's all the same," I said, "I'd like to pass on the opportunity of spending another night in the sheriff's department motel. Just did that. The room service is good but the beds are horrible, and I prefer to visit the ladies' in private and when I want. Myrtle was great about giving us bathroom breaks, but the restroom at the sheriff's department is still used mostly by men."

"They have a cleaning service, don't they?" Gertie asked.

"Yeah, but they come in the morning. We were there overnight. That's a whole day of male usage. Besides, they have a Bible in there."

Gertie nodded. "Reading material."

"Bathroom reading material should be *Guns & Ammo* or *Hot Rod* magazine or for here, something on fishing. Who stays in the restroom long enough to read the Bible?"

"It's probably Carter in there praying about you," Ida Belle said.

"Good point," I said.

I pulled into Gertie's driveway and she climbed out. "I'll do the shower and change thing and dig something out of the refrigerator, then I'll head over to your place. I assume Carter won't have a problem with us being in the same house as long as we're inside."

I shook my head. "I'm pretty sure Carter would prefer we reside in different states, but that's not my problem. I'm starving too. Bring whatever you've got. It's bound to be better than what I can come up with."

Gertie gave me a thumbs-up and headed up the sidewalk. Ida Belle looked over at me. "Are you planning on gaining any domestic skills now that you're not running around killing people for a living?"

I shrugged. "I don't know. I mean, sometimes I think I should learn how to cook a couple of my favorite things at least, but then I figure Francine or Gertie will cook them for me and mine would never be as good, so why bother. I've made it to this age without starving, and trust me, until coming here I hadn't had a decent home-cooked meal since my mom died."

Ida Belle nodded. "I suppose your dad wasn't much of a cook."

"My dad was the king of takeout. Where do you think I got the habit? Granted, in DC there's a ton of choices. In Sinful, I'm limited to Francine's opening hours and friends who will take pity on me." I looked over at her. "What about you? I don't think I've seen you cook anything except on the grill."

"It's not really my thing. Neither is sewing. I mean, I'll put a button back on or fix a hem, but I don't want to do it for sport, and I don't see anything relaxing about it regardless of what Gertie claims. I tried to make a shirt once. Gertie pestered me about the cost of buying in the store versus the cost of material until I figured I ought to give it a try."

"How did that go?"

"I outgrew the shirt before I finished sewing it."

I smiled. "How old were you?"

"Fifteen. But I figured it was a clear indication of how things were going to be. I can do wonders with duct tape, though."

"My preferred method of dealing with missing buttons and loose hems was to buy cheap clothes and replace them when something went wrong. The CIA had to cover a lot of my wardrobe costs anyway. God, the things I had to wear...makes me cringe just to think about it."

"What kind of things?" Ida Belle asked. "Thick camo in the desert? Those awful hiking boots?"

"Worse. Designer dresses and heels."

Ida Belle laughed. "Yeah. I can see that."

I pulled into her driveway and she hopped out. "See you in a little while," I said.

She gave me a wave and headed inside. I put Walter's truck in gear and started for my house, thinking about everything that had happened since I'd returned to Sinful. A dead fisherman, a night in jail, a friend up for murder charges, and a defrocked nun. It was pretty impressive for only two days, even for me. At this rate, I might not make it a week as a regular civilian.

I managed the drive to my house without incident, which I gave myself a brownie point for, then headed straight for the shower. I had bits of cake on me and had worked up a sweat trying to chase down Gertie the Flying Nun-Stripper. Merlin greeted me as I walked in the door, which was strange. So strange that I stopped short and stared.

He meowed. That loud, piercing meow that only an irritated cat can manage.

I frowned. I'd fed him this morning before I left the house and he'd eaten everything, then gone outside for a bit to do his business. But ever since the summer heat had rolled in, he preferred sleeping inside on the couch or on my bed to sleeping outside. Or maybe he was on alert since Godzilla had chased him up the tree. Regardless, he hadn't shown much interest in being outdoors.

The only other time he got this peeved was when something wasn't right in the house. Like when I'd replaced the doormat in the kitchen because Bones had chewed the ends off and it kept shedding fibers on the floor. Merlin had protested for a week by refusing to step on the new rug. I'd had to let him out the front door, which was a real hassle. But less of a hassle than an angry cat who has to pee locked up inside your house.

I automatically reached for my hip, but my gun wasn't there. Damned civilian living. Fortunately, I kept a spare in the rooms I occupied, so all I had to do was make it to the end table by the window and I had a nice nine-millimeter tucked in the drawer. If someone was inside, they'd heard me come in. I hadn't exactly been quiet about it, but then, I hadn't had any reason to be.

Now I did.

I crept over to the end table and slid open the drawer, reaching inside for the gun.

"You looking for this?" Mannie's voice sounded from the hallway.

I whirled around and saw him standing there, an amused look on his face and my nine dangling from his finger.

"Jesus, you scared the crap out of me," I said.

He handed me the gun. "I find that extremely hard to believe. I couldn't even scare the cat. He's as ornery as you."

"I'm going to take that as a compliment."

He grinned. "Maybe I meant it as one."

I looked around him toward the kitchen. "You got anyone else stashed in there?"

"No. The Misters Hebert are busy with prior obligations, but they asked me to come speak to you."

"I have beer and cookies in the kitchen."

He stood back and waved me past. "The more I get to know you, the more I like you."

"Really?" I asked as we walked into the kitchen. "Then how about you tell me how you keep getting into my house? Because I've checked and there's no sign of entry. I'm not exactly a layman, so either you're that good or you can walk through walls."

Mannie took a seat at the kitchen table and tilted his head to one side. "I suppose I could leave you thinking I'm that good, but I have too much pride in my actual work to claim something I didn't do. Marge's locksmith is a cousin of Big and Little. He might have furnished them a key."

I sat two beers on the table and took a seat. "Remind me to change my own locks."

"Do you really think that would matter?"

"Not in your case, but you're not who I'm worried about."

He frowned. "You're worried about someone?"

"No. I just meant that if someone else was trying to gain access to my home besides you, that would be a problem."

His expression relaxed. "But your previous situation is resolved, correct?"

"Yes. Completely."

"No chance of someone else picking up the torch?"

"No way. The organization is in shambles, with a bunch of Ahmad's top men fighting for control. Word is none of them are happy with the heat Ahmad brought onto them with his vendetta. Don't get me wrong—if one of them saw me on a street, they probably wouldn't hesitate to shoot, but no one is motivated to come looking."

"Good. If anything ever changes, you let me know. I'm always available for backup."

I grinned. "I think I have more backup here than I did with the CIA."

"It's southern Louisiana. Land of many hidden skill sets."

"Lord, isn't that the truth. And a lot of them really scary. Well, I'm sure you didn't come all the way over here to have a beer, so what's up? Is everything okay with Big and Little?"

"The Heberts are well. I'll relay that you inquired. But they are a bit concerned. They always have an ear to the ground, so to speak, and have heard about the fisherman who was poisoned yesterday."

"Wow. They've got really good ears or good ground. The police haven't even released the cause of death."

"But yet you are not the least bit surprised, which tells me you were already aware of that fact. I assume Ida Belle's ladies are on the job. They probably knew it was murder before he drew his last breath."

"Close enough. What's the Heberts' interest in this?" I was certain they weren't associated socially in any way, and I couldn't fathom Hooch trying to strike a business deal with them.

"Mr. Carre contacted the Heberts last week about obtaining money."

"As in a loan? The man who made perpetual excuses to get out of work had the nerve to ask the Heberts to lend him money? Was he drunk?"

"I'm pretty sure Big asked him the same thing. Mr. Carre wasn't interested in a loan but in an exchange. He claimed he would sign over the rights to property that would cover the amount he wanted."

"What property? Ida Belle said he lived in some shack out in the bayous. What was he asking for—a hundred bucks?"

"Half a million."

I almost dropped my beer. "Pennies?"

"Dollars."

"And they're sure he wasn't drunk?"

Mannie put his hands up.

"Property in Sinful? Is there a gold mine here? Or diamonds?"

"There's oil but you can't exactly dig a hole and harvest it for sale. Besides, mineral rights are closely guarded."

"Then I don't get it. I mean, let's just indulge the fantasy for a moment that Hooch had property worth that kind of money. Why not just sell it outright? If he wanted money from the Heberts then he knows they're not doing it for free. So if he wanted half a million, he'd need property worth, what?"

I looked at Mannie, who was silent for a couple seconds, then he leaned forward. "Let's just say eight hundred thousand. Maybe more."

"Wow! That's some serious profit."

"There's appraisal, legal and administrative costs and facilitator's fees. It adds up. The Heberts don't exactly take on simple transactions. There's a steep cost for the risk they assume."

That kind of fee was on the wrong side of legal, but then, the people who went to the Heberts for money weren't the type that could afford to turn them in.

"But it also makes my point," I said. "Why take a three-hundred-thousand-dollar hit? Why not sell the property and pocket it all?"

Mannie frowned. "I don't know, and the Heberts said Mr. Carre was very vague about why he needed the money quickly. You have to understand, it's against their policy to ask too many questions. That's the reason people come to them in the first place."

"Sure."

"Nonetheless, when the Heberts heard of Mr. Carre's demise and the manner in which he exited, it raised some questions. When they got word that your friend had been arrested, they grew concerned. I'm sure that whatever reason Mr. Carre needed that money is directly tied to his death. The Heberts felt so as well, which is why we're having this chat. They did not want to see your friend railroaded for something she wasn't responsible for."

"That's not going to happen. I've already got her released from custody and if the ADA has a lick of sense, he won't touch pursuing charges with a ten-foot pole. But there's still the problem of local talk."

Mannie nodded. "She has to live here. I understand she wants to open a business as well. That kind of speculation tends to linger unless something is definitively resolved."

I sighed. "Yeah. One of the many hazards of small-town living."

"Right up there with undressing nuns."

I stared. "Is there anything you don't know?"

"Unfortunately, plenty. This summer's crime spree proved that even the Heberts don't have their pulse on everything, and neither do Ida Belle and her crew. But a half-naked nun story tends to make the rounds rather quickly."

"I suppose it would."

He rose from his chair. "I don't want to hold you up any

longer, and I apologize for once again showing up without calling first. But the Heberts wished for you to have the information as soon as possible, and they don't like to relay such things on cellular devices."

"Their assumption being that I was about to stick my nose into police business?"

"No use fighting DNA."

"Ha! You think Carter would buy that one? That I'm physically unable to mind my own business because of my DNA?"

"Carter is no fool. I don't think he'd believe it, but he might accept it in passing because of his feelings for you."

"Yeah, well, he's a little peeved at me right now."

"And that will likely be an ongoing place you two visit, but it will never be boring."

I perked up a bit. "I guess it is more interesting to fight over undressing nuns than something mundane like taking out the garbage." I looked up at Mannie. "What about you? Is there a Mrs. Badass tucked away somewhere?"

Mannie grinned. "I have not yet found my match. I didn't have the time or inclination when I was serving. And the sort of women I encounter as part of my job now aren't the type I'd roll the dice on."

"Makes sense. Well, if you're ever interested in going older, I know Gertie would love a run at you."

He laughed. "I'd worry about my longevity dating Ms. Hebert. Although she does seem to have quite an interesting collection of explosives."

"Just what a man looks for in a woman."

"It was good seeing you again, Fortune. If there is anything we can do to assist with this, please let us know. "

"Tell the Heberts I said thank you. And thanks for delivering the information."

"It was my pleasure. Good to have you back."

He gave me a nod and exited. I leaned back in my chair and marveled over how the politest of people always seemed to be the most deadly. Except me. I was as abrasive as heavy-grit sandpaper.

Eight hundred thousand dollars.

What the hell did Hooch own worth that kind of cash? And why did he need the money so badly he was willing to pay top dollar to get it now?

For something that had appeared as simple as an out-of-condition drunk having a heart attack, this was shaping up to be as convoluted as everything else I'd encountered in Sinful. I chugged down the rest of my beer and hurried upstairs for a quick shower. Gertie and Ida Belle would be arriving soon, and we had a lot to discuss.

CHAPTER THIRTEEN

"HALF A MILLION DOLLARS?" Gertie snorted. "He's lost the plot. Or I guess I should say he'd lost the plot. Either way, no one in their right mind would give Hooch a half-million dollars regardless of the collateral. That goes ten times over for the Heberts."

She shoved a chicken casserole into my oven and started buttering a big loaf of French bread. Ida Belle and Gertie had arrived ten minutes earlier, and I'd just finished filling them in on Mannie's impromptu visit.

Ida Belle frowned. "I have to agree with Gertie's assessment. The Heberts are not the people to acquire money from unless one is in dire straits, but to approach them with that kind of request is lunacy even beyond what I thought Hooch capable of."

"What in the world would he need that kind of money for?" Gertie asked. "The man has never owned anything worth more than a couple thousand bucks. Hell, I don't think he even knew how many zeroes were in five hundred thousand."

"It certain makes you wonder," Ida Belle said. "Clearly our friend Hooch wasn't the run-of-the-mill redneck we thought he was. He had something going on. Something that led him to believe his property was worth a lot of money."

"Or he was insane enough and desperate enough to try to convince the Heberts that was the case," Gertie said.

"Is anyone that insane?" I asked.

"Well, this is Sinful," Ida Belle said. "But I agree. Even the least intelligent among us knows not to get on the wrong side of the Heberts."

"Okay," I said, "so if we assume he wasn't that insane and actually thought he had property worth that amount, that still doesn't tell us why he'd approach the Heberts for the money. Why not sell the property and pocket way more?"

"I can only think of two reasons," Ida Belle said. "First, he didn't want people to know what the property was worth. A sale would have produced public records and then all the people he stiffed on jobs would have lined up for repayment."

Gertie nodded. "And I heard Hooch liked to gamble, so he might have owed bookies and the like."

"What's the second reason?" I asked.

"He needed to leave quickly and quietly for some reason far more urgent than monies he owed," Ida Belle said. "With that kind of cash in hand, it would be easy to disappear."

"So either he wanted to skip out on his debts," I said, "or he needed to skip out on something worse. But what? If something big was going on with Hooch, could he have really kept it a secret in Sinful?"

Ida Belle shook her head. "At one time, I would have said no. And I would have been wrong. I mean, I've always believed you never really know a person, but this past summer was a rude awakening for me when it comes to just how much I didn't know about my town and the people in it."

"People work really hard to keep the kind of things we've exposed a secret," I said.

"Yes, but most aren't all that good at it," Ida Belle said. "Some of this has been happening for years, and right under our noses. If you'd told us last year about all the things that have happened the last few months, I would have laughed off half of it."

"But the other half?" I asked.

"Well, I have a lower opinion of human beings than a lot of people," Ida Belle said.

"I can appreciate that," I said. "So we have to assume that Hooch had more going on than you would have ever guessed. But surely someone knows something. So where do we start?"

Ida Belle's phone rang and she glanced at the display and frowned. "It's Walter."

She answered and did one energetic "really" and several "uh-huhs," then ended with a "thanks." She placed her phone on the table and looked at us.

"Hooch's ex-wife and son just walked into the General Store," she said.

Gertie's eyes widened. "What? Seriously? She swore she wouldn't step foot back in this town."

"If you remember correctly," Ida Belle said, "she swore she would never set foot back in this town as long as Hooch was here."

"Fair enough. Dead doesn't count as here," I said. "So what's the story? Did Walter get any information out of her?"

"Not much," Ida Belle said. "Just that Carter had tracked her down looking for Hooch's son. He's next of kin, so he's in charge as far as decisions go on burial and such. She came with him to help. He's in his twenties. Probably doesn't know the first thing about planning a funeral."

"Especially for a father he barely knew," Gertie said. "Junior couldn't have been six, maybe, when Margarita left."

"I don't suppose Hooch left a will," I said.

"I doubt it," Gertie said. "Most people around here don't. Wills are for those with a lot of assets and kids that will fight over them."

"But if he really had property worth half a million..." I said.

"She's right," Ida Belle said. "If Junior inherits anything of value, we have to take a harder look at him and Margarita."

Gertie shook her head. "But if no one in Sinful knew Hooch had something of value—assuming he really did—how in the world would the son he hasn't seen in well over a decade know?"

"I don't know," Ida Belle said. "But you watch enough of those forensics shows to know if you follow the money, you usually find the answers."

"So first up is figuring out if the property story is true," I said. "I assume we can get the details on Hooch's property online?"

"And we still have our other list of suspects," Gertie said. "I know following the big money trail usually gets the answer, but we still don't know for certain that Hooch had anything of value, and if he did that anyone else knew about it."

"You're right," I said. "We can't ignore the personal angle. It's still possible this was all over some botched construction job or someone who felt scammed or cheated by Hooch and his crappy business ways."

Ida Belle nodded. "While a half a million is definitely an amount that might spark a murder, the reality is a couple thousand could do it as well, given how little some people have."

"Exactly," I said. "It's all relative. So we check everyone."

I grabbed my laptop off the kitchen counter and started a search. "First up, Hooch's property holdings."

With guidance from Gertie and Ida Belle, I searched the local parish and several surrounding parishes, but the only property that came up with Hooch's name was the piece he was living on.

"But it's just like every other shack on the bayou, right?" I asked.

"As far as I know," Ida Belle said. "I'd think if he had built a mansion on it, we'd have heard about it by now."

"And we'd have seen an oil derrick," Gertie said.

"I thought mineral rights were a weird deal here," I said. "Would Hooch even hold them?"

"Someone does," Ida Belle said. "You can sell the surface property and hold the mineral rights, but they revert to the new owner after ten years. Unless the land is put in use. Once a well is drilled, the ten years starts all over."

"So how are people keeping mineral rights forever?" I asked. "I thought you said it was practically impossible to get them nowadays. And people are still building. I know sometimes the building is somewhat sketchy, but it's still a structure. They can't all be squatters."

"It's because of the leases," Ida Belle said. "Estates won't sell the land, so no reversion. But they'll do long-term leases of the land that are transferable if the person sells the property."

"So people still own the structure, but not necessarily the land it's sitting on," I said. "Isn't that risky?"

Ida Belle shrugged. "I'm talking about leases for fifty or a hundred years."

"I see," I said. "Sorta like some properties in Hawaii. I saw that on a television show."

"Maybe," Ida Belle said. "I haven't been in the market for property in Hawaii so I'm not sure if it works the same."

"Probably a lot more expensive to lease there, and I'm going to guess the view is probably a heck of a lot better," Gertie said. "Leases are negligible here. Not a lot of people want to lease some of this land, especially the campsites. Too off the beaten path, hard to get utilities, hard to sell if you need to clear out."

"A lot of the camps are on long-term leases of the land," Ida Belle said. "The oil companies lease the land, too. The mineral rights–holder negotiates the terms, but it usually includes a share of the profits from any drilling that occurs on the property."

"So since Hooch bought the property rather than leasing it," I said, "and more than ten years ago, doesn't that mean he owned the mineral rights?"

"Unless an oil derrick was erected at some point by the previous owner and we didn't notice, it's a good possibility," Gertie said.

"So it *is* possible that Hooch owned property worth half a million or better," I said.

"It's possible," Ida Belle said, and pointed to my screen. "But not overly probable. That's a small piece of land. And assuming there's oil, he'd still have to find a company interested in drilling. It's not like there's a shortage of oil here."

"How would he find out if there was oil?" I asked.

"Geologists and geophysicists inspect the land and use special equipment to see if there's a probability that it contains oil," Ida Belle said. "Based on their findings, you then pitch to an oil company and see if they're interested in drilling. The testing isn't cheap, though, and convincing an oil company to drill isn't like selling a used car. The companies invest serious money in equipment and manpower to drill. If they come up empty, everyone loses."

"But if they come up full?" I asked.

"Then some people may never have to worry about working," Ida Belle said.

"You know a lot about this," I said.

Gertie rolled her eyes. "Why do you think she never talks about her previous profession? Ida Belle is an oil baron."

"Please," Ida Belle said. "It's nothing that dramatic. And I worked. I just didn't take anything overly seriously after the military. I inherited some land and a little money, so I rolled the dice and spent it on testing. The dice roll paid off. But I'm not a baron. I'm not even rich. I made some decent money until the land went dry, and I was smart with investing and never liked debt, so I'm in good shape."

"That's very cool," I said. "If you were that good at investing, we might need to talk. I have to do something with my inheritance. It's been dumped with some dude in DC, but I honestly don't know if he's doing a good job."

Ida Belle nodded. "I'm happy to take a look at your investments. I am no expert, but I don't do badly. And I know some people I can refer you to if you'd like to change managers."

"Okay," Gertie said, "now that the *Forbes* part of our discussion is complete, can we get back to murder?"

"Right," I said. "Sorry." But I was still processing this new information I had on Ida Belle. She was one layer of mystery after another. I wondered how long I'd have to live here to know even half of the woman's life.

"I say we take a look around Hooch's property and see if there's any sign that testing has happened," Gertie said. "At least then we'd know where he was coming up with that half a million request."

"Testing won't give you a dollar amount of worth," Ida Belle said.

"And you think Hooch knew that?" Gertie said. "He probably just picked the biggest number he could think of that he figured would support him forever and that's what he used."

"Sounds like the way Hooch lived, ten thousand could have supported him forever," I said.

Ida Belle sighed. "Probably true. You know Carter is going to be covering his place with a fine-tooth comb."

"And he's not going to want us messing with his investigation," Gertie said. "Blah, blah, blah. So what? We sit here and wait for things to happen to Ally?"

"I'm not saying that," Ida Belle said. "I'm just saying that we might want to give him time to take a look and clear out before we go tromping down there, especially since we've been ordered to sit still the rest of the day."

I frowned. I hated when the man I had strong feelings for was also the biggest obstacle in the way of helping a friend. It sometimes felt like my constant state of existence in Sinful was being torn between two obligations.

Oh well. One of those obligations was looking at having her future destroyed. The other was looking at being annoyed for a while. Guess which one trumped?

"I suppose Deputy Breaux will be by to make sure we're complying with orders," I said. "So I have to agree with Ida Belle. I think we should check out the property, but now probably isn't the best time."

"Checking it out at night might be safer as far as the Carter angle is concerned," Gertie said, "but it's going to be harder to spot anything, and getting out there in the dark might not be the picnic you imagine."

"Since when is anything in Sinful a picnic?" I asked. "A picnic with ants and mosquitoes and the occasional alligator maybe."

Gertie grinned. "But it's never dull."

———

WE FINISHED up lunch and did some Googling on Margarita

and Junior but didn't turn up much of anything. I thought it was a little strange at first, but then Ida Belle pointed out how many people were in the world and most of them didn't have an online presence. I supposed unless one was highly successful, famous, a criminal, or enamored with what they ate every day, there was probably no reason for them to appear in a basic internet search.

Since we were more or less on house arrest and didn't really have anything to work on until Walter showed up, we decided to use some of the time wisely and take a nap. Gertie was stretched out on the couch with Merlin at her feet. Ida Belle and I occupied the recliners. Everyone but me was snoring, including the cat. But despite having little sleep the night before and not good sleep at that, I couldn't get my mind to stop whirling long enough to doze off.

Finally, I gave up and headed back into the kitchen. If I couldn't sleep, I might as well eat. I had some leftover cobbler and decided if I was going to be awake for a while, I should make some coffee and perk myself up a bit. I was just about to sit down when I heard a knock at the front door. It was rather a polite knock, so that meant it wasn't Carter. Maybe Walter had headed off from work early.

I hurried to the front door before the knocking woke everyone up and swung it open. Deputy Breaux stood there, a somewhat anxious look on his face.

"I'm really sorry," he said, "but Carter insisted I check on you."

I waved him into the living room where he could witness the snoring firsthand. "All inside and accounted for. Tell Carter his house arrest is in full effect."

Deputy Breaux shuffled a bit. "You're not really under arrest, which is why I'm kinda uncomfortable with this whole thing. But Carter has seniority..."

I patted him on the shoulder. "Don't worry. I don't hold Carter's insecurities against you."

He blushed. "Oh, I didn't say nothing like insecurities."

"You didn't have to. Tell me, why didn't you just peek in a window?"

He swallowed. "Carter told me to do just that, but I figured you probably know ten ways to kill me with just household items alone."

"At least," I said. "But this house came with an arsenal, so I wouldn't have to work that hard. There's also the illicit dynamite that Gertie has in her purse. If all of that fails, I could throw the cat on you. He's tough."

He gave me a slightly pained look, which I attributed to the arsenal and the dynamite, but it might have been the cat comment. A lot of people were rightly afraid of cats. I was just about to offer him something to drink or maybe a snack when a thought crossed my mind.

Carter's asking Deputy Breaux to check up on us didn't really surprise me, although I thought it was a bit of overkill. And Deputy Breaux's discomfort didn't really surprise me, especially given his newly acquired information about my former profession. But the checkup had come sooner than I'd expected, and Deputy Breaux seemed more nervous than I imagined he would be.

Something was up.

"So," I said, "what innocent person is Carter about to harass that he doesn't want us to know about?"

The dark red flush that flooded Deputy Breaux's face was a dead giveaway. "Uh, no one. I mean, Carter doesn't harass people. We're cops. We question people because, uh, you know, that's what cops do. And we're cops. So we, uh, do that."

"Who is it? He sent you here to prevent me from getting in the middle of another interview. Ida Belle and Gertie are on my couch. I exchanged texts with Ally just minutes ago and she was about to go back to bed. So who? Come on, Deputy. I'm going to find out anyway. Either you tell me now or Ida Belle's phone starts ringing in a couple seconds. Regardless, the secret is going to be out."

He gave me a pained look. "Walter. He's questioning Walter."

"What?" Of all the names I'd expected to hear, Walter wasn't even on the list. He was Carter's uncle, for Christ's sake. And while I had no doubt Walter was capable of killing someone in self-defense, there was no way he would waste his time and future on someone like Hooch.

I didn't even bother asking any more questions because there wasn't a thing the good deputy could say that would make sense. Instead I stalked over to the recliner and shook Ida Belle. "Wake up. Carter's gone bat-crap crazy."

Ida Belle opened one eye and stared at me. "I'm gonna need more than that."

"You're too loud," Gertie grumbled. "Take it to the kitchen or something. People are trying to get their beauty rest."

"Carter is questioning Walter!" I shouted.

CHAPTER FOURTEEN

Both of them bolted upright as if they'd been shot.

"Are you kidding me?"

"There's no way!"

They both started talking at once.

I held up my hand to stop the barrage. "The good deputy was sent here to make sure we stay put while Carter does his dirty work. How many are in favor of ignoring a direct order from Deputy LeBlanc?"

Ida Belle's and Gertie's hands shot up along with mine. Deputy Breaux stared at us for a second, then slowly raised his hand.

"Please don't tell Carter," he said.

"Some say the fear of God is the beginning of wisdom," Gertie said. "I think the fear of women is the beginning of wisdom. At least for men."

"What makes you think God's not a woman?" Ida Belle asked.

"Because she would never have allowed men to invent pantyhose," Gertie said.

"Good point," Ida Belle said, and pulled on her tennis

shoes. "Well, let's go raise some hell. I mean, it's been at least an hour or two. We don't want to get rusty."

I looked over at Deputy Breaux. "We were already gone when you got here."

I thought he would faint from relief.

"Well, go on," Gertie said. "Get out of here before someone sees you and tells Carter we were still here."

Deputy Breaux shot out of the house like a bullet. We waited until he'd pulled out of the driveway to jump in Walter's truck and hurry into town. I screeched to a stop in front of the sheriff's department, a move that got me an approving nod from Ida Belle, then we hurried inside. The new day dispatcher, a local young man who had his sights set on being a deputy someday, jumped up when we entered.

"Can I help you ladies?" he asked, his voice polite but strained.

"We need to speak to Carter," I said. "It's urgent."

"Um, he's not here right now," the dispatcher said. "Can I give him a message?"

There was something about the way he delivered the first sentence that sounded rehearsed.

"Are you sure he's not here?" I asked. "Because I'm guessing he's in his office with Walter."

His strained look turned into full-blown panic. "I can't let anyone go back there. Deputy LeBlanc gave strict orders."

"You carry a gun, Gavin?" Ida Belle asked.

His eyes widened. "No, ma'am. I just answer the phones and stuff."

"This is Louisiana," Ida Belle said. "Most people carry a gun shortly after learning to walk."

"Some before," Gertie said.

"Anyway," Ida Belle continued, "your job does not necessarily dictate whether or not you're packing."

He sighed. "Carter won't let me have a gun. He makes Deputy Breaux frisk me every day when I get to work. It's embarrassing."

"Good. Then throw a stapler at us when we walk past," Ida Belle said. "Because nothing short of a bullet is going to stop us, and that way you can tell Carter you tried."

He brightened. "Hey, maybe then he'll realize I need to have a gun."

"Yeah, that'll do it." Ida Belle rolled her eyes and stalked off toward Carter's office. Gertie and I fell in line and let her lead. I figured as Walter was Ida Belle's man—whether she acknowledged that fact or not—she was the one who ought to do the talking. As the girlfriend of the man causing all the trouble, I figured keeping my mouth shut was my best course of action. Of course, that didn't mean I'd actually be able to accomplish it.

I could hear heated voices as we approached Carter's office but could only make out the last thing Carter said before we arrived.

You should have told me.

Ida Belle glanced back at us, clearly angry, then grabbed the doorknob and shoved Carter's office door open. Neither of the men so much as flinched at the flying door, which told me just how intense their conversation was. Walter's jaw was clenched and he barely glanced at us when we entered. Carter took one look at us and sighed.

"This is official police business," Carter said. "And the three of you are disobeying a direct order by leaving your homes."

"Oh, stuff your direct order," Ida Belle said. "Everyone who knows anything knows you can't tell us where to stay unless we're under arrest. So unless you want to arrest us and babysit the jail again tonight, I don't want to hear another word from you. I'm a little old to be grounded and certainly not by someone young enough to be my grandchild."

Carter looked over at me with a 'why do you allow this to happen' look. I shrugged. No way I was getting in between Ida Belle and the object of her anger, even if I was sleeping with him.

"Now, Ida Belle," Walter began, "I appreciate you ladies coming down here in my defense, but it's not necessary."

"I beg to differ," Ida Belle said. "I think questioning you like a common criminal is unnecessary. I think your own nephew questioning you is a serious conflict of interest. If he'd had a casual conversation with you at the store, like he should have done, we wouldn't be here. But to insist you come to the sheriff's department for an official interview is beyond the pale."

Walter put his hand up to stop her, which was probably a good idea as I could tell she was just getting started. "I came here voluntarily. Sort of. I didn't want customers to overhear our conversation."

"Then that conversation could have waited until you got home tonight," Ida Belle said. "Given that Carter is family, no one would have thought twice about him stopping by your house, but hauling you into the sheriff's department sets a whole different tone. And that tone gets gums flapping in this town."

I could tell by the slightly guilty shift in Carter's expression that Ida Belle had struck a nerve. I didn't like to think that people would suspect Walter of something just because Carter had questioned him, but I'd also been exposed to enough narrow-minded Sinful thinking to know that some might do exactly that. Walter's business depended on having the trust of the community. Sure, it was far more convenient to buy right here on Main Street, and Walter didn't do like a lot of other small grocers and jack up the prices, but the reality was, people could drive a couple miles out of town and do their shopping if they took a mind to it.

"I understand your point," Carter said.

Ida Belle blinked. Clearly, agreement was not the expected response.

"Then why did you do it this way?" she asked.

"Because I didn't have time to wait for him to close the store," Carter said. "And besides, I needed an official record of what he had to say."

Something was up. Carter's tone, which I'd expected to be both annoyed and belligerent, had a sense of urgency to it that wasn't in keeping with what we knew about the situation.

"Someone called the state police," I said.

Carter frowned and I knew my statement was a direct hit.

"Who?" Gertie demanded. "Who would do such a thing?"

Ida Belle's shoulders slumped. "You have to ask?"

"Celia," I said.

"But why on earth would she do that?" Gertie said. "When her own niece is one of the chief suspects? I mean, we all know better and I'm sure Celia does as well, but the state police won't know better. They'll just go with motive and opportunity and Ally, conveniently, has both."

"No one ever said Celia was bright," Ida Belle said and looked at me. "She probably heard you were thrown in the clink with Ally and thought it was because you were also a suspect. She'd do anything to get you out of Sinful, especially now that you've made your residency permanent."

"Regardless of Celia's reasoning," Carter said, "the state police have informed me that as soon as they have availability, they are sending an officer to 'supervise' my work because of the conflicts of interest I have. He'll be here within the hour."

"So you had to talk to Walter before they got here to get

him on record or they'd be in the room with you doing it later," I said. It was a sucky situation for all involved, but it made sense.

"But why talk to Walter at all?" Ida Belle continued to push, clearly still not satisfied. "He had no beef with Hooch and he was on the dock all morning handing out passes. He was never near the lunches when they were being prepared and wasn't manning the table where they were handed out."

"I supplied the water," Walter said.

"But it was in a big tub of ice," Gertie said. "We pulled our own bottles out. How in the world could you have targeted Hooch when you didn't control who took what bottle?"

"Maybe he wasn't targeting Hooch," I said. "Maybe he just wanted to kill someone, and that was the easiest way to do it without having his hand directly on the trigger."

Ida Belle gave me a look of total dismay.

"I'm not saying that's what I think," I said. "But the state police will have all kinds of theories that have nothing to do with what we know about Walter."

"His friends were in that tournament," Gertie said. "Surely that counts for something."

"The first suspect in a murder is the spouse," I said. "What does that say?"

"Okay, stop." Carter rose from his desk. "We all know Walter had nothing to do with Hooch's death. But he supplied the water so I needed to ascertain chain of ownership, then dispersion. I've done that, so Walter is free to leave, as are the rest of you."

I could tell by the set of Walter's jaw that his conversation with Carter was far from over, but I also suspected that the argument we'd walked in on wasn't about Hooch's drinking water. The conversation might have started that way but it had gone another direction. One that neither of them wanted to talk about.

One glance at the suspicious look Ida Belle cast at both of them before we walked out let me know that she wasn't buying their story, either. As we headed down the hallway, I looked over at Ida Belle, who gave me a barely perceptible shake of her head. It wasn't until we exited the sheriff's department that I remembered we were in Walter's truck.

"I suppose we could leave the truck here and walk home," I said. "Now that we're all properly dressed."

Ida Belle shook her head and opened the passenger door. "Take me to Bomber Bruce's to get my SUV. We're going to need it later. Then take the truck back to your place. We still need to talk to Walter about Ricky."

"And then we can grill him on what really happened in there," Gertie said, and climbed into the back of the truck.

Ida Belle looked at her friend. "You noticed something off too?"

"Are you kidding me?" Gertie asked. "You could cut the tension with a knife. No way that was over water bottles, state police or no."

"Something's definitely up," I said as I pulled away from downtown. "But it might not have anything to do with Hooch's murder. Walter and Carter are family. It could be a family matter."

"Could be," Ida Belle agreed. "But I haven't seen those two look daggers at each other since Carter was a smart-mouthed teen."

"He's completely full of crap on that official questioning thing, too," Gertie said. "He could have asked Walter about the water right there in the store in front of God and everybody. Probably would have been better for Walter if he had, given that they're related. Witnesses and all."

I nodded. "Carter said 'you should have told me' right before we opened the door. Could either of you make out anything they said before that?"

They both shook their heads.

"And that sentence could apply to just about anything," Gertie said.

"Maybe Walter did have a bad business dealing with Hooch," I said. "One he kept quiet."

Ida Belle shrugged. "I suppose anything is possible, but if Walter attempted business with Hooch, it never even got started. If he'd had work done at his house or at the store, we would have noticed."

"What about a camp?" I asked. "Does Walter have one?"

"Of course," Ida Belle said. "Most everyone has a camp, but you've seen them. They're not the sort of structures you usually pay to have work done on."

Gertie nodded. "Mostly you just buy scrap lumber and keep piecing them back together until a hurricane washes the whole thing into the bayou. Then you start over."

"Makes sense," I said. "Well, I guess we'll have to wait until Walter comes to pick up his truck."

"If he comes," Gertie said. "He'll be expecting the third degree. He might send someone else."

"It's pay me now or pay me later," Ida Belle said. "He knows he can't avoid us forever."

I nodded. Walter wasn't the type to avoid trouble, but he wasn't the type to volunteer for it, either. From what I'd seen, he tried to keep a low profile. Not exactly easy in Sinful and when you had a thing for Ida Belle, but he managed to stay off the radar most of the time. It would be interesting to see if he showed or if he sent his lackey Scooter to fetch his vehicle.

It would be even more interesting to see what he would fess up to if he came himself.

CHAPTER FIFTEEN

AT SIX FIFTEEN, Scooter pulled into my driveway and Walter climbed out of his truck and gave him a wave as he drove off.

"Show's on," Gertie said, and rubbed her hands together.

"Maybe we should all move away from the window and not jump him as soon as he walks in the door," I said.

Ida Belle waved Gertie away from the window. "Let Fortune answer the door. It's her house and Walter is sweet on her anyway."

I frowned.

"Like a daughter sweet," Ida Belle clarified. "He's really taken a liking to you. If Carter screws things up, Walter might disown him."

Gertie nodded. "There's been talk."

"Which you haven't told me a thing about," I said. "But it will have to wait until after we quiz Walter. Take a seat, he's coming up the porch."

I hung back in the living room and waited for him to knock, then I took my time walking the three steps to the door. I swung it open and gave Walter a big smile.

"Come in for a bit," I said. "Ida Belle taught me how to

make sun-brewed sweet tea this afternoon and I have some chocolate peanut butter cookies that Ally made."

Walter stepped inside and gave Gertie and Ida Belle a nod.

"You just want to ply me with sugar in an attempt to get me to talk," he said.

"Yep," I said. "Is it working?"

"I'll let you know after I have a cookie," he said, and smiled.

I looked over at Ida Belle, who nodded. So far so good. Walter didn't seem strained or unwilling to talk. Getting information out of him might be easier than we'd anticipated. We headed into the kitchen and I grabbed the container of cookies and some napkins while Gertie served up the tea.

We waited until Walter had taken his first bite before starting in.

"Did you catch any flak at the store over Carter questioning you?" Ida Belle asked.

Walter shook his head. "A lot of people were curious, of course, and they danced around the subject trying to get information out of me. But I don't think anyone believes I killed Hooch."

"Good," Ida Belle said, and I could tell she was satisfied that he was telling the truth. At least so far. "Then we'll get right to pumping you for information without dancing. I know you never liked to dance."

"Now, that's not true at all," Walter said. "I just never wanted to dance with anyone but you, and you never liked to dance."

"You two can have this age-old argument later," I said. "Lay it out for us. What do you know about Hooch's murder? People aren't going to be as kind to Ally as they are to you."

Walter frowned. "I'm afraid that's a fact. There's a lot more going against poor Ally, even though we all know the girl couldn't hurt a fly."

"We have to help her," Ida Belle said. "You know what happens here if your name isn't cleared. How many years did Marie catch grief over Harvey going missing? It was a million times worse when the body finally surfaced."

Gertie nodded. "Marie was tough and a good bit older when all this came down on her. I don't think Ally can take it in stride like Marie did."

"You think she'll leave Sinful?" Walter asked, looking worried.

"If Carter never figures out who killed Hooch, yeah," Ida Belle said. "She's already lived in New Orleans before and has some restaurant connections. It wouldn't be hard for her to find a job or a place."

"Crap," Walter said, and I could tell he was genuinely troubled. "I guess I hadn't taken my thinking that far. I just figured Carter would find out who did it and the town would move on to the next scandal."

"And that's what we all hope will happen," I said. "But we'd like to hedge our bets."

"You mean you want to butt your nose into police business," Walter said.

"So what if we do?" Ida Belle said. "You got a problem with us helping out a friend?"

Walter held up his hands. "No problem here. Heck, I've helped you more than once with your investigative shenanigans. And you know how fond I am of Ally. If there's a way to get this cleared up and soon, I'm all for it."

"Good," I said. "Then tell us everything you know."

"I'm afraid there's not a whole lot to tell," Walter said. "I furnished the water but I dropped it off at the dock still in the cases. Scooter brought the tubs and the ice and put all that together, but he was right there in the open with a ton of people milling around."

"The water doesn't sound like a good distribution method," I said. "I think someone would have noticed if Scooter had removed caps and poured something in one of the bottles."

Walter put his hands in the air. "And that's exactly what I told Carter. I know he still has to question the boy, but I hope he doesn't get him riled up. Last time Carter asked Scooter questions, he bungled two oil changes—forgot to put the plugs back in."

"Why does Carter make him so nervous?" I asked.

"It's not Carter, per se," Walter said. "It's cops, in general. Scooter's dad died in prison. Scooter still believes he was framed and that the cops didn't do their job."

"Any chance of that?" I asked.

"No way."

"Not a chance in hell."

"He was guilty as sin."

They all spoke at once.

"Well, don't just sit there all silent," I said. "Tell me what you think."

Walter shook his head. "Scooter's dad was bad news from the crib. The only person who refused to believe it was Scooter. The truth is, he was caught on video robbing a convenience store and he shot the cashier. The guy lived, but I'm pretty sure getting shot shouldn't fall in the job description of a minimum-wage position."

"Poor Scooter," I said. It was strange how much of an effect our parents could have on our lives, even when they were gone. Even when they weren't all that great human beings. Which reminded me of the first reason we'd wanted to question Walter. "Hey, we heard Hooch's ex and his son showed up in your store today."

Walter nodded. "Almost didn't recognize Margarita. Bleached her hair blond and she's had a bit of work."

"Plastic surgery?" Gertie shook her head. "She always was a bit vain."

"Who are you kidding?" Ida Belle said. "If you could find a doctor who would operate on prehistoric creatures, you'd be on the table having everything from top to bottom lifted, stretched, or sucked smaller."

"I was thinking of something noninvasive, like Botox," Gertie said. "Just to lift my face a little."

"I'm going to lend you a physics book," Ida Belle said. "You can read up on these two concepts called gravity and time."

"I think you look just lovely," Walter said to Gertie. "I don't know why you'd want to mess with perfection."

Gertie stuck out her tongue at Ida Belle, who rolled her eyes.

"Anyway," I said. "Margarita had some work done and you almost didn't recognize her. That sounds like more than a bit. What was different?"

"Her face was stretched tight," Walter said, "like those older actresses you see whose faces don't move anymore when they smile."

"They all look like the Joker," Ida Belle said.

"And her lips were all puffed up like she'd been stung by a bee," Walter continued. "And uh, the other thing women do." He flushed a pretty shade of pink.

"Breast lift?" I asked.

"I don't know about any lifting but they were a sight bigger. I'm not the kind of man who goes around looking at women's chests, mind you, but she was wearing a top that could have gotten her arrested in a place like Sinful. It was hard not to notice."

"Margarita never had any chest to speak of," Gertie said. "Used to stuff her bra with toilet paper."

"Good Lord," Walter mumbled and rummaged through the cookie container.

"What?" Gertie said when Ida Belle stared at her. "I'm just backing the man up. She pulled some out at church one day when Junior sneezed. If she didn't want everyone knowing, then she should have carried tissue in her purse like everyone else."

Ida Belle shook her head and looked at Walter. "What did she say?"

"We exchanged the usual greetings and she asked about Carter and Emmaline. I said I was sorry about Hooch's death and asked if there was anything I could do. She said I could pray he had some life insurance so they could afford to bury him."

"Sounds like Margarita," Gertie said.

"Practical?" I asked.

"I was going with cold," Gertie said, "but in this situation, I can see how practicality would apply."

"There was certainly no love lost between Margarita and Hooch," Walter said. "Not by the time she left. And that's all on him. Margarita was a nice enough girl, but she was also naive. She should never have married Hooch."

Ida Belle nodded. "I think once she got a few years behind her, she realized that. What about Junior?"

"Good-looking boy," Walter said. "Must have taken after Margarita's family because he sure don't look like Hooch's. About six feet tall and a solid build. Said he works construction, so I guess he might have gotten that gene from his father. He had the tan and the muscles for it, anyway. He didn't say much, but then, what could we expect him to say? He had to drop everything to come to Sinful to bury a man he didn't know by that man's deliberate choice."

"But Margarita took Junior with her when she left," I said.

"Parents still have rights," Walter said. "Even fathers. Even if they're a lousy father and don't pay support. Courts still say they have rights. Everyone knows the truth is Hooch didn't care to see the boy, so he didn't bother to try."

"Can't really blame him for being quiet then," I said. "What's he supposed to say?"

Ida Belle glanced over at me and I knew that she'd caught something in my tone. I'd tried for nonchalant, but apparently I hadn't been completely successful. Lousy, dead fathers were kinda a sore spot with me. I needed to remind myself not to let it color my judgment. Regardless of how crappy a father or a contractor Hooch was, neither was a reason for someone to kill you.

"Can't imagine he'd have much more to say than he did," Walter said. "Margarita said Carter had searched Hooch's house but hadn't found a will or any other legal documents."

"No surprise there," Gertie said.

"No, but it complicates things," Walter said.

Ida Belle nodded. "As only Louisiana can."

"So does everything go into probate then?" I asked.

"Succession," Ida Belle said. "That's Louisiana's version of probate. And the answer is yes for some things, maybe for the rest. Real estate goes into succession because you need a change of deed. Vehicles can go through a lesser process and title can transfer by affidavit. Personal property that isn't worth anything to speak of usually just transfers to next of kin without much pomp and circumstance."

"Ha!" Gertie said. "You make it sound so simple, but this state is all about the drama. If someone dies with more than one kid, bet your heinie the fight is on. We've seen more than our share."

"True," Ida Belle agreed, "but in this case, there is only one child, so no drama."

"So how long does succession take?" I asked.

"Might as well ask how high is high," Gertie said. "Best case, a couple months."

"Worst case?" I asked.

"People he owes money to file claims against his estate," Ida Belle said. "Then there's no telling how long it could be tied up."

I glanced at Ida Belle and frowned and she gave me a barely imperceptible shake of her head. She didn't want to say anything in front of Walter, but she knew exactly where my train of thought had gone. Potential debts were one of the reasons we'd deduced Hooch was trying to sell out to the Heberts rather than go about things openly.

"So Margarita and Junior can collect the things in Hooch's house?" I asked. "I'm assuming he doesn't have any antique furniture or Da Vincis lurking around in there."

"Not likely," Walter said. "I was there about a month ago to deliver some lumber. Hooch's truck was broken down, again, and he had a hole in his roof he needed to patch before the next storm. The furniture looked about as good as something you'd find sitting on the curb for trash pickup. Nothing hanging on the walls but stuffed dead things."

"No velvet Jesus?" I asked.

"No," Walter said. "But he had beer cans hanging from a Christmas tree in the corner of his living room."

"You were there in August," Gertie said.

Walter nodded. "Looked like this wasn't the first August that tree had seen, either. Probably been there for years."

"So Junior will be able to load up anything worth keeping and take it with him?" I asked.

"Yes, but not quite yet," Walter said. "Carter says the house could be part of a crime scene and it's off-limits until he gives the word."

"How is that?" I asked. "Hooch died in his boat."

"Which is also a crime scene," Walter said. "My guess is Carter's going overboard because of this state police thing."

I nodded. "Did they show up before you were done with Carter?"

"No," Walter said. "They called and said they were delayed in getting someone out and it would likely be tomorrow. Honestly, I doubt they'll ever send someone out. I think they're just yanking his chain."

"Making sure he goes out of his way to do everything by the book since the threat of them getting involved is hanging over his head," Ida Belle said. "That sounds about right."

"I bet Margarita isn't happy about the holdup," Gertie said. "She'll just see it as Hooch screwing with her from the grave."

"I got the impression she wasn't thrilled about any of it," Walter said, "but I'm pretty sure being delayed longer than she expected didn't thrill her."

"Why should it matter?" Gertie said. "Not like she was going to sleep in the same bed that Hooch had been sleeping in. Hell, she'll probably have a priest perform an exorcism before she enters the house. She can help Junior make arrangements for the funeral, then they can head back home until Carter says everything is clear."

"I got the impression she was just wanting it all settled so they could move on and close this chapter forever," Walter said. "They're staying at the motel for a couple days, hoping Carter gets things wrapped up enough for them to start all the legal stuff."

"I feel sorry for Junior," Gertie said. "Hooch wasn't much of a father but as long as he was alive, there was always that hope that he might change his mind and try to be."

"A little late now," Ida Belle said. "The boy's grown."

"Still," Gertie said. "It probably would have meant something to him to know his father gave a damn."

"Maybe," Ida Belle said. "Or maybe he decided long ago that his father wasn't deserving of any mental space."

There was an edge to her voice that I didn't hear often, and I remembered the comments she'd made in passing about her own father. About how he'd wanted a son but Ida Belle had been his only child. I wondered how much of her childhood had consisted of her trying to fit into a role that biology would never allow her to assume. I could appreciate the dilemma. It was one of the many things Ida Belle and I had in common.

Walter rose from the table. "Well, ladies, I have a steak marinating and a dog waiting to be fed, so I'm going to leave you to whatever it is you're doing that I don't want to know anything about."

"That's it?" Ida Belle said.

Walter looked confused. "That's all I know."

Ida Belle narrowed her eyes at Walter. "Things sounded kinda heated in Carter's office when we arrived. Sounded like a lot more than an argument over bottled water."

Walter looked down at the ground for a couple seconds, then back at Ida Belle. "I'm not happy about some of the choices my nephew has made recently. I get that he has a job to do, but I disagree with the way he has to go about it."

"And what did Carter think of your disapproval?" Ida Belle asked.

"He wasn't impressed with it," Walter said. "My nephew is a stubborn man. I don't expect he'll admit he's been wrong a time or two, but that doesn't mean I'm going to stop pointing those times out."

Ida Belle nodded. "I wouldn't expect any less. I'm sorry he wasn't interested in hearing what you had to say."

Walter nodded, the tension slipping from his expression. "I know there's no point in my telling you not to stick your nose in, what with Ally in the mix and all, so instead, I'll just tell you to be careful."

"We're always careful," Gertie said. "Why do people think we're not careful?"

Ida Belle stared at her. "Seriously?"

Walter smiled. "That's my cue. You ladies have a nice night."

I handed Walter his keys and walked him to the door, raising my hand as he climbed in his truck. Then I headed back into the kitchen and plopped into my chair.

"You buying that?" I asked.

"No way," Ida Belle said.

Gertie looked confused. "What did I miss?"

"Walter lying," I said. "Or to be fair, more like leaving out a big chunk of the truth."

Ida Belle nodded. "I have no doubt he had words with Carter over you and Ally spending a night in jail, but that wasn't what they were fighting about when we arrived."

"Carter said 'You should have told me,'" I said. "That doesn't fit the narrative of Walter complaining about the way Carter handled Ally and me."

"Nor does it fit the water bottle scenario," Ida Belle said, "because everyone knew Walter supplied the water. It was hardly a state secret."

Gertie clapped her hands. "Two mysteries! It's like Christmas came early."

"Yeah," Ida Belle said. "One being slightly less dangerous than the other."

"I don't get it," Gertie said.

"One is a murder," Ida Belle said. "The other is probably a family matter."

Gertie's eyes widened. "Oh. I see. Yeah, the murder might be the less lethal. Getting in the middle of family business, especially Southern family business, was never a good idea. So what do you think is going on?"

Ida Belle shook her head. "No idea. But it must be something good for Carter to be that mad."

"And something he doesn't want anyone else to know about since he hauled Walter to the sheriff's department to confront him," I said. "Twenty bucks says that had nothing to do with Hooch's murder, regardless of the state police excuse."

"If Carter pulled police rank to question Walter about family business, he's really got his underwear in a knot," Gertie said. "Carter never blurs those lines."

Ida Belle laughed. "Are you kidding me? Carter's been blurring those lines since Fortune blew into town."

"That's different," Gertie said. "He's having sex with Fortune. Men lose their minds over sex. Some women, too. I remember this hot navy guy I met in Japan—"

"Nope!" Ida Belle held up her hand. "I am not about to listen to the hot navy guy story again. The first time almost sent me to therapy."

"That was over fifty years ago," Gertie said.

"I promise you, hearing it now would be worse," Ida Belle said.

Gertie crossed her arms over her chest. "Well, maybe I'll just have Fortune over one night for a retelling and you won't be invited."

"Do I have to be invited?" I asked.

"Et tu, Brute?" Gertie asked.

"I'm more of a leave-it-to-the-imagination sort of girl," I said.

"I wouldn't even imagine," Ida Belle said. "Not if you plan on eating again anytime soon."

Gertie gave her the finger.

"In other news," I said, "if Carter declared Hooch's property a potential crime scene, then that makes checking it out an even bigger problem. I imagine there aren't fifty entrances to the place, and there's always a chance that Carter will have the ones that do exist watched."

"Or just be sitting on the front porch himself," Ida Belle said. "I wouldn't put it past him if he really thought there was something of value inside, but in this case I don't see it."

"Maybe Hooch has money stuffed in his mattress," I said. "I mean, there has to be some reason that Carter won't allow his son into the house. The murder didn't happen there and I don't think anyone would buy that Hooch poisoned himself, so the preparation of the poison didn't occur there either."

Ida Belle nodded. "It is interesting and makes one wonder. Usually the police only control access to property if it's part of the investigation or there is likely to be pilfering by relatives before the courts settle things up. But in this case, there's only the one child."

"Carter must know something," I said.

"You don't think you could get it out of him?" Gertie asked.

"Not even if I had him handcuffed to a chair and was standing there naked with a gun to his head," I said.

"I have to agree," Ida Belle said. "Carter's not going to give up information to Fortune. One, because he's serious about his job and the responsibilities that go with it. Two, because he knows we'll use that information to insert ourselves into his investigation."

"He's just prolonging the agony," Gertie said. "We're in full insertion mode anyway."

"Why don't you call him up and tell him that and see if he changes his mind," Ida Belle said.

"Well, you don't have to get condescending," Gertie said. "Anyway, this doesn't change my mind. I still think we need to check out Hooch's property, and it's best to do it before Junior douses it with gas and lights the whole thing on fire."

"Hold on," I said. "We were going to check out the ground for signs of oil exploration. No one said anything about breaking into Hooch's house."

Gertie rolled her eyes. "And do you think Hooch would have stored any paperwork from oil companies outside? Come on, if Hooch really had property worth the kind of money he asked the Heberts for, then there will be some indication of it inside his house."

I threw my hands up and looked over at Ida Belle. "I can't get through to her. You try."

Ida Belle slowly shook her head. "I agree with her. In theory, anyway. Hooch had a huge distrust of banks and the government so I guarantee you he didn't have a safe-deposit box. Anything he had to document the value of the property would be in his house."

I sighed. "Fine. Then we'll trespass and break and enter on a property that the police have specifically designated as off-limits. What could possibly go wrong? How are you planning on getting there? You buy a teleportation device off of eBay?"

"Not yet," Gertie said, "but I keep looking for one."

Ida Belle shot her a worried look, then looked back at me. "There's two ways in—road or bayou. One road, one bayou."

Gertie shook her head. "That's not true."

"They built a new road to the middle of nowhere?" Ida Belle asked. "God carved out a new bayou?"

"Of course not," Gertie said. "But we could parachute in. Bomber Bruce said we could do it anytime for free."

"And hike out?" Ida Belle asked. "Or would you prefer a midnight swim in alligator-infested bayous? Walter won't be next door with a truck. I swear that whole skydiving thing has scrambled your brain even worse than usual."

"I guess I forgot about that whole extraction part," Gertie said.

"Hey, why worry about the small details?" I asked. "I personally vote for road. The thought of taking an unplanned dip in the bayou in the middle of alligator lurking time is not anywhere on my agenda. Not tonight or ever."

"No one said anything about taking a dip," Gertie said.

"No one had to," I said. "It's us. It's bound to happen. Besides, no way we can approach by water without the sound of the engine echoing across the water. And since boating at night is reasonably limited, anyone watching Hooch's house will hear us coming a mile away."

"I have an idea," Ida Belle said. "Pull up a satellite image of Sinful."

I grabbed my laptop and pulled up the image.

"Move northeast," Ida Belle instructed, "and zoom in. There. That's the road to Hooch's place."

"Is that thing at the end of the road that looks like an abandoned building his house?" I asked.

Ida Belle nodded. "But see over here?" She pointed a bit west of the road. "There's another road that runs parallel. They're about a quarter-mile apart when you exit the highway, but the gap narrows a bit toward the end."

"So you're thinking take the first road and then hike through the woods to Hooch's place?" I asked.

"Exactly," Ida Belle said.

"What about this?" I pointed to a shack at the end of the road Ida Belle suggested using. "Who lives there and how handy is he with a shotgun at night if he hears people on his property?"

"That's Young Huck's place," Gertie said. "He owns all the property from the highway clear to the bayou."

"*Young* Huck?" I asked.

"As opposed to Old Huck, his father," Gertie said. "Young Huck is only eighty."

"Only?" I asked. "I assume his father has passed?"

Gertie shook her head. "If he'd passed, we could just call him Huck. Old Huck lives in New Orleans in one of those retirement homes. He likes daily poker and the ladies."

"So how strict is Young Huck about trespassing on his land?" I asked. "Because I really don't want to deal with some old guy with shaky hands and faulty eyesight shooting at me."

"Don't worry," Ida Belle said. "I can handle that end of things."

"Okay," I said. "I guess that could work. I mean, nothing says 'good time' like hiking through a Louisiana swamp on a hot September night."

I mean, what could be better? A sketchy road among the bayous of Louisiana. A hike through woods with any number of creatures that could maim you, while wearing long sleeves to ward off mosquitoes the size of prehistoric birds. Then we search a property that is likely being guarded by law enforcement, and attempt escape without being arrested.

I smiled. Better than a good thriller and a case of beer.

CHAPTER SIXTEEN

IT WAS close to midnight when we drove out of town in Ida Belle's SUV. We'd taken the back way around downtown and driven with no headlights until we reached the highway. So far, there had been no movement along the way, but it was Louisiana and we were about to trek through the woods, so all bets were off on the quiet continuing.

"So explain to me again about the rifles?" I asked.

"It's our cover," Gertie explained. "We're hunting possums."

"Why would we do that?" I asked.

"We wouldn't," Ida Belle said. "Some people like them but I think they taste like death. But we need a reason to be out in the middle of the woods at night with weapons, and this is the one that fits. There's no hunting season for possum and it's one of the few things you can hunt at night."

"Uh-huh," I said. "And we brought Bones with us, why?"

"Because you can only hunt at night with a dog," Gertie said.

"He's a thousand years old," I said. "We had to lift him into the truck. I seriously doubt he's up to a trek through the woods."

"Doesn't matter," Ida Belle said. "We can always say we brought him to hunt and he got tired or injured."

"Or just refused to wake up," I said, speaking louder than usual in order to be heard over his snoring.

"Regardless of the reason," Ida Belle said, "we have our cover. And it's one that even Carter can't argue with."

"Don't we have to have permission from the owner of the land?" I asked. Surely you couldn't randomly shoot things on other people's property. Not even in Louisiana.

Ida Belle nodded. "It so happens that I have a standing agreement with Young Huck to hunt his land. I gave him a call this evening to let him know we'll be out there and he might hear gunfire."

"So basically, like any other night in the woods of Sinful," I said.

"More or less," Ida Belle said. "But he won't call the police about it since I warned him ahead of time."

"Or come out on the porch and start firing his own weapon," Gertie said.

"That's important," I agreed.

"Hang on," Ida Belle said. "It's off-roading time."

Technically, it was considered a road, like many other dirt paths through the Louisiana wilderness, but the term was applicable in the loosest form possible. I grabbed on to the door handle and braced my feet on the floorboard, trying to keep from bouncing off the seat every time we dipped in and out of the huge holes. When we hit a flat stretch, I glanced back and saw that Bones still hadn't stirred. I was fairly sure he'd been completely airborne a time or two, but apparently it hadn't fazed him.

Finally, the bone-jarring ride came to an end when Ida Belle pulled into a tiny clearing. I could see a sliver of light through the trees and figured that must be Young Huck's place. I worried for a minute that he was still awake, but given his age, he might have been asleep since early afternoon and considered midnight morning. He was probably drinking coffee and wondering why the sun wasn't up yet.

"Let's get this show on the road," Gertie said. "Or off the road, as the case may be."

We climbed out and went around to the back of the truck. I killed at least fifty mosquitoes in those ten steps. I'm pretty sure I tripped over one of their carcasses. Ida Belle opened the back of her SUV and doled out the .22 rifles. Gertie pulled on a backpack, which she claimed was extra ammo. Based on the look she gave Gertie, Ida Belle wasn't any more convinced of that truth than me, but apparently neither of us wanted to check the bag. Besides, Gertie was expecting just that sort of check and had probably hidden the real contraband somewhere on her body. No way was I frisking a senior citizen to confiscate a stick of dynamite. It wasn't like it would make a difference anyway. She seemed to have an endless supply.

Ida Belle handed out the flashlights and shook Bones a couple of times for good measure. He flopped over, farted, and continued to snore. She lowered the back window on the SUV and filled a bowl with water.

"In case he wakes up," she said.

"More likely, he'll keep sleeping and five million mosquitoes will get in that water and breed ten million more of them," I said, and waved at the woods. "Lead the way."

Ida Belle checked her compass and we set off into the woods, perpendicular to the road. With the dense brush and minimal light, it was slow going. So slow that I began to wonder if we'd arrive before morning. Finally, Ida Belle put her arm out to stop us.

"Turn off your lights," she said.

Gertie and I clicked off our flashlights and squinted into the inky black. I couldn't even make out Ida Belle and I knew she was only inches in front of me.

"Reach out and grab the back of my shirt," Ida Belle said. "Gertie first, then Fortune. I'll get us to the road. Remember to lift your feet as you walk."

"What the heck are you talking about?" Gertie asked. "I always lift my feet to walk. Everyone does."

"Lift them like you're marching," Ida Belle said.

Gertie and I bumped around until we'd formed a single line behind Ida Belle, then she started to inch forward. I hoped she had a great memory because no way could she possibly see anything. The trees were close together and full of moss, blocking out any chance of moonlight guiding our way.

Finally we moved forward a couple of steps, then stopped.

"Stop kicking me in the butt," Ida Belle said.

"I'm not kicking you," Gertie said. "That's my knees."

"Well, march lower then," Ida Belle said.

"This would be easier if we had night-vision goggles," Gertie said.

"Then you shouldn't have dropped Fortune's and broken them," Ida Belle said. "Can't exactly pick up a new pair at the General Store."

"If I hadn't dropped them," Gertie said, "I would have fallen out the window."

"Then you shouldn't have been spying on Cindy Thompson in her backyard," Ida Belle said.

"I wasn't spying on Cindy," Gertie said. "I was spying on that hunk of a guy she's dating. They were totally naked in the swimming pool. I bet Susan has no idea her high school daughter is cavorting with naked college guys in their pool when Susan's at choir practice."

"And we're not going to tell her," Ida Belle said.

I grimaced and wished I could have brought my noise-canceling headphones. Gertie had fessed up to dropping my night-vision goggles, but she hadn't gone into details then. I wished she hadn't now. We continued and counted twenty steps before Ida Belle stopped again.

"There," she said. "Look straight ahead."

I stepped to the side and peered around her. The tree line ended and I could see a bit of moonlight shining over an open area. I hoped it was the road, or even better, Hooch's front lawn. We stepped up to the edge of the trees and took a look. I could make out a structure about twenty yards to our left that had to be Hooch's place.

Bingo.

I scanned the area surrounding the structure but didn't see a vehicle or any telltale lights to indicate that someone was lurking around.

"No car," Gertie said.

"I don't see any light or movement," I said, "but we need to get closer to be sure."

"I agree," Ida Belle said. "Deputy Breaux or someone else Carter drafted could have come by boat. Might even be around back if they're walking the perimeter."

"Or sitting quietly in the dark if they're wanting the element of surprise," Gertie said.

"Can one really sit quietly in the dark with the mosquitoes around here?" I asked. "Wouldn't you hear slapping or cursing?"

"Let's find out," Ida Belle said. "Stay just inside the tree line until we can get a better look at the house."

We took a step back into the woods and began the slow

creep toward the shack. At least we had a bit of moonlight this time. It wasn't much, but any amount of light was better than the inky black we had before. And my eyes were adjusting rapidly. I could see some distance, even in the dim light. But as we moved closer, I never caught sight of another person. Finally, we stopped directly in front of the structure.

"Nothing," Gertie said. "Maybe we got this all wrong. Maybe there's nothing in there that Carter's worried about in regard to the case. Maybe he's just covering his butt for the succession courts."

Ida Belle nodded. "Seems that way. If Carter suspected there was evidence in the house, he would have posted someone here."

"He doesn't have that many people, though, and he's not about to call the state for help," I said. "He and Deputy Breaux were working all day."

"And Sheriff Lee can't hardly stay awake past 6:00 p.m.," Gertie said.

"He could have gotten some backup from another department close by," Ida Belle said. "Worst case, he would have jacked Sheriff Lee up on coffee and had him sitting here. All he really needs is a deterrent. Anyone with nefarious business in mind usually sets their eyes on law enforcement and heads the other way, even if they're sleeping."

"So it looks like we're clear," I said. "What's first?"

"Inside," Gertie said. "If we can find paperwork from any geological studies, we don't have to poke around in the dirt looking for signs of movement. Besides, there's probably fewer mosquitoes inside."

I pulled a small set of lock-picking tools out of my back pocket, motioned for everyone to put on their latex gloves, then handed Ida Belle my gun as we walked up onto the porch. "I'm going to need some light," I said.

Ida Belle turned on her flashlight and directed it at the lock. "Keep lookout," she said to Gertie.

I made quick work of the old, cheap lock and we headed inside, closing and locking the door behind us. Ida Belle shone her light around the small space and I blanched.

"It looks like an episode of *Animal Head Hoarders*," I said.

"And beer cans," Gertie said. "Hasn't he heard of recycling?"

"I'd settle for a trash can," Ida Belle said, "but it appears our friend Hooch wasn't big on clearing or cleaning."

"This is why I always bring gloves," I said. "It's not all about the fingerprints."

"How do you want to divvy this up?" Gertie asked.

"There's three main rooms," Ida Belle said. "Gertie, you take the bedroom. I'll take the kitchen, and Fortune can take the living room."

"Why do I have to take the bedroom?" Gertie groused.

"Because Fortune and I are the better shots," Ida Belle said. "So if anyone comes through that door that needs shooting, I want one of us on the other end of the gunfire."

Gertie headed off to the bedroom without argument, but then, she couldn't really argue against reality. I shone my flashlight around the living room, trying to decide which pile of junk to start with. Finally, I figured I'd begin at the television console and work my way around the perimeter of the room, then tackle everything in the middle.

Thirty minutes later, I'd gone through stacks of old hunting magazines and shaken two years' worth of old *TV Guide*s to make sure nothing was stuck in the pages. The only thing I had left was the drawer on the end table. I pulled it open and found twelve television remotes.

"Good Lord, he really doesn't throw anything away," I said.

"Some of the food in this pantry expired two years ago," Ida Belle said. She turned to look at me. "Anything?"

I shook my head. "Not a single personal piece of paper anywhere. I mean, besides food wrappers. The man lived on Twinkies."

Ida Belle nodded. "It was darn near impossible to lay eyes on him that he didn't have one in his hand. Been that way since he was a kid."

"You find anything, Gertie?" Ida Belle headed for the doorway to the bedroom that was off the kitchen.

"Bunch of girlie magazines," Gertie said. "I accidentally stuck my hand in a pile of dirty underwear. I'll bleach it when I get home, even though I'm wearing a glove."

"Yuck," I said as I stepped up behind Ida Belle and peered into the bedroom. It made the living room look like paradise.

"Why didn't you notice it was underwear before you shoved your hand in it?" Ida Belle asked.

"It was balled up under the bedcovers," Gertie said. "What kind of laundry system is that?"

"The disgusting man kind," Ida Belle said. "Anything personal—cash, legal documents, deed?"

"A plastic container of quarters in the nightstand," Gertie said. "Maybe a couple bucks' worth. And this box of old letters and some photos shoved under the bed." She handed Ida Belle a shoebox.

I looked over as Ida Belle riffled through the letters and photos. "These letters look old," she said.

"They are," Gertie said. "I looked in all the envelopes to make sure something else wasn't slipped inside, but it looks like correspondence from one of Hooch's relatives during the First World War."

"I never took Hooch for the sentimental type," Ida Belle said.

"More likely he's the never-throw-anything-out type," I said.

"True," Ida Belle said. "Are you almost done?"

Gertie nodded. "I just have that wardrobe left."

She headed to the end of the bedroom and flung open the doors of a huge wardrobe that stood in the corner.

"Jesus H. Christ, it's a skunk!" Gertie screamed.

CHAPTER SEVENTEEN

GERTIE WHIRLED AROUND, tripping over her own feet as she tried to flee the room. Ida Belle and I dashed for the front door and ran outside into the middle of the lawn.

"He got me!" Gertie ran out on the porch, flailing around like she was warding off an attack of birds.

"He's right behind you!" Ida Belle yelled. "Get off the porch!"

"I can't see," Gertie said. "The fumes are killing me." She took off running but missed the steps by a good five feet and fell straight off the porch and into a set of unkempt hedges. The skunk scurried down the stairs and hurried off under the house.

Gertie thrashed around in the bushes and finally crawled out. We probably should have helped her out, but with the skunk lurking just under the house and Gertie already stinking to high heaven, neither of us was anxious to get in the mix.

Finally, she crawled out of the bushes and staggered to her feet. Ida Belle and I both covered our noses as she walked up.

"That is horrible," I said.

"How was I supposed to know there was a skunk in the

wardrobe?" Gertie said. "Point of the matter, why the hell was a skunk in the wardrobe?"

"I couldn't even begin to guess," Ida Belle said, "but it's a good thing you opened it up. The poor thing could have died in there before Carter got around to letting people in the house."

"That skunk is not a poor thing," Gertie said. "And it would have served Carter right if he'd taken the shot himself with the way he's acting lately."

"Regardless, we have a problem now," Ida Belle said. "First off, we have to retrieve our guns and your pack and close that door. Then we have to figure out how to get you home. I'm thinking about strapping you on the roof of my SUV."

"I'm not riding on the roof," Gertie said.

"Well, you're not riding inside, either."

I shook my head and hurried into the cabin to retrieve our belongings while the two of them sorted out the travel arrangements. I wasn't excited about the prospect of getting into a vehicle with Gertie, but I couldn't see strapping her to the roof as a viable option either. I mean, it was if no one saw us, but we rarely managed to do insane things without someone seeing.

As I grabbed Gertie's pack, I glanced over at the wardrobe. The entire bedroom reeked of skunk and I was going to guess the wardrobe had gotten a good dosing, but Gertie hadn't had a chance to check out the contents without fleeing. What if the important thing we were looking for was inside? We'd already gone through all this trouble. No point in leaving empty-handed.

I pulled both doors completely open and shone my light inside. At the back of the wardrobe at the bottom, I saw a hole that went straight through the wardrobe and the wall. That explained the skunk occupation. It also gave him a way to come back in and refire, which meant I needed to hurry. I riffled through the drawers but all I found was a meager supply of holey underwear and socks.

The hanging garments were also sadly sparse. A couple pairs of blue jeans, some stained T-shirts, a couple of flannel button-ups, and a camo jacket. A box of shotgun shells sat in the corner of the wardrobe, and I wondered briefly where Hooch's gun was as I hadn't seen it during my search. But then, he might have had it with him during the fishing rodeo, which meant Carter had confiscated it. Or Carter might have taken it when he checked Hooch's house to ensure no one helped themselves to a free firearm. He had enough problems with the ones that were bought and paid for.

I checked the pockets of the jeans and came up with nothing but more Twinkie wrappers, but in the jacket, I found a piece of paper. It was folded over and over until it had formed a small square. I unfolded it and directed my flashlight on it, figuring it was probably nothing, but my pulse shot up when I saw the sender.

Lassiter Drilling Services.

"Mr. Carre,

We received your email and are interested in speaking with you. Please contact us at the following number at your convenience to arrange a meeting."

THEN THERE WAS the contact information.

I placed the letter on the bed and took a picture of it with my phone. I would remember the details, but it never hurt to have proof for everyone else. Unless, of course, Carter found a reason to take my phone. Then I'd have to explain why I had a pic of a personal document addressed to Hooch, taken after midnight at a time when Hooch's house was under the control of the sheriff's department.

No big deal.

I stuffed the letter back where I'd found it, closed the wardrobe, and hurried outside with our belongings. I shoved Gertie's pack at her and divvied up the rifles.

"We need to get out of here," I said as I pulled off my gloves and motioned to them to do the same. "That was an awful lot of yelling. If Carter has anyone nearby, they're going to come running."

I figured telling them about the letter could wait until we were safely back in my house. I didn't want any more delays. Not out here in the woods with the mosquitoes and skunks and the potential for arrest.

Gertie pointed her finger at Ida Belle. "Well, tell her I'm not about to—"

I clamped one hand over Gertie's mouth and held up a finger. "Someone's out there," I whispered, and clicked off my flashlight.

"Where?" Ida Belle asked as she extinguished her light. Gertie had turned hers off with all the flailing, so now we were back in the dim moonlight. I pulled them toward the tree line, then paused just inside it.

"On the road," I said. "I heard the sound of footsteps on shell."

A lot of the roads in Sinful had shells dumped on them from time to time. They made a different sound than gravel, and I was certain I'd heard someone walking on them.

"Stay here," I said.

I crept out of the trees and hurried down the tree line until I found the road. Then I skirted the edge of it, hiding in the shadows as much as possible and staying in the grass to avoid making a sound on the shells. I could hear someone ahead of me hurrying away. I picked up my pace and stepped on a branch. It snapped with a crack that sounded like a gunshot in the still night air. The footsteps ahead of me took off and I sped up to a run. When I reached the first bend in the road, I saw a shadowy figure jump into a truck about fifty yards ahead. Seconds later, the truck took off, no lights on.

I hurried back to where Ida Belle and Gertie were and told them what I'd seen.

"That's not Carter's people," Gertie said.

"No," Ida Belle agreed. "Someone else wanted a peek at Hooch's place. One person or two?"

"I'm not sure," I said. "Only one person on the road but there could have been another in the truck. I couldn't make it out in the dark. You think it was Junior?"

"Maybe," Ida Belle said. "But why? We're here looking for some indication of the property Hooch offered up to the Heberts, but Junior wouldn't know about that. For that matter, neither would Carter. I can't imagine Hooch wanted the fact that he had something valuable to get around, so he wouldn't have been blabbing about it."

"Maybe he let something slip when he was drunk," I said. "If someone overheard and knew how to contact Margarita or Junior, they might have felt they needed to know."

"Before or after he was murdered?" Ida Belle said.

"Good question," I said. "Assuming it happened at all."

"There's one way to find out," Gertie said. "Hooch did all his public drinking at the Swamp Bar."

"No one at the Swamp Bar is going to talk to us," I said. "Especially now that Hooch has been murdered. I'm sure it won't take that little tidbit long to make the rounds. It's easier to keep underwear on a prostitute than it is to keep a juicy secret in this town."

"God, isn't that the truth," Ida Belle said. "Still, it might be worth a shot, and you know how much I hate the Swamp Bar."

"Why? You're not the one constantly humiliated there," I said.

"Yes, but that doesn't mean the potential isn't there for it to happen next time," she said.

"Well, we can hash this out indoors, with AC, and with no mosquitoes," I said. "Let's get out of here."

Ida Belle pulled out her compass, we all clicked on our lights, and we headed into the woods. Since we weren't worried about being seen this time, we moved at a faster pace and using a broader spread of light. We were two-thirds of the way back to the SUV when a branch cracked.

Everyone froze. The crack had been loud, signaling that the branch wasn't small. Further signaling that whatever had broken it had some size to it. I didn't think alligators would be this deep into the woods away from the water, but I wasn't willing to bet on it. Ida Belle had told me there were feral hogs in the woods, and they were definitely heavy enough to break a good-sized branch. They were also not known for their pleasant temperament. We'd made it this far without having to shoot something, and I was really hoping we wouldn't have to start.

A second branch broke, this one much closer.

"It's behind us," I said. "I mean almost directly."

"Like it's following us?" Gertie asked.

I nodded.

"Do you think the guy on the road could have doubled back?" Ida Belle asked.

"Maybe, but he'd have to be a good tracker to pick up our trail, at least in the beginning. I think we should get out of here."

I didn't like the circumstances—unknown terrain,

unknown assailant or assailants, unknown motivation. Way too many unknowns.

We set out at a slow jog, Ida Belle in the lead. I followed last, listening for any signs of pursuit. Seconds after we began, I heard the steps...heavy crushing steps. But not from two legs. This was definitely four, and something a lot heavier than a human.

"Run!" I yelled as the roar of the bear ripped through the still night air.

Gertie whirled around and aimed her rifle at the sound of the roar, but when she squeezed the trigger, nothing happened. Her eyes widened and I shoved her in the back. "Go!"

We all took off at a dead run. I'd read that when you encountered a bear you shouldn't run, but that didn't seem to make a lot of sense when you were actually being chased by a bear. Ida Belle and Gertie surprised me by setting a good pace, but we were in the bear's house and I could tell he was closing in.

"There!" Ida Belle yelled as we burst out of the trees.

We came out of the woods north of where we'd parked, and the SUV was nowhere in sight. But directly ahead was a cabin. Young Huck's place. Free of the brush, we increased pace and ran for the cabin, all of us yelling as we went. The front porch light on the cabin clicked on and a man stepped onto the porch with a shotgun.

Six foot even. A hundred and sixty pounds. Nothing young about him.

"Who's there?" he hollered and leveled the shotgun at us.

"It's Ida Belle and friends! A bear is chasing us!"

Young Huck ran down the steps toward us. "Where?"

"There!" I waved a hand behind me as we ran past Young Huck and into the cabin.

I heard the shotgun blast behind me but I didn't slow to check. Instead we all sped into the cabin then slid to a stop inside the doorway and looked back. Young Huck's shot had missed, and the bear was barreling right for him.

"Run!" Ida Belle yelled.

With a surprising amount of agility and speed, Young Huck spun around and ran for the cabin. As soon as he'd crossed the threshold, we slammed the door and threw the dead bolt. But that didn't deter the bear. He rammed into the door and I saw the doorframe begin to split.

"Upstairs!" Young Huck yelled, and headed for a ladder at the back of the cabin. I was pretty sure I'd seen this scene in at least ten of the horror movies that Gertie had made me watch, and it had never ended well for the people climbing the ladder. Of course, they'd had a two-legged pursuer, not a bear, so unless this was an escaped circus bear that could climb ladders, we would probably be good.

The bear slammed into the door again and the walls of the cabin shook as I scurried up the ladder behind the other three. Okay, maybe we were in trouble if he tore the whole place down. I stepped off the ladder and Young Huck clicked on a lantern. I'd expected to be in an attic, but instead, we were on what appeared to be an observation deck, complete with roof. Or a sniper tower, depending on your perspective. I suspected Young Huck was probably using it for more of the latter than the former.

"What did you do?" Young Huck asked. "Did you startle him?"

"We didn't do anything," I said. "We never even saw him until he started chasing us. He'd been following us for a while, though. I heard something behind us but we didn't realize it was a bear until he roared."

"No reason for a bear to follow you unless you've got something he wants," Young Huck said. "You bag anything while you were hunting? Smells like someone took a skunk hit. I hope you ain't thinking of eating that. Even I don't go for skunk."

"Gertie got sprayed by a skunk," Ida Belle said. "It was an accident. And we haven't bagged anything."

"Maybe he's rabid," Young Huck said.

I looked over at Gertie, who had been suspiciously silent and now wore a guilty look. "What?" I asked her. "You know something. What is it? You wearing bear pheromone perfume or underwear made of rabbit fur?"

She pulled off her backpack and unzipped it.

"What is that smell?" I asked.

She reached inside and pulled out a dead possum.

"I thought we might need it for our cover," Gertie said.

"Your bag is leaking," Ida Belle said.

"I had ice in it," Gertie said. "It's hot as heck out here. Meat would have been spoiled before we could even get it home."

"It spoiled anyway," Ida Belle said. "That's why the bear was chasing us. He probably smelled it from three parishes over."

The bear took another shot at the door and this time I heard it split from the frame. He was inside!

Young Huck clearly had zero idea what we were talking about, but I don't think he cared to figure it out. "Throw that thing on the lawn before that bear tears my house down!" he yelled.

CHAPTER EIGHTEEN

GERTIE LIFTED the possum by the tail and we all ducked, and she swung it around before tossing it off the roof.

"What the hell?" Carter's voice sounded from below.

We all stared at one another in horror, then leaned over the railing to see Carter standing there with the dead animal draped across his shoulder.

"Run!" I screamed.

Carter stared up at us, but his confusion only lasted long enough for the bear to catch the scent of decaying possum and come barreling out of the cabin. Carter took one look at the charging beast, grabbed the possum, and threw it as hard as he could into the woods. Then he set out running for the cabin. The bear hesitated for a second, then launched into the woods after his dinner.

A couple seconds later, Carter stepped off the ladder and onto the deck. His shirt was wet where the possum had draped across it and I imagined the smell wasn't all that grand either, but since I was standing next to Gertie, I wouldn't know. The skunk was beating out the dead possum in the odor wars.

"What the hell is going on here?" Carter asked. "I'm on my

way to do a drive-by on Hooch's place and I hear gunfire. Then I find you people feeding bears."

"We were hunting possum," Ida Belle said. "We wanted to teach Fortune some local stuff."

"Hunting on private property?" Carter asked.

"I have a standing agreement with Young Huck that I can hunt his land," Ida Belle said.

"That's true enough," Young Huck said. "Never said anything about staking out my roof though."

"We'll renegotiate our terms next week," Ida Belle said.

"So you were teaching Fortune how locals hunt," Carter said. He picked up Ida Belle's rifle and checked it, then repeated the process with mine and Gertie's.

"These rifles aren't even loaded," he said.

"I never intended to shoot a possum," I said. "I don't like their beady eyes."

"Don't look at me," Ida Belle said. "The taste is awful. I just use it to push brush out of the way. Gertie's the big hunter in the group."

"What?" Gertie said, looking confused. "I loaded my rifle. I swear I did."

"I figured it might be safer for her to load when she needed to shoot," Ida Belle said.

"You unloaded my rifle?" Gertie asked. "No wonder I couldn't shoot the bear."

"Thank God I unloaded your rifle," Ida Belle said. "All you would have done is pissed the bear off and he would have eaten Young Huck's house trying to get at you."

"So let me get this straight," Carter said. "You decided to teach Fortune about hunting, with unloaded rifles, and in the middle of the night."

"Best time to hunt possum," Gertie said. "You know that."

"Yes. I also know you're supposed to do it with a dog," Carter said.

"We have Bones with us," Gertie said.

Carter glanced around. "Did the bear eat him?"

"Do you really think we'd let the bear eat Bones?" Ida Belle asked. "He was getting tired, so we headed back to the SUV. We'd gotten him in the back when the bear charged us. We were standing in the middle of the road and the bear ran between us and the SUV. So we hauled butt to Young Huck's house yelling for help."

I nodded, marveling a little at Ida Belle's lying skill set. I was good but I could definitely learn a thing or two from this woman. "Young Huck must have heard us, and he ran out with his shotgun and fired at the bear."

"Dead people could have heard you," Young Huck said.

"Anyway," Ida Belle said, "the bear didn't slow. Not even a little bit. Then we all ran inside and when the bear started tearing down the door, we climbed up here. We speculated about why the bear was chasing us and that's when we remembered that Gertie was still wearing her backpack with the possum in it. So we had her toss it before the bear tore the house down. That's when you arrived."

Carter narrowed his eyes. "If you two had no intention of shooting anything and Gertie's rifle wasn't loaded, who killed the possum in Gertie's backpack?"

"I hit it with my truck on the way here," Ida Belle said. "Gertie didn't want it to go to waste and she had ice packs in her backpack, so..."

"*So* now, we're all up to speed," I said. "Can we go home now? Because hunting sucks."

Carter stared at us for several seconds. I'm sure he knew it wasn't the whole truth and probably guessed that we'd been snooping at Hooch's place, or attempted to. But unless he decided to track our footsteps and the bear tracks, there was no way he could prove we were lying. I was going to hazard a guess that he didn't really want to know. Because if he knew for sure that we'd been on Hooch's property, then he'd have to do something about it.

Which made keeping him in the dark a favor to him. At least, that's the way I was looking at it.

"Huck?" Carter asked. "Your door is pretty mangled. Do you want some help getting it back up?"

"No, thanks," Young Huck said. "I've got some plywood next to the porch. I'll just nail it shut and use the back door until I can get it looked at."

"Get any supplies you need from Walter," Ida Belle said, "and tell him to put it on my bill."

Young Huck gave her an appreciative nod.

"Then if there's no other dead animals to be tossed at charging bears," Carter said, "I'd like to move this party back to Sinful where we can all get a shower and some sleep for what is left of the rest of the night."

"Great," Ida Belle said. "I don't suppose you'd do me a favor?"

"I'm not really in a favorable mood," Carter said. "What is it?"

"Could you give Gertie a ride back in the bed of your truck? She got sprayed by a skunk just before the bear started chasing us."

Carter shook his head. "You guys are 0 for 2 with the wildlife. Maybe you should take up indoor hobbies that don't include firearms or explosives."

"The bear was indoors," Gertie pointed out.

"Fine," Carter said. "I'll take Gertie home in my truck." He pointed his finger at Ida Belle. "You will drop Fortune off at her house and proceed directly to your own. All three of you will lock the doors behind you and you will not emerge until at least an hour after daylight. I need sleep. I have a murderer to catch. And the three of you are costing me sleep, energy, and brainpower."

"I bet you're okay staying up all hours of the night with one of us for other reasons," Gertie said, and gave Carter a wink.

"All right," I said. "Hunt's over. Let's go home. And no more hunting for me. Unless mosquitoes become extinct. I'll probably look like I have the measles on my face tomorrow."

Carter gave me one last lingering look, and I figured there were about a million things he'd like to say to me, and most of them not positive. Whatever. With me staying in Sinful, he had a lifetime to chew me out. As long as I didn't have to sleep on that cot in jail again tonight, I was perfectly happy to go home and come up with fifty excuses to never leave my house after dark again. At least, not until it was so cold there were no mosquitoes. Assuming such a thing happened at all. More likely, the mosquitoes in Louisiana had evolved to some status that allowed them to move about more like zombies. You probably couldn't really kill them without cutting their heads off.

"Let's go," he said to Gertie and pointed to his truck.

"I don't want to ride in the bed of the truck," Gertie groused as they started walking. "This road is horrible. I'll have bruises all over my butt tomorrow."

"There's a couple of life jackets back there," Carter said. "You can sit on them, and maybe use the bouncing time to rethink the choices you make and the company you keep."

"What the heck are you talking about?" Gertie asked. "I keep the best company in this town."

"And yet," Carter said, "you always appear to come out on the short end of things when the three of you get together."

"That's because I'm a warrior," Gertie said. "You know, charge first, ask questions later."

"How'd that warrior thing work out with the skunk and the bear?" Carter asked.

Ida Belle looked over at Young Huck. "I'm really sorry about your house. Take a good look around tomorrow and give me a list of anything else that was damaged. I'm happy to take care of it all. You might want to look out for that bear, too. Once he's found a meal..."

Young Huck nodded. "I have my ways of dealing with a lazy bear."

"Hey," I said, "out of curiosity, why did you build a deck on top of your house? I don't see you as the type of guy who likes to spend time gazing at the sunset."

Young Huck grinned. "Ain't interested in no sunsets, that's for sure. But you gotta have high ground when hurricanes come."

I stared. "But that's like twelve feet, and a good surge would knock the whole structure down. You see how the bear shook it."

"Been living in that house for sixty-two years," he said. "Ain't left for a storm yet and ain't planning to. If God wants to take me, then he's welcome to it. I just hope he's got enough beer stocked. The ice chest up there only holds a twelve-pack."

Ida Belle grinned. "Let me know about the damage."

We set out down the road for Ida Belle's truck. Carter and Gertie had pulled away while we were talking to Young Huck.

"Should have caught a ride with Carter back to the SUV," Ida Belle said.

"Nah. I think Carter and I need some time apart. Besides, if I smelled that skunk for a minute longer, I was going to hurl."

Ida Belle looked over at me. "You and Carter have had a rough start to the rest of your life together."

I shrugged. "It is what it is. I used to worry about it, but what's the point? I'm not going to change who I am and as soon as I'm legit, we'll have every right to be poking our nose into things. Carter knows I'm not going to sit around watching television or fishing or doing whatever other innocuous thing he can think of. I'm made just like him. He's not doing any of those things."

"He is when he's off work," Ida Belle said. "But I get your point. Hard for the man to argue when you're cut from the same cloth."

"We'll have our arguments, I'm sure. But at least now it's better than in the beginning...before he knew."

Ida Belle nodded. "At least now he knows you can defend yourself. And likely a small city."

I grinned. "Depends on the layout and my options for weapons."

We reached the SUV and checked on Bones. He was upside-down, all four legs in the air, snoring so loud he sounded like a chain saw. Ida Belle closed the back of the SUV and we headed out.

Then I remembered the letter. "I found something in the wardrobe," I said.

"Really? I thought you were taking a while just to retrieve our things."

"I knew Gertie didn't have a chance to search it and I didn't want to leave things incomplete." I told her what I'd found and showed her the pic I'd taken.

"So it looks like maybe there is some oil on the land," Ida Belle said. "That's interesting. But you didn't find anything else?"

"No."

"So we don't know how much oil we're talking about or if Hooch even contacted the drilling company, much less if they made him an offer."

"I guess we'll have to contact them and find out. We'll have to play it off as something else, though—grieving widow, attorney for the deceased, something."

Ida Belle nodded. "We'll figure out something and make a call tomorrow. I keep a burner phone. We can use that."

"Cool. I probably need to stock up on burner phones, with that whole PI thing and all."

"Wait until you have your license. Then it's tax-deductible."

I nodded and yawned. "I cannot wait to get some shut-eye. This has been one of the longest days of my life."

"Going to be lovely for me listening to that all night," she said, and pointed to Bones.

"How does Marie stand it?"

"She wears those noise-canceling headphones," she said. "Got the idea from you."

"You're welcome to borrow mine," I said. "Should be quiet at my place. Merlin doesn't make noise unless he's pissed off or hungry."

"No worries. I'll stuff my ears with cotton and turn on the television. That should drown him out well enough."

"Well, if you change your mind—"

My cell phone ringer went off, and I frowned as I pulled it from my jeans, hoping there wasn't already a Gertie issue at hand. I glanced at the display and felt my back tighten.

"It's Ally."

I answered, but she was talking so fast and was so stressed, I couldn't make out what she was saying. "Slow down," I said. "Take a deep breath and repeat that."

I heard an intake of breath and then the exhale.

"Someone threw a rock through my living room window,"

she said. "It had a note that said 'Murderer get out.' How could people believe I killed someone? I've lived here almost my whole life. These people know me."

"Did you call the sheriff?" I asked.

"Yes. Myrtle said Carter would be here in a few minutes, but there's a hole in my window and it's the middle of the night. I'm scared, Fortune. This had to be someone I know. How could anyone who knows me be this mean?"

"I'm on my way. Gather up some things. As soon as you're done with Carter, you're coming to my house."

"No! I can't bring my problems to you. That's not fair."

"Life isn't fair. Either you come to me or I start sleeping on your front porch."

There was a couple seconds of silence, then a quiet, "thanks."

"I'll be there in a few minutes," I assured her before disconnecting.

I explained the situation to Ida Belle, who'd already assumed there was an emergency and had been pushing far past the speed limit ever since we'd turned onto the highway. She cruised through downtown Sinful at a fast clip and pulled up to the curb at Ally's place. Carter's truck was already in the drive. There was no sign of Gertie, so I assumed he'd dropped her off first.

Ida Belle and I rushed to the house and went right inside. Carter was standing in the living room, holding an evidence bag with the rock in it. Ally was sitting on the couch but as soon as we came in, she launched forward and threw her arms around me.

"Thank you for coming," she said.

I looked over her shoulder at Carter as I hugged her, and he gave me a grim look.

"Of course I came," I said as she released me. "Did you pack some things?"

"I didn't," she said. "I forgot. Let me go grab a toothbrush and change clothes at least. I'm still in my pajamas. And with Carter in my house. The tongues will be wagging tomorrow."

"To hell with people and their tongues," Ida Belle said. "And to hell with changing clothes. It's bedtime and you're properly dressed. No sense in putting on something fancy to go to Fortune's house and go back to bed. Just grab a set of clothes for tomorrow and a toothbrush and call it done."

Ally nodded, seeming somewhat relieved to receive orders from an older woman. I suppose it was that whole child-mother thing. She headed upstairs and I turned to Carter.

"Well?" I asked.

He showed us the rock. "Typical of any rock found in the woods around here." He turned the bag around and showed us the note. "Typed. I'll run it for prints, but I don't expect I'll get anything."

Ida Belle shook her head. "And I'm sure no one saw anything because it's the middle of the night and they were all asleep."

"I haven't had a chance to ring doorbells," Carter said, "but that's what I'm expecting to hear. I probably won't bother canvassing the neighbors until tomorrow. No sense waking up the whole block to find out they were all asleep."

I nodded, understanding how frustrated Carter was at the situation because it held little chance of resolution and was almost definitely done by a local. Sinful residents liked to pretend the town was some sleepy little Southern hamlet with eccentric characters and mostly good people. No one liked a reminder that hateful people called it home as well.

"It's good you're taking her to your house," Carter said. "She won't be able to rest here. Not yet."

"Especially not with that broken window," Ida Belle said.

"I'll call someone about it tomorrow," Carter said, "but it will probably take some time to get it replaced. In the meantime, I'll board it up for her."

"And she'll stay with me until this entire mess is over," I said.

Carter nodded and gave me a rueful smile. "Cuts a bit into date night, but I'll feel better about this if you're keeping an eye on her."

Ida Belle snorted. "Please. You don't think there's any real threat against Ally. Just some nasty coward flinging rocks in the middle of the night. What you do think is that having Ally in her house will keep Fortune from doing things you don't necessarily approve of."

The tiny flash of guilt in Carter's expression let me know that Ida Belle's comment had hit the mark. He recovered quickly, but it was too late. He'd already given himself away.

"Carter knows better than to think anyone influences my decisions," I said. "Right?"

He sighed. "Unfortunately, that is correct."

"You wouldn't be even remotely interested in me if I were a pushover."

"But I'd have a lot less worry," he said. "And I wouldn't be hauling off skunk-infested senior citizens in the middle of the night."

"There are a handful of available young women here who fit your bore-me-to-death description," Ida Belle said. "Of course, I notice that you never bothered to ask any of them out..."

"I'm ready," Ally called out as she hurried down the stairs with a tote bag.

"Then let's get you back into bed," I said.

"I'll be by Fortune's sometime tomorrow to talk to you,"

Carter said. "And don't worry about your window. I'll get it addressed."

"Thanks," Ally said. "Do you have any booze?" she asked me as we left her house.

"Of course," I said. "I'm an official Sinful resident now. I thought that was a requirement."

Ally hesitated for a second before climbing into Ida Belle's SUV, then jumped when Bones let out a big snort. She glanced into the back of the SUV, then frowned.

"I'm sorry," she said, giving me a look of dismay. "You and Ida Belle were having date night, or whatever you call it when you're doing things that Carter doesn't approve of. And since you arrived at my house together, I gave you away."

"Carter was already aware that we were out cavorting," I said. "Don't worry about it."

"You're sure?" she said. "I don't want to cause any problems with you guys, especially since you were probably out tonight doing something to help me."

"Actually, we were hunting," I said. Might as well keep up the charade.

"Hunting?" Ally looked confused. "Is that why you have Bones?"

I nodded.

"Did Carter buy it?" she asked.

Ida Belle laughed. "About as well as you did. But he's got nothing on us, so don't worry about it. We're all sleeping in our own beds tonight, although Gertie might need to burn her sheets and mattress tomorrow. She had a run-in with a skunk."

"Oh no." Ally giggled. "It seems Ms. Hebert is always having a mishap."

"Funny," Ida Belle said. "We pointed out the same thing."

Ida Belle pulled into my driveway and Ally and I climbed out.

"I'll call you in the morning," I said.

She gave me a nod and a wave and we headed inside.

"You can take whatever room you'd like," I said. "The bed in the back guest room is more comfortable than the bed in Marge's room."

"You mean your room?"

I laughed. "Yeah. I guess I should look into replacing the mattress now that it's mine. I think Marge probably had that one a while. It's still strange though. Anyway, go ahead and take your stuff up. I'll bring you a big shot of whiskey."

"Are you going to bed too?" she asked.

"I've got to take a shower first, but yeah, eventually." I put my hand on her shoulder. "Don't worry. I've got you covered."

Ally smiled. "You know, that statement would have made me feel better before, but now that I know the real you, it adds a whole other layer of meaning."

"There's nothing in Sinful that's a match for me, except maybe Carter if we're talking hand-to-hand combat. Get some rest. No one is going to bother us."

Ally gave me a hug and headed upstairs. I could tell by her slow tread that she was exhausted and a bit defeated. I understood why she'd feel that way, but I didn't agree. All the rock had done was make me even more determined to find out who had killed Hooch and completely clear Ally's name. I imagine it had done the same for Carter.

Bottom line—the murderer didn't stand a chance.

CHAPTER NINETEEN

CARTER SHOWED up around eleven thirty the next morning. Ida Belle and I had already decided that church today was off our to-do list. She promised to call Gertie early enough to fill her in on the situation with Ally before she started getting dressed. Between the late-night hunting and rocks through windows, I was happy to skip out on service this week. Besides, Francine's cooler was broken and the fact that there was no banana pudding had already circulated. Therefore, my running skills weren't needed.

I answered the door, still half asleep, and shuffled off into the kitchen. He followed me and took a seat at the table as I put on a pot of coffee.

"Did I wake you up?" he asked. "You never sleep this late."

"Well, when you spend a good majority of the night listening to Ally toss and turn, and you move back and forth from the couch to the recliner trying to find a comfortable spot, it takes a while to actually fall asleep."

"Why didn't you sleep in your room? You don't think anyone is going to bother you here, do you?"

"No. But I think Ally felt safer knowing a former CIA agent was downstairs with a gun. Or two."

"Gotcha."

"I don't suppose you found out anything from the neighbors."

"No. Didn't expect to."

"Do you think they're telling the truth?"

"Yeah. This isn't gang territory, where people are afraid to speak out of retaliation. If one of them had seen something, they would have told me."

"Probably did it on foot anyway," I said. "Then scurried off into the woods like a good little coward." I sighed. "I don't get this whole small-town thing. It's like some people want to believe the absolute worst about someone. And the nicer the person, the more they want it to be true."

"There's some truth in that."

"But why?"

"I don't know for sure. Maybe inferiority. They know they're not as 'good' as someone else, so they like seeing the people they picture as better than them taken down a bit."

"So basically, they want everyone to wallow in the mud with them so they can pretend to be better than what they are."

"Something like that."

"That's crappy."

"It is, but it's also not restricted to small towns. I saw plenty of it in the military. It's everywhere, Fortune. It's just more obvious in small places and it's something you never would have noticed before."

"Maybe not." I'd moved away from people after my mom died, and my career had been my only focus until now. Things like this had probably been going on around me but I hadn't paid attention. Mostly because other people weren't really on my radar. Not unless they were on my insertion team. Or a target.

"So what do you do now?" I asked. "And please don't give me the whole 'police business' speech. This is Ally. I'm not going to back off."

"I know. But even if I wanted to tell you my business, the truth is I don't have anything to tell. I'm stumped. I have a list of people who had reason to have a grudge against Hooch, but not one that I think would lead to murder. And since most of the grudges are months or years old, it seems odd to think someone would wait that long."

"I guess opportunity is a bit of a problem as well what with half the town having access to the food or water at the fishing rodeo. I mean, it might have been a risk to do it out in the open but with so many people milling around the café and the dock, wouldn't it have been impossible to do it without someone noticing? Maybe they just don't know what they saw."

Carter nodded. "I'm not giving up. Someone knows something. Sooner or later, the truth will surface. It always does."

"I hope it surfaces soon. Too many rocks through windows and Ally might leave. I don't want that to happen. It would be a big loss. To the town. To Francine. Mostly to me."

Carter reached across the table and squeezed my hand. "I'm not going to let that happen. I'll figure this out."

I nodded. I didn't doubt his dedication or his belief in himself. But Carter didn't have the same connections I did. Couldn't really, as they were criminals. I felt a tiny bit guilty for not telling him about Hooch's request for money from Big and Little, but there was no way I could betray that trust. Carter would rush right in to question them and that would be the end of my working relationship with the Heberts. I owed them too much to put them in the middle of things. Besides, I had no doubt Carter would search Hooch's house before he allowed people in and find the letter from the drilling company. He'd put two and two together and start taking a closer look at Junior and anyone else who stood to gain if Hooch struck the oil lottery.

But no matter how convinced I was that all of us were doing everything we could, I couldn't help but feel that we were completely overlooking something.

Something big.

———

ALLY CAME DOWN RIGHT after Carter left. Since he didn't have any information for her, he'd elected to leave her sleeping and had asked me to bring her up to speed on the neighborhood questioning when she got up. She looked as if she'd had a rough night, which was fitting since I was positive that was the case.

"You want anything to eat?" I asked. "I have breakfast stuff. I'm no gourmet, but I can manage eggs and toast."

Ally poured herself a cup of coffee and smiled. "I must look awful for you to volunteer to cook."

I shrugged. "You look how I expect you to look, given the situation. I'm sorry, but I'm not good at the whole lie-to-make-you-feel-better girlie thing. I can try harder, but I seriously doubt I'll ever be any good at it."

She laughed. "Everyone needs that person in their life who will always be honest with them. Well, I mean, honest excluding that whole CIA thing. That one was outside of your control."

I felt a bit of relief sweep through me. My friendship with Ally was important to me, and now that I was going to be around for a long time, I didn't want to do anything to jeopardize the only peer relationship I had. Peer as in age. In everything else, I was more like Carter, or Ida Belle if I needed to go for the female version.

"Oh good," I said. "Because while I'm really good at lying—I mean really, really good—I don't want to do that with you. But I do reserve the right to leave things out. For your own good."

"I assume you're talking about that whole treading-on-Carter's-toes thing that you, Ida Belle, and Gertie do. I get it. I can't be in trouble if I don't know anything. More importantly, I can't get you into trouble."

She frowned. "But can you at least tell me if you're finding anything about Hooch? I know that's probably where you were last night. I don't need the details. I just want to know that you found something, anything. I'm sorry. I'm going on and I'm putting pressure on you and that's not fair."

I sat down at the table next to her. "I was a CIA agent. Trust me, there is no way you can ever put as much pressure on me as the federal government."

"Ha! Yeah, I suppose the rest of us are amateurs facing that comparison."

"Well, they have had a lot of experience. Anyway, to answer your question, we have discovered some things that need further checking but we don't have anything concrete just yet." I reached over and squeezed her arm. "We're not going to give up until we figure this out. Neither is Carter."

She nodded. "I know. I've got the best people in the world looking out for me. It will all turn out just fine. I know that, but I can't stop worrying about the what-if."

"Leave the worry to me."

"You eat worry for breakfast."

"Exactly. And speaking of which, would you like some?"

My cell phone rang and I checked the display. Ida Belle.

"I'm on my way to pick you up," Ida Belle said. "Margarita and Junior are at the café."

"Great!" I jumped up from the table. "Gotta run. It's one of those things I can't talk about. Help yourself to anything. I'll be back later."

I ran upstairs and threw on clothes and shoes and grabbed my gun and hauled butt downstairs. Ida Belle was just pulling up in my driveway and I yelled a goodbye to Ally before hurrying outside. Gertie was in the back seat but her smell had carried all the way up to my sidewalk.

I wrinkled my nose and made a face.

"She smells like a French whore," Ida Belle said. "Did you have to bathe in perfume?"

"It was either that or smell like tomato paste," Gertie said.

"Perhaps Italian whore would be more appropriate," I said. Gertie was indeed a fairly awful combination of obnoxious perfume, tomato paste, and the faint whiff of skunk.

"I'll have to put an air purifier in this vehicle to get the smell out," Ida Belle said.

"Oh, stop your whining," Gertie said. "Just roll down all the windows and drive like you usually do. The smell will flee out of terror."

I grinned. "If you went just a little faster than that, you might be able to turn back time to before Gertie got sprayed."

"You two are hilarious this morning," Ida Belle said. "I've already filled Gertie in on the drilling company letter and the rock through Ally's window. I heard Carter was at your house earlier. Did he find out anything?"

"Do those followers of yours report to you every time Carter's truck is in my driveway?" I asked.

"Just when they think I need to know," Ida Belle said.

"Oh, well, as long as they have a reason for being nosy tattletales," I said.

"They're Southern women," Gertie said. "They don't need a reason. So did he find out anything or not?"

"Of course not," I said. "Everyone was asleep. So what's the play on Margarita and Junior?"

"We go to eat," Ida Belle said. "Gertie and I exclaim over not seeing them in forever and proceed to pump them for personal information just like any other self-respecting old Southern woman would do."

Gertie nodded. "Sometimes the stereotypes come in handy."

"Okay. Then you take the lead. I'll just watch the reactions. If someone's lying, I'll know."

Ida Belle parked and we headed into the café. I let out a sigh of relief that I'd called it correctly. Without banana pudding on the menu, Celia's group had opted out of eating lunch there. With all her current issues with Gertie, it was probably better that they didn't occupy the same space for a while, especially after Celia had attended a religious ceremony.

I scanned the patrons and spotted an older woman and young man I didn't recognize sitting at a table against the wall. The other customers were giving them sideways glances but going out of their way not to make eye contact, so I figured that had to be them.

Middle-aged woman. Five foot six. A hundred forty pounds. No obvious physical ailments but horrible muscle tone. Face stretched too tight. Lips too big. Makeup too dark. Clothes a little too tight and too low. But prettier than I'd expected. No threat at all.

Male. Early twenties. Five foot eleven. A hundred eighty pounds. No obvious physical ailments. Excellent muscle tone. Mismatched socks. One red logo. One green logo. Could probably hold his own in a basic street fight, but no threat to me.

Ida Belle and Gertie strode right up to the table and gave them smiles.

"Margarita," Gertie said. "It's been too long. You look great."

Margarita looked up at us and smiled. "Ida Belle and Gertie. I never thought I'd see you two again and yet here we are. You two haven't changed a bit. How are you?"

"Doing well," Ida Belle said. "You're looking good yourself. I take it your time after leaving Sinful has been good."

"The best," she said.

Gertie looked at Junior. "I haven't seen you since you were a boy, and now here you are all grown up. I'm really sorry about your father."

Junior looked down at the table and nodded before looking back up at us. "Thank you." He seemed more embarrassed than upset.

Margarita gave her son a sympathetic look. "Junior is having trouble figuring out what to feel, I'm afraid. He didn't have a relationship with his father to speak of. Hadn't even spoken with him for probably ten years or better, but you don't get to pick your parents, and blood is blood, so..."

Gertie nodded. "Still a loss."

Junior squirmed. "I just want to get this over with, you know? And get back to my job. I know how to handle things there."

"What do you do?" Ida Belle asked.

"Junior works construction," Margarita said. "He's the youngest foreman at the company."

"That's great," Gertie said. "Are you still painting? You were quite the artist, even as a young child. Such great perspective and use of color."

Junior blushed a bit. "That's awful nice of you to say. I still paint some, but I don't have as much time for it now."

"Junior's done some simply beautiful paintings for my house," Margarita said, and pulled out her phone. "Here's one hanging in my dining room, and this one is over the fireplace in the living room."

I leaned and looked at the pictures. I was no art expert, but I liked what I saw. One was a landscape of a beach with seagulls flying in the distance and seashells in the foreground. It was very serene. The other was of the French Quarter. The detail was so elaborate, it almost looked like a photograph rather than a painting.

"Those are incredible," I said. "You are very talented."

Junior barely mumbled a thanks and dropped his gaze down to the table. Margarita looked up at me and frowned.

"I'm sorry," I said. "My name is Fortune. I'm a friend of Ida Belle and Gertie."

She gave me a nod.

"And what about you?" Gertie asked Margarita. "How have you been? Is there a new Mr. Margarita?"

"Definitely not," Margarita said. "Hooch pretty much put me off men forever. Do you know he never paid a single dime in child support? Owes me more money than he's probably made in the last ten years. When I left here, I swore I would concentrate on raising my son and I did. Now that he's on his own, I suppose I have the time to pursue someone else, but honestly, it just doesn't appeal."

Ida Belle nodded. "There's a lot worse things than being single."

"Being married to a cheater is one of them," Margarita said.

Gertie's eyes widened. "Hooch cheated?"

"As often as he could find someone willing," Margarita said. "The last one was the final straw. Some cocktail waitress in the French Quarter. He didn't even bother to hide it. Used to come home reeking of cheap perfume." She gave Gertie a quizzical look and sniffed.

"I'm sorry," Ida Belle said. "We had no idea. You were right to leave. For that and a lot of other reasons. I suppose you're here to take care of the service and settle up the property and stuff?"

Margarita frowned. "That's the goal, but it seems we're on hold for a bit until Deputy LeBlanc deems it okay for us to enter Hooch's house. I don't expect he's got anything worthwhile inside, but we still have to get a look at it before we can list it for sale. As for the service, it will be the cheapest one that can be arranged. Lord knows, Hooch spent every dime he made, so no counting on help on that end. And I'm not going to let Junior pay for some expensive funeral. My boy works hard. Hooch doesn't deserve a cut of his earnings."

I looked over at Junior, who started to say something, then must have thought better of it and just shook his head and looked back down at the tabletop again.

"Maybe you'll luck out and he'll have money stuffed in his mattress," Gertie said.

Margarita laughed. "The only thing Hooch is likely to have stuffed in his bed are dirty clothes. The man was always a pig."

I remembered Gertie's comment about the dirty underwear in the covers of Hooch's bed. Apparently, some things never changed.

"Maybe he struck oil," I said. "Isn't that a thing down here? You have to excuse me, I just moved here from up north."

"Best I remember," Margarita said, "that patch of land Hooch lived on was so small you could spit from one side to the other. If there's oil, it probably wouldn't be enough to refill the reservoir on my Cadillac."

"Oh well," I said. "You can always hope."

"I'm all out of hope when it comes to Boone Carre," Margarita said. "I was out of hope the day I left him and I had no interest in generating any more. My boy and I just want to get this mess taken care of and get on with our lives the way they've been for years now—without any thought of Hooch."

"I don't blame you," Ida Belle said. "Well, if there's anything we can do, please let us know. Everyone in Sinful knows your history. They'll do you right down at the funeral home. I know it's not much, but we still try to take care of folks down here."

"Thank you," Margarita said. "You ladies were always kind to me, even back when I didn't have a lick of sense."

"You were young and had your reasons for the choices you made back then," Ida Belle said. "Sometimes we have to work with what we've got until we figure out something else."

Margarita stared at her for a moment, and I wondered if she was remembering that young girl, fleeing an abusive father. Only to hook up with an abusive, cheating husband.

Finally, she nodded. "I'm just glad I figured out something else before I raised my son to be like his father." Her eyes clouded with tears and she sniffed. When she glanced across the table at Junior she sobered, pulling herself together once more.

"Well, we'll let you get back to your breakfast," Ida Belle said. "And please, let us know if there's anything we can do."

"Of course," Margarita said.

We headed to our usual table in the back and I realized that everyone in the café had stopped talking to listen to the exchange. I hazarded a guess that as soon as they left the café, cell phones would be buzzing.

We slid into our seats and waited until a server took our drink order to start talking.

"Well, that was interesting," Gertie said, her voice low. "Did you know Hooch was cheating?"

Ida Belle shook her head. "I had no idea. He must have

kept it in New Orleans. If he'd had a run at anyone in town, we'd have heard about it."

"If he'd had a run at anyone in town, they'd have told him to stick it," Gertie said.

"All the more reason to take that show on the road," Ida Belle said. "He could tell whatever lies he wanted in New Orleans."

"You definitely can't blame her for leaving," I said.

"So you think she was telling the truth?" Gertie asked.

"About that? Sure."

Ida Belle narrowed her eyes. "But you don't think she was telling the truth about everything."

"She was lying about not dating," I said.

"I figured as much," Gertie said. "The surgery, the makeup, the clothes. A woman doesn't bother that much unless there's a man in the picture."

"But why lie about it?" I asked. "She left Hooch forever ago."

"Probably doesn't want Junior to know," Gertie said. "Young man, feeling his oats. He'd probably have something to say about anyone his mother was interested in. I've seen it over and over again with the widows here in Sinful when they take up dating again."

Ida Belle nodded. "Grown sons can be horrible babies about their mothers, especially when it comes to men and the possibility of sex."

"That makes sense," I said. "I can see Carter being a total pain if Emmaline dated. She doesn't, right?"

"She's gone out a time or two with some old college friends from New Orleans," Gertie said. "But she hasn't dated anyone seriously since Carter's dad died."

"Hence why Carter is still walking around free and carrying

a badge," Ida Belle said. "I pity any man who attempts a romantic relationship with Emmaline."

Gertie sighed. "It's a shame, really. She's a beautiful woman and such a great person. She deserves someone special in her life besides her son."

"I imagine if Emmaline decides she wants some company, she won't have any trouble making it happen," Ida Belle said.

"Someone please warn me if you even get an inkling that's going to occur," I said. "I'll go on extended vacation or something."

Gertie nodded. "You don't want to have to back up Carter when he declares no one is good enough for his mother. I understand."

"No," I said. "I don't want to have to back up Emmaline and tell Carter it's none of his business."

Ida Belle raised an eyebrow. "Smart. But since Emmaline's potential dating future is not on our current agenda, can we get back to the business at hand?"

"I think our business just came to a dead end," I said. "At least on this end of questioning. If Hooch had an oil deal in the works, Margarita didn't know anything about it."

"I agree," Ida Belle said. "If Hooch really had something of value, he didn't let on about it to his son. Junior would have told his mother. That's where his loyalty lies."

"So what now?" Gertie asked.

"Ricky Marks is the only real unknown," I said. "I think it's time we found out a bit more about him."

Gertie immediately brightened. "So we're going to the Swamp Bar?"

"Well, you already smell like you're going," I said. "It would be a shame for all that perfume to go to waste."

CHAPTER TWENTY

IT WAS close to 9:00 p.m. when I jumped in Ida Belle's SUV for our trip to the Swamp Bar. Carter was working late again, and since Ally was staying with me, I didn't have to worry about him dropping by later on. I'd spent most of the after-noon trying to figure out another way to get information on Ricky Marks, but the Swamp Bar was his only known hangout. If we wanted to get eyes on him, that would be the most likely place. Especially as we couldn't exactly drive out to his rented farmhouse in the middle of nowhere and proceed to quiz him without looking a tiny bit suspicious.

Since Ricky was young and to the best of our knowledge, single, Gertie had suggested I wear something sexy and play the half-drunk bar patron and see if I could get him talking. I figured pretty much everyone in Sinful knew I was dating Carter by now and even if Ricky wasn't up on the local gossip, someone in the bar would warn him off. Instead, I wore jeans, a sports bra, a T-shirt, and tennis shoes. Not even remotely sexy, but I could fight or run in them quite nicely.

"Ally okay?" Ida Belle asked as I climbed in the passenger's seat.

I nodded. "She knows better than to ask anything. She's watching a movie right now and has promised to lock up everything before she goes to bed. She's got a pistol with her in the living room and one in her bedroom."

"You don't think anyone's going to bother her at your place, do you?" Ida Belle asked.

"It would be stupid to," I said. "But Sinful has coughed up a big share of stupid."

"That's true enough," Ida Belle said.

"The bigger question is what about Carter?" Gertie asked. "Are things still tense between the two of you?"

"It's gotten a little better," I said. "But then, we've hardly seen each other, so that's kinda the default. Plus, his mind is 100 percent on the case, so that doesn't leave him as much time to be irritated at me."

"He's going to need stock in Xanax if he continues to let you bother him," Gertie said.

"He'll get used to it eventually," Ida Belle said. "I've been friends with you for a hundred years and I haven't shot you yet."

"That's because I'm superhuman," Gertie said. "Stronger than steel. Faster than lightning."

"So fast a skunk in a wardrobe got you," Ida Belle said.

"That was a fluke," Gertie said.

"You have an awful lot of fluke for a superhuman," Ida Belle said. "In fact, one might argue that you have an awful lot of fluke for a regular human."

"Anyway," I interrupted. "What's the plan? It's not like we can stroll in without someone knowing who we are. Not anymore. That whole mess with the poacher that went down at the Swamp Bar was big news and you two were the main witnesses."

"But no one knows you were there," Gertie said, "so you weren't in the news or the local gossip."

"Yeah," I said. "I'm just going to throw out a guess that announcing on Main Street that I'm a former CIA agent who just relocated permanently to Sinful has probably made the rounds."

"That's true," Ida Belle said. "It was an unfortunate loss of cover, but it was bound to happen when Fortune made her home here. Not only will she not be able to fool men into talking to her, it's highly likely that most of them will be afraid of her."

Gertie threw her hands in the air. "So what is the point then? If no one will talk to any of us, this whole thing is a waste of time."

"Maybe not," Ida Belle said. "Hooch wasn't well liked. That might be enough to get some gums flapping."

"Look," I said. "Maybe we'll get nothing here. I say we go inside and check the temperature of the room. If someone appears open to talking, then we try them out. If no one does, then we make our exit and figure out another way to get the scoop on Marks."

"That's a sound plan," Gertie said. "I baked a coffee cake today, so worse case we go back to Fortune's early and have shots of whiskey and coffee cake."

"I'm voting for shots of whiskey and coffee cake regardless of outcome," I said.

"Me too," Ida Belle said as she pulled into the parking lot.

As per usual, she parked at the end and backed in, just in case we had to flee in a hurry. That had sorta been our standard fare.

"Looks busy," Gertie said.

"Only bar in town," Ida Belle said. "When is it not?"

I climbed out of the SUV and took a long look at the

building that was my nemesis before starting across the parking lot. Gertie was practically skipping. I had the fleeting thought that she should probably conserve her energy for the exit but decided that I was going to think positive and this time, we were not going to have to flee.

The music blared out of the bar and into the parking lot and I sighed as we walked up the rickety wooden steps and headed for the front door. Live band. With music that loud, there was no way we'd be able to have a conversation. We'd be lucky to leave there without partial deafness. I pulled open the door and stepped inside. Smoke left a haze in the entire building and I felt my eyes water a bit.

I glanced around and spotted a couple open stools at the bar, so I headed that direction. Couples usually occupied the tables. Singles were at the bar and that was where we would be more likely to find someone drunk enough to talk. I slid onto the stool and motioned for Gertie to take the one next to me.

She shook her head and leaned close to me. "I see my plumber over at the dartboards. I'm going to say hi and see if he'll talk."

"Do not play darts," I said.

"I can't," Gertie said. "I'm banned for life from the dart-board, remember?" She hurried off for the darts area and I shook my head.

Oh, I remembered. All too well. I just hoped Gertie respected the ban and kept her paws off the darts. The last time she'd handled them, she'd almost caused a riot and had narrowly escaped by stealing a boat.

"I'm going to take a lap," Ida Belle said. "See if I can spot Ricky anywhere."

I gave her a nod and she headed off into the crowd. I pulled my cell phone out of my pants pocket and shoved it in my sports bra. It was easier to feel it vibrating there, especially when the stool was shaking from the loud music. I was just about to pray for a power outage when the song ended and the lead singer announced they'd be taking a short break. He stepped off the stage and the jukebox fired up, but it wasn't half the volume of the band.

I was scanning my options at the front of the bar when I heard someone call my name. I looked over behind the bar and saw one of the bar owners, Whiskey, give me a nod.

"Beer?" he asked.

"Please. I'm sorta surprised to see you here."

He nodded and pushed the beer over to me. "I got lucky. Cut a deal with the DA for testimony. I have to pay a steep fine for the poaching and I got a couple years' probation, but it was a lot better than what I'd hoped for."

"I'm glad," I said. Whiskey had gotten caught up in a poaching-murder case back in the summer and had almost taken a bullet. Unfortunately, while he hadn't been the perp of the major offense, he was guilty of some lesser crimes.

"Carter put in a good word for me," he said.

"Really?" That was somewhat surprising. Carter was all about right and wrong, to the point of things being almost black and white.

"My dad's pretty sick," he said. "Cancer. He doesn't have very long."

"I'm sorry."

He nodded. "Carter's mom volunteers at the church to deliver meals to people who can't get out or do for themselves, so I figure he found out from her. Never said anything to me, but the DA told me the judge had gone easier on me because of a conversation she'd had with the arresting deputy. I tried to thank him, but he pretended he didn't know what I was talking about."

"That sounds like Carter. While we're handing out thanks,

I need to thank you again for not ratting me out for being here."

He smiled. "At first, I thought maybe you had warrants out and were looking at jail time. Then I heard you and Carter had a thing, so I thought you were trying to avoid relationship problems. Can't have a criminal and a cop together. Doesn't work out too good for the cop, you know?"

"Probably not."

He leaned over the bar. "But then I heard you were actually CIA. That true?"

"Former. I'm retired now, unemployed, and a new Sinful resident."

"So were you down here undercover, on some secret mission or something like that?"

"Something like that."

He nodded. "You can't talk about it. I get it. That's badass. But then I find myself wondering what you're doing in my bar. Because let's face it, you and your lady friends usually bring trouble with you."

"Or we're here because this is where trouble hangs out."

He smiled. "Maybe."

"The truth? We're trying to figure out who killed Hooch."

"Why? Shit, Hooch ain't the kind of guy anyone is crying over."

"Probably not, but my friend Ally is a suspect and she's being harassed by some anonymous douchebag cowards who like to throw rocks through windows."

He frowned. "The cute little waitress from Francine's?"

I nodded.

"Well, hell, that's ridiculous. Even if she had a reason to kill Hooch, that girl is about as dangerous as a box of kittens."

"Yeah, but you know what this town is like. If Carter

doesn't figure out who killed Hooch, then Ally will keep getting harassed."

"People suck."

"We're in agreement there. So anyway, we know Hooch hung out here, so we thought we'd come and see what the talk was. Assuming anyone will talk."

"Anyone in particular you looking at?"

"We don't have any reason to suspect anyone, but I was wondering about Ricky Marks. No one seems to know much about him, but we heard he hangs out here some."

Whiskey nodded. "Yeah, he's in here fairly regular, or at least, he was."

"When was the last time he was here?"

"The night before the fishing rodeo." Whiskey looked around and leaned across the bar. "He's been in here steady since he came to town. I've tried to talk to him a time or two, but he never said much about himself. Then lately, he had questions, and you know how questions in a bar go."

"Makes the patrons suspicious."

"You got it."

"What was he asking about?"

"Not what. Who—Hooch."

"Really? That's interesting. Did he ever let on to why he was asking?"

He shook his head. "I asked once, and he made some noise about thinking he recognized him from a job in New Orleans, but he was lying. Hell, Hooch don't work here. No way he's going to drive all the way to New Orleans to piss people off with his lousy work ethic."

"Yeah, that doesn't sound very likely."

"No, it doesn't. And I'll tell you something else. That night —the night before the rodeo—Ricky got into an argument with Hooch."

"Had he ever talked to him before that night?"

"Not that I'd seen."

"What was the argument about?"

"I have no idea. He said something to Hooch and they went outside. I was curious so I walked up front and looked out the window. They was arguing something fierce. Hooch's face was all red and he was almost shaking. Ricky looked mad as hell."

"You couldn't hear them?"

"No. Window was closed and the jukebox was going. I started to step outside but then I figured I was probably better off not knowing. Sometimes knowing is a liability you don't need."

I nodded. "Did you see them leave?"

"Hooch pointed at the kid and said something, then stomped across the parking lot and tore out of here like he was on fire."

"What did Ricky do?"

"Punched the No Swimming sign on the dock. Sign's made of metal so it made out better than Ricky. He jumped around a bit and I figured he was cussing, then he got in his truck and left. Haven't seen him since. You think he did it?"

"I have no idea, but it sure looks like he had a problem with Hooch."

"Yeah, him and a bunch of other people. Wasn't no shortage of people wanting to take a poke at him. That fishing broad he's been seeing cracked him with a beer bottle a couple weeks ago."

"Dixie? Not Dixie?"

"Yeah, that's the one."

"Hooch and Dixie were...dating?" I had to force myself to say the last word.

He shrugged. "Don't know if it was official, but they came

in here together some and based on their behavior, whatever it was went beyond fishing buddies."

"Fascinating. I wonder why she hit him."

"My experience, women get mad over a lot of things, but they only get violent over one of them. Another woman."

Which would fit with what Margarita said about Hooch being a serial cheater. "Hey, I don't suppose Hooch ever mentioned coming into money, did he?"

"Hooch? Money?" He laughed. "Half the time he was in here, he hit somebody up to cover his beer. Hooch drank away money as quick as he got his hands on it. Hey, it was nice talking to you but I better go serve the natives before they get restless. The beer's on the house."

"Thanks," I said as he walked off to handle two impatient-looking men at the other end of the bar. I glanced around and saw Ida Belle next to the bandstand talking to a large gentleman wearing overalls and no shirt. Both of them appeared relaxed so I assumed things were going as she wanted. I spotted Gertie hovering at the edge of the darts area, but her hands were empty so I didn't have to worry. Not yet, anyway.

I scanned the rest of the bar. Most of them I'd seen at some point in time, but I didn't really know any of them. Not well enough to plop down and strike up a conversation anyway. And then I spotted a lone figure sitting in the corner.

Dixie.

Granted, we'd never officially met, but women had that whole bonding thing over crappy men. At least, that's what I kept seeing on television, so it must be right. I grabbed my beer and threaded myself through the crowd until I reached her table.

"You mind?" I asked and pointed to the empty chair next to her.

She glanced up at me and scowled. "What do you want?"

I took that as permission to sit and dropped into the seat next to her. "Just looking for a spot away from the general maleness of the room."

"Then you better try your house, because men aren't going to ignore you just because you're sitting in the corner with me."

I studied her, a bit confused, because I was certain she didn't know me. But she'd delivered that statement with a lot of anger that I could probably warrant if she gave me a minute or two but hadn't warranted yet.

"I'm Fortune," I said and stuck out my hand. "I don't think we've met."

She glanced at my hand but didn't make a move to shake it. "I'm sure we haven't."

"I'm sorry, but have I done something to offend you?"

She sighed. "All you Barbie bitches are alike. You go out to a bar full of men then complain when they hit on you. What are you expecting?"

I retracted my hand before I used it to throat-punch her. "Barbie? I assure you there is nothing about me that warrants the title of Barbie. I'll allow the bitch part."

"Blond hair, blue eyes, probably live on lettuce and air. Definitely a Barbie."

"Not unless they make Lethal Barbie. Out of curiosity, is your problem with me or with men looking at me?"

"Look, I don't even know you, but with women like you around, women like me don't get a second look. So I guess my problem is with both of you, although I suppose you can't help the way you look." She gave me an up and down assessment. "And you sure didn't go out of your way to look hot."

It was an accurate statement, but somehow, she managed to make it sound like an insult. But since I wanted information, I figured I'd let it slide. "Maybe because I just wanted a beer and didn't feel like sitting alone at home."

She stared at me for a moment, a little suspicious, but finally, curiosity won out. "Man trouble?"

"What other kind is there? You?"

"Nah. My man trouble is all over."

"That's good. What did he do?"

"He died."

I stared at her, attempting to feign surprise. "Oh! I'm so sorry. Wait, you don't mean that fisherman guy, do you?"

She nodded. "Hooch."

"But I thought he was your competition. I mean, that's what I heard people say anyway."

"When it comes to competitive fishing, even Jesus would be my competition, although I wouldn't expect to beat him. I'm in it to win and to win every time. But you can't spend all your time fishing."

"No. I guess not. I'm just a little surprised. I didn't know Hooch well, but what I did know didn't portray him as highly desirable. I guess I have to wonder what you saw in him."

I knew it was possible that my question would make her mad, but I couldn't help asking.

"It's easy for you to say something like that," she said. "You could have your choice of any man in Sinful. But a woman like me...our options are somewhat limited. Hooch wasn't a good catch—and I would know—but he was someone to pass some time with. And we could talk about fishing. Like you said, it was better than sitting in my house alone."

I studied Dixie as she spoke. She'd attempted to sound nonchalant—almost businesslike with her delivery—but her voice had broken just a tiny bit on the last sentence. She'd cared more for Hooch than she was letting on.

"I'm sorry for your loss," I said.

She shrugged. "He was already a loss before he died. I'd ended it a couple weeks before."

"Can I ask why?"

"Same reason as always."

"Another woman." I made it a statement rather than a question.

She looked over at me and nodded. "You too, huh? I guess the leopard really doesn't change his spots. I'd been warned, but I chose to ignore it. I got him back, though."

"You cheated on him?"

"No. Better. I took his fishing spot in the rodeo. He'd already baited it with fish he'd caught the week before. Thought he was going to screw me in the bed and out of it. But I showed him."

"I bet he was fit to be tied," I said, now understanding why Hooch had been so mad when he confronted Dixie on the lake. "Did you know her? The other woman? I mean, it sucks no matter what, but when you know them, it's worse."

"Nah. Hooch never dipped his wick in the same pool at the same time. He did all his catting around in New Orleans. I don't know who she was, but I caught him on the phone with her. He addressed her as Andy, but it was a woman's voice. Probably some perky twentysomething with daddy issues."

"Looking for a paycheck, probably."

She snorted. "Well, she was looking in the wrong place. Among his many other admirable traits, Hooch was lazy and spent a dime if he had a nickel." She rose from her chair and looked down at me. "I think I've had enough socializing for one evening. Good luck with your situation."

I thanked her but she had already started walking away. An interesting woman. And an angry one. So Hooch had cheated on her and she'd clocked him over the head with a beer bottle and stolen his fish. The question was, had that been enough? Or had she taken things to a whole different level?

As Dixie disappeared into the crowd, Ida Belle appeared in front of the table. She slid into the chair that Dixie had vacated. "You get anything?"

"Plenty. If I knew what any of it ultimately meant, life would be grand. What about you?"

She nodded. "We'll compare notes when we leave, which we should probably consider doing soon. So far, nothing bad has happened, and I'd really like to get out of here before it does."

"I am all for that. Where's Gertie?"

"Still over by the dartboards," Ida Belle said, and lifted an arm to wave.

I spotted Gertie standing behind a burly guy wearing camo. She caught sight of Ida Belle's wave and nodded. We rose and headed out. When we were about halfway across the bar, the jukebox cut out and I heard a man talking loudly.

"I know you," he said. "You're that crazy woman that assaulted a nun."

"Uh-oh," I said as I turned around and saw the camo guy pointing at Gertie.

Six foot two. Two hundred fifty pounds. Not in great shape, but enough muscle tone to be a problem in a tight environment.

"That was an accident," Gertie said.

Camo staggered a bit and blinked to help his focus. I could tell he was easily a six-pack past rational thought, assuming he was capable of it in the first place. I hurried in their direction, hoping I could intervene before Gertie got ideas of her own. But since the jukebox wasn't playing, everyone had stopped dancing and was now crowding toward the fight, making moving through them a slow process.

"That nun was my great-aunt," Camo Dude said as he stepped right in Gertie's face. "She had to be sedated."

"I'm really sorry," Gertie. "But you need to step back."

"Or what?" he asked.

Oh no!

I couldn't see her reach, but I knew that tone. Something was coming out of the purse of doom. There was no way I was going to get to her in time to stop it. All I could do was pray that it wasn't something that would take down the entire bar.

A second later, the screaming started. And it wasn't Gertie.

CHAPTER TWENTY-ONE

I SHOVED the remaining cluster of spectators to the side as Camo Dude started to twitch. I knew that motion. I made a big launch at Gertie's hand and grabbed the Taser from her. Camo Dude staggered backward as I clutched Gertie's arm and yanked her through the crowd. Ida Belle hurried in front of us, paving the way. I saw Whiskey standing at the bar, grinning, and lifted a hand to wave as we hurried outside.

I released Gertie's arm on the porch and we ran down the steps. As soon as our feet hit dirt I heard the door of the bar slam against the wall and Camo Dude hollering behind us.

"Run!" I yelled.

Ida Belle had already started sprinting ahead of us. As the getaway driver, it was important that she reach the vehicle first and prepare to launch us out of the swamp. This was one of those times when her ridiculously fast vehicle and her penchant for wanting to test its limits came in handy. Gertie and I took off after Ida Belle. I could hear running behind us. I just hoped Camo Dude was too drunk and out of shape to pursue us at any speed.

Ida Belle already had the SUV running when we reached it.

I jumped inside and saw Camo Dude closing in on us at an alarming rate. Gertie jumped into the back seat but before Ida Belle could tear out of there, Camo Dude jumped on the front of the SUV.

This was so not good.

I could practically see steam coming out of Ida Belle's head. I knew there was no way Camo Dude could have damaged the vehicle. It had this huge brush guard on the front that could take down a small water buffalo without so much as creating a dent. But that wasn't going to prevent Ida Belle from taking it as a personal assault on her baby.

"I got this," Gertie yelled and pulled a .45 out of her purse.

I reached back over the console to grab the gun. At the same time, Ida Belle punched the gas. As the SUV launched forward, I flew into the back seat, still clutching the .45. I managed to right myself and saw Camo Dude clinging to the brush guard. Actually, hanging on for dear life was a better description at this point. His eyes were wide and all the color had drained from his face.

"I think he's learned his lesson," I said, not even sure we were actually on the road. "You can let him off."

Ida Belle whipped the SUV around a set of trees so fast the back tires lost traction, which was both impressive and a little scary given that it was a four-wheel drive vehicle. Suddenly, a set of headlights blinded us and Ida Belle slammed on the brakes. I launched back over the console and crashed into the dash before falling into the passenger floorboard.

"Uh-oh," I heard Gertie say as I scrambled to right myself.

I looked out the windshield and saw Camo Dude splayed out on the hood of the vehicle that had blinded us. And Gertie's disclaimer made perfect sense.

Carter stepped out of his truck and went to check Camo Dude. I held my breath until he twitched, then let it all out in a whoosh as Carter helped him off the hood and sat him down on the side of the road. Then he strode for my window. I pressed the button to lower it as he stepped up next to the vehicle and glared.

"You want to tell me why you're driving around with a man as a hood ornament?" he asked.

"He chased us out of the bar and jumped on the front of my SUV," Ida Belle said.

Carter raised one eyebrow. "And you thought driving at the speed of sound with him perched on the front was a good idea, then slamming on the brakes was a good idea?"

"Well, he's not on the front of my vehicle anymore," Ida Belle said.

"You could have killed him," he said.

"I seriously doubt it," Ida Belle said. "I wasn't going that fast, and besides, you know how drunks are. They don't break when they fall. Besides, if he didn't want to be taken for a ride, he shouldn't have jumped onto my personal property, potentially damaging it."

Carter closed his eyes for a moment and sighed. "And would you like to tell me why he decided to take an unscheduled ride on your front bumper?"

"He was chasing Gertie," I said.

"Of course he was," he said.

"The defrocked nun is his great-aunt," I said.

Gertie leaned over the console. "I told him it was an accident, but he wouldn't let it go, even after I Tasered him."

"You what?" Carter asked.

I clamped a hand over Gertie's mouth. "Even after she apologized," I said.

"That crazy bitch assaulted a nun," Camo Dude yelled. "I want you to arrest her and the other one for running me over."

Carter turned around. "Shut up or I'll arrest you for drunk

and disorderly and private property damage. See how that works?"

Camo Dude grumbled a couple of expletives, but I noticed he didn't try to rise from his spot.

"I don't suppose you're going to tell me what you were doing at the Swamp Bar?" Carter asked.

"Having a drink," Ida Belle said. "That's sorta what bars are known for."

"But that's not the reason you three are known for going," he said. "Look, I got a call about a disturbance here and if I'd known you guys were here, I wouldn't have even bothered to make the drive."

"What if we needed help?" Gertie said.

"Ha!" Carter laughed. "I think you've got that reversed. When you guys are at the Swamp Bar, it's everyone else who needs help. Go. Leave. Before I change my mind about arresting you and throw you in the clink with the nun's nephew."

"What are you arresting me for?" Camo Dude asked.

"I'm just giving you a place to sleep it off," Carter said. "Then you can rethink attacking seniors over that situation with your aunt."

"My aunt is a senior," Camo Dude said.

"And she has God in her corner," Carter said. "Do you think he needs your help?"

———

IDA BELLE MADE the drive to Sinful in record time. Because Ally was at my house, we elected to meet at Ida Belle's. Normally, we would have picked Gertie's because she was more likely to have tasty baked goods, but Ida Belle and I figured her house probably still held the faint smell of skunk in the morning and took a pass. Ida Belle had a package of Oreos, so that was good enough.

Gertie put on coffee to brew and Ida Belle placed the cookies and some napkins on the table. I grabbed some cookies and popped a whole one in my mouth.

"Did anyone get anything?" I mumbled, my mouth full of cookie.

They both nodded. I pointed at Ida Belle. "You're up," I said.

"I was talking to one of the guys I deer hunt with sometimes," Ida Belle said. "He said Hooch was in there drunk a couple weeks ago, bragging about how one of these days, he'd buy all of Sinful, including the bar."

"I guess the term 'inflation' was lost on him," I said.

"There were a whole lot of things lost on him," Ida Belle said. "Anyway, the guys ribbed him about making up stories but he stuck by his tale."

"Did any of them believe him?" I asked, wondering if Ricky had started asking about Hooch before or after he began bragging about his big payday.

Ida Belle shook her head. "Which is why none of them asked for details. Of course, now that he's been murdered, they're all wondering."

"I think everyone's wondering," Gertie said. "My plumber said basically the same thing. Hooch claimed he was going to be rich soon and was going to spend the rest of his life sitting on a beach in Costa Rica with a cold beer and a hot woman."

"That's more affordable than buying all of Sinful," I said.

"Not the hot woman," Gertie said. "A hot woman can cost a fortune, especially if she has to hang out with a guy like Hooch. But that's not the most interesting part. My plumber said he used to talk to a hotshot driver for the oil companies while he was working on a commercial job at the motel and that guy dated Margarita."

"I knew she was lying about the dating," I said.

"How did her name even come up?" Ida Belle asked.

"My plumber told the driver where he was from, and the driver said he used to date a woman from Sinful and gave her name. My plumber remembered her, of course, and asked how she was doing. The driver said he guessed she was doing okay but he didn't like the company she was keeping."

"What kind of company was that?" Ida Belle said.

"He said she took up with some biker dudes," Gertie said. "She claimed they were just friends but she spent a lot of time down at their bar. The driver was on probation so he decided to cut ties with her. He was afraid something her friends were up to might fall out on him."

Ida Belle shook her head. "It doesn't really surprise me that Margarita gravitated toward a rough bunch. Between her dad and Hooch, she's probably locked in on a type."

"Also explains why she didn't want Junior to know," Gertie said.

"I don't understand," I said. "I would think she'd learn what type of men to avoid because it always brings her heartache."

"You would think that," Gertie said, "but people tend to crave the familiar, even when it's not good for them."

I frowned. Was that what I was doing with Carter? Gravitating toward a man like my father? That was a particularly upsetting thought and one I'd have to process when I was alone and not trying to solve a murder.

"Did you get anything?" Ida Belle asked me.

"Boy, did I."

First, I told them about my conversation with Whiskey and Hooch's fight with Ricky Marks. When they were done exclaiming over that one, I launched into my chat with Dixie.

"Dixie was dating Hooch?" Gertie said. "Talk about getting hit by one out of left field."

Ida Belle nodded. "I definitely did not see that one coming."

"So this information is great," I said, "but it's also a problem."

"Because now we have two really good suspects," Ida Belle said.

"You don't really think Dixie killed Hooch for cheating on her, do you?" Gertie said. "I mean, it's Hooch. Hardly the loss of the century."

I thought about Dixie's expression when she called me a Barbie bitch and explained how women like her didn't have the same options as women like me. "Maybe it was enough of a loss to Dixie," I said.

"Anything is possible," Ida Belle said. "So what now?"

"Bed," I said, and rose from my chair. "Then tomorrow, we figure out a way to get the scoop on Ricky Marks. He's the big unknown."

———

IT WAS AN UNEVENTFUL NIGHT. Or I guess I should say the rest of the night. Or early morning if you wanted to get really specific. I managed to sleep until eight, then headed downstairs where I found banana nut bread and the coffeepot staged. All I had to do was press the button. Ally had left me a note saying she had the early shift at the café and would see me later.

I sent Ida Belle and Gertie a text and suggested we have breakfast at the café and then chat with Walter about Ricky

Marks, as he was the only person we knew who had interacted with him on a regular basis. I heard back from both of them within seconds and we arranged for Ida Belle to pick us up in thirty minutes. That gave me plenty of time to consume the pot of coffee and at least a quarter of the banana nut bread. I promised myself I'd eat something healthy at the café.

I was waiting on the porch when Ida Belle pulled up. We all looked a little worse for the wear but considering how badly things could have gone the night before, we were doing all right. Ida Belle made the short drive to the café and Ally waved us to our usual table at the back and hurried off to get our drink orders. Margarita and Junior were sitting at the table next to ours. They both looked tired and frustrated.

We took our seats and extended morning greetings to Margarita and Junior. They were polite but unenthusiastic in their response.

"I take it things aren't progressing?" Ida Belle asked.

Margarita sighed. "I'm afraid not. We just came from talking to Carter. Apparently, Hooch owed people money and they plan on putting liens on the estate."

She laughed. "Estate. It sounds funny even using that word in reference to Hooch. Anyway, the cops don't want any liability, so they're sending an appraiser out tomorrow to see if there's anything of value inside the house. I imagine they'll come back with a recommendation to burn it down."

"I'm sorry this has become more difficult than you imagined," Ida Belle said.

"Sort of the story of my life when it comes to Hooch," Margarita said. "I guess I shouldn't have expected any different."

"Do you need help making the funeral arrangements?" Ida Belle asked. "Gertie and I would be happy to assist."

"Thank you, but Junior and I will handle that today.

Hooch didn't leave any instructions regarding his death so we've elected to have him cremated. It sounds crass, but it's the cheapest way to go. We'll pour his ashes in the bayou. That's where he loved to be most, so now he can rest there forever."

Ida Belle nodded. "Well, if there's anything else we can do... Both Gertie and I have spare rooms if you'd like to get out of that hotel. I can't imagine it's all that comfortable."

"The beds are horrible," Margarita said. "I'll probably need a chiropractor when I get back home, but hopefully, it's only for one more night. As soon as the appraiser sees there's nothing of value, we can list the property and let the courts settle up with those Hooch owed money when it sells. If it ever sells. I hope no one is holding their breath."

"I can't imagine they would be," Gertie said. "Not if they knew Hooch well at all."

"If they knew him that well," Margarita said, "they wouldn't have put themselves in a situation where Hooch owed them money."

"That's true enough," Ida Belle said.

Margarita shook her head. "I'll just be glad to get back home. Both Junior and I need to get back to work. Sitting here isn't paying the bills."

"Well, at least let us get your breakfast," Ida Belle said. "Then we'd feel like we're doing something."

Margarita smiled. "That's the one thing I miss about Sinful —the graciousness. You don't see much of that in cities."

The door to the café opened and I looked up to see Carter walk inside. He scanned the room and headed right toward us.

"What now?" I asked, my voice low. I elbowed Ida Belle, who looked over and frowned as she spotted Carter approaching. He did not look happy.

I was just running through a list of potential excuses, for

what, I had no idea, when he stopped in front of Margarita and Junior.

"I'm really sorry," he said, "but there's been an incident at the motel. Several of the rooms were broken into this morning, yours included. We need everyone to check and see if anything's been taken."

"Good grief!" Margarita said. "Like we need more trouble."

"I can give you a lift if you'd like," Carter said.

"No," Margarita said as she rose. "We were finished anyway. We'll drive."

Carter nodded. "The state police will meet you there. I'm sorry to interrupt your breakfast."

"Thank you for picking up the tab," Margarita said to Ida Belle. "You ladies have a nice day."

Junior gave us a nod and they hurried out of the café. Carter watched them leave, then turned back to us. "I trust you have recovered from your night of flinging men from your vehicle?"

"As there was no damage to my SUV, I slept quite well," Ida Belle said. "Thank you for asking."

Carter nodded. "Unfortunately, there is the small matter of the dent in the hood of my truck. I assume I can forward the repair bill to you."

"I'll take it," I said. "I'm already buying a mirror anyway. No use having to split things up."

"What happened at the motel?" Gertie asked.

Carter shrugged. "Petty theft, looks like. A couple people reported their rooms were broken into while they were at breakfast. Margarita and Junior's room was one of them. The front desk clerk had seen them leave earlier and gave me a call, figuring they might be here taking care of things."

"Was anything taken?" Gertie asked.

"The usual. Some money lying around. A cell phone. A

wedding band." Carter shook his head. "That guy's in a world of trouble. He wasn't there with his wife."

"Ouch," Ida Belle said.

He gave us all a hard look. "I don't suppose I could convince you to stay home today and knit or something?"

"You will never convince me to knit," I said.

"You know what I mean," Carter said.

"Yes," I said, "and you know we're not about to agree to that."

He sighed. "At least try to keep from stripping people, especially religious people. And no more riding around with guys on your brush guard."

"I think we can probably manage those two," I said.

"Probably?"

"I don't want to make any promises I might not keep."

He turned around and walked away, still shaking his head when he left the café.

"That was smart," Gertie said. "You never know when we might need to run over someone or take their clothes."

Ida Belle stared at her for a second, then looked back at me. "So after breakfast, we talk to Walter?"

"That's the plan," I said. "But I'm afraid I don't have anything after that."

"That's easy," Gertie said. "We spy on Ricky at his place."

"He's renting a farmhouse," Ida Belle said. "The acreage surrounding it is all cleared for crops. We couldn't get within a half mile of that place without being spotted. And if you suggest we parachute in, I swear to God, I'll shoot you before you get your breakfast."

"Surely Fortune has some spiffy telescope from Marge's collection that can see that far," Gertie said.

"Several," I said. "But none of them see through walls. It's a million degrees out here. Even if he happens to be off work on a Monday, why in the world would he be outside? It's a rented house. He has no repairs to make. No crops to work."

"Fortune's right," Ida Belle said. "It's far more likely he's at work, but even if he isn't, the best we could hope for is to catch a glimpse of him through a window. I hardly think that would be worth sneaking through fields and collecting a crap-ton of bugs and itchy grass."

"We could always break in," Gertie said. "Take a look through his things."

"No way," I said. "It is one thing to break into a dead man's house. The risk of someone shooting you is a lot lower. But I'm not about to stroll into the house of a man who's alive and probably packing."

"So what if Walter doesn't know anything?" Gertie asked.

"Then we figure out another way to get information," I said. "One that does not involve breaking and entering."

CHAPTER TWENTY-TWO

WALTER WAS CHECKING out a customer when we walked into the General Store, but the place was otherwise empty. We milled around until the customer left, then headed to the counter. He looked up with a smile that faltered a bit as we approached.

"I know that look," he said. "Do you need bail money? An escape vehicle?"

"Only information," I said.

He snorted. "Like that's any less dangerous. Who are you locking in on this time?"

"Ricky Marks," Ida Belle said.

"Ah." He nodded. "I wondered when someone would make their way around to him."

"Why?" I asked.

"Because he's new and he keeps to himself," Walter said. "That tends to make people speculate more, not less. Best you come into a place like Sinful and hand everyone the story of your life in a binder. Preferably with charts and pictures."

"I see," I said. "So if you keep to yourself and don't mix

with the locals, everyone assumes you have something to hide."

"That's because you usually do," Gertie said.

"Since I'm kinda the queen of secrets," I said, "I'm not about to throw stones. So what do you think Ricky is hiding?"

"I honestly don't know," Walter said. "He's a tough one to figure out. He comes once a week for supplies and always buys the same thing—bread, lunch meat, frozen entrées, two bags of chips, three packages of cookies, and a case of Dr Pepper."

"Based on his diet, he might be hiding diabetes," Ida Belle said. "But I don't see anything out of the ordinary about it. Not for a single guy."

"Nope," Walter said. "That's pretty standard fare for those of us not fortunate enough to have a lady to cook us a good meal or to take out to dinner. Just maybe not in that quantity."

"Surely he's said something," Gertie said. "You talk to everyone. Don't tell me you haven't gotten a personal tidbit or two out of him."

Walter nodded. "A couple. He works for a drilling company."

"Do you know the name?" I asked.

"Lassiter, I think," Walter said. "There's a ton of those smaller outfits around, so I'm not sure I got that right."

I looked at Ida Belle, who frowned. The letter we'd found in Hooch's house was from Lassiter Drilling. Strange coincidence or something else?

"He's from New Orleans," Walter continued, "but he's assigned to this area for a year or so and was tired of the commute. His lease was up on his apartment, so he decided to get a place closer to work. But rentals are very limited, and he didn't like the motel. I got the impression he likes the farmhouse because there's no people around to have to deal with."

"What about family or friends?" Ida Belle asked. "Any out this way?"

He shook his head. "Doesn't know a soul that I'm aware of. Said his mother died back a bit from cancer. Didn't mention his father, so I took that to mean he was either dead as well or not in the picture."

"Any reason to think he knew Hooch?" I asked.

"None offhand." Walter stopped talking and frowned.

"What?" Ida Belle said.

"Nothing really," Walter said, "it's just that when he was in here a couple weeks ago, he was looking at the flyer for the fishing rodeo. When I checked out his goods, I noticed him looking at the pictures here of previous years' winners. I asked him if he was interested but he said he didn't have a boat."

"If he's only here for a bit and usually lives in the city, a boat wouldn't be a good investment," Ida Belle said.

"No, it wouldn't," he said. "But I saw him at the dock the day of the rodeo. I didn't think about it at the time—there was so much going on. But it seems a little strange now."

"You mean given his reclusive tendencies and the fact that he wasn't taking part in the rodeo?" I asked.

He nodded. "But who am I to say anything? Maybe he got bored sitting in that house alone. Or lonely. No shame in either."

"Of course not," Gertie said. "He goes to the Swamp Bar some as well."

"He asked about whiskey," Walter said. "Was surprised the town was dry. I guess he could get two fixes at a time in the bar."

"Maybe three if he found a willing floozy," Gertie said.

Walter blushed. "Yes, well, that's a bit out of my territory."

"Floozies aren't out of anyone's territory," Gertie said. "That's sorta the point."

Ida Belle cleared her throat. "All talk of floozies aside, is there anything else you can tell us?"

He shook his head. "Sorry, but that's all I've got. You don't think he killed Hooch, do you? I mean, he didn't even know the man."

"There's been some talk," Ida Belle said. "Hooch has been drunk-bragging about cashing in some big payday."

"Doesn't sound very likely," he said.

"No, it doesn't," Ida Belle agreed. "Yet Hooch is dead and someone was sneaking around his place the other night."

Walter raised his eyebrows. "And you know this how—you know what? Never mind. I think this is one of those times where the less I know the better."

"Agreed," Ida Belle said.

The bells above the door jangled and two women made a beeline toward the counter holding shopping lists. We retreated to the far end of the store while Walter took care of them.

Ida Belle pulled out her cell phone and motioned for us to step outside. "I'm calling that drilling company," she said. "Who was that contact?"

I accessed the picture and she dialed, then introduced herself as a court clerk and explained that Mr. Carre had died and she was verifying assets. She needed to know if he had a legal agreement with the company to drill on his property and if so, what it entailed.

The assistant put her on hold and a couple minutes later, a manager got on the line and verified that they had done a cursory review of Hooch's property but didn't consider it large enough to pursue exploration at this time. They were keeping his information on file and wanted to maintain open lines in case they changed their mind in the future.

"So that's that," I said. "The whole oil thing doesn't sound overly promising. Surely Hooch wouldn't have approached the Heberts about money over something this flimsy."

"I don't think even Hooch was that foolish," Ida Belle said.

"Which means Hooch thought he had something else worth that money," Gertie said. "But what?"

Ida Belle nodded. "If we can't figure out what Hooch was trying to sell, we're probably not going to figure out who killed him. I refuse to believe the two things aren't related. Not after finding out Hooch was blabbing at the bar. It's too much of a coincidence."

"I agree," I said, and frowned. Then I snapped my fingers. "Hooch's house!"

"We've already checked his house," Gertie said.

"But tomorrow, the appraiser will," I said.

"But there weren't any valuables," Gertie said. "We checked everything."

"We checked everything inside the house," I said. "But what about outside?"

Ida Belle nodded. "It would be just like Hooch to bury whatever it is in a hole."

"But we don't even know what we're looking for," Gertie said. "We can't go dig up every spot of dirt around his house."

"We don't have to," I said. "The reality is, we don't care about Hooch's valuables. Our goal is to catch his killer."

Ida Belle brightened. "And if that person killed Hooch for his valuables, then he'll believe his last chance to recover them is tonight."

"How do you know he hasn't already?" Gertie said.

"Because I chased him away the night we were there," I said. "I think we disrupted that search. Then after all the racket we made, Carter had someone guarding the place day and night."

"They were probably biding their time," Ida Belle said.

"Thinking it would all blow over soon and they could waltz right in.

I nodded. "But they weren't counting on the courts getting involved so soon and an appraiser being sent. Their time is up tonight. Which means all we have to do is spread word around town about the appraiser and then wait at Hooch's house for his killer to arrive."

Gertie grinned. "You're a genius. But if it's all the same, I'd still like to find Hooch's valuables. If for no other reason than to sneak them out to Junior. With the appraiser and all, it feels like he's getting the short end of the father stick all over again."

I sobered a bit. I did feel sorry for Junior. Hooch definitely didn't deserve any fatherhood awards, but if he really had something worth all that money, then he could have tried to make a little bit right. Instead, he'd been plotting to sell off and disappear, his last big FU to his son.

"It would be nice to help Junior out," Ida Belle said, "but even if we discovered what Hooch was hiding, and even if it was actually worth something, we'd still have to turn it over to Carter. Giving it to Junior would only make him a criminal, and if whatever it is really values out as high as Hooch claimed, then it would be hard for Junior to hide that sort of windfall."

Gertie sighed. "I guess if we could find out Hooch was running his mouth about coming into a fortune at the Swamp Bar, anyone else could as well. Man, I wish someone hadn't murdered him. I'd punch him in the face."

"I'd aim lower," Ida Belle said.

I pointed to the General Store as the two women exited with their bags. We hurried back in and Ida Belle went straight to the counter and got on with the business at hand.

"We need to ask another favor," she said.

"What kind of favor?" Walter asked.

"The easiest kind for you," Ida Belle said. "We need you to spread some gossip around town." She told Walter about the appraiser who was due to arrive the next morning to review the contents of Hooch's house.

"And I suppose you want me to make extra sure Ricky gets this information?" he asked.

"Yes," I said. "Can you do that without it appearing odd?"

"Heck yeah," Walter said. "He's got a special order that I can call and update him on. It's completely normal for me to yammer on about something. Hooch's murder is big news in a small town. He won't think anything of an old man gossiping. Neither will anyone else, for that matter."

"You think you can get decent coverage?" I asked.

He nodded. "Got a few of Sinful's biggest tongue-waggers coming in to pick up orders today. By this afternoon, everyone in town will be up to date on everything happening with Hooch."

"That's awesome," I said. "Thanks for helping." I studied him for a minute. "You're not going to ask why, are you?"

"Just guessing produces enough worry," he said. "Now you guys have to promise me something."

Ida Belle gave him an apprehensive look. "What?"

"That you won't get yourselves killed," he said. "I'm kinda fond of you three. I'd miss having you around."

I smiled at him. If I were older, I would so have a run at Walter. And while I completely understood Ida Belle's reasoning for not getting involved with him, I didn't necessarily agree with it. Maybe all this humanity was making me a romantic. Or Gertie's constant hints and forcing me to watch chick flicks.

Or, God forbid, I might be becoming a girl.

CHAPTER TWENTY-THREE

WE WAITED until dark to head out and I said a quick prayer of thanks that despite the fact that it was cloudy, it wasn't raining and there was still a good bit of moonlight to operate by. I didn't think anyone would attempt to get into Hooch's house until much later, but I wanted us in place just in case the killer got impatient and moved in sooner than expected. Carter had informed me earlier that Deputy Breaux would be watching Hooch's place tonight and he would personally be checking in on him. I figured that was to nix any ideas we might have had of taking a peek at Hooch's property again.

I was growing fond of the young deputy. I didn't see him as a huge challenge to entry. Unless he spent the night inside the house, which I doubted, it would be a fairly simple matter for someone to enter from one of the windows while the deputy was on the opposite side of the house. If they searched with a penlight, that would drastically reduce the possibility of being spotted inside because of a light source.

Of course, that was assuming the killer was smart and patient, and my experience so far was that most couldn't manage both. At least, not when under pressure. I was counting on the impatient part kicking in and leading to some stupid decision-making. It was the stupid thing that got them every time.

We parked close to Young Huck's house. Ida Belle had already called him ahead of time and let him know we'd be lurking around his land so he wouldn't mistake us for the bear and take a shot at us. She said he was okay with us using the land but his deck was off-limits. I couldn't really blame him. We had essentially invited a bear into his house.

This time, I'd gone through Marge's stock and brought a FLIR camera with us. I wasn't so much worried about getting discovered by Deputy Breaux or even the killer, but I definitely wanted to avoid the bear. The forest was so dense the FLIR wouldn't provide a whole lot of benefit, but it would probably be good enough to alert us to the bear's presence before we heard him coming.

We traipsed across the woods as we had before and slowed up when I got a signal of heat on the FLIR. It wasn't moving, so we inched forward until we were right at the edge of the tree line. I checked the screen again and pointed to the end of Hooch's porch where Deputy Breaux was sitting, leaned against one of the posts holding up the roof.

"He probably shouldn't lean on that," Gertie whispered. "The whole mess might come down on top of him."

"Looks like he's in place for a while," I said. "We might as well get comfortable."

Ida Belle nodded. "There's a log just a bit over and behind us. We'll have a view of the house and the road but still be covered by those bushes. If they approach by boat, we'll hear it coming. So unless they approach by foot on the back side of the house, the FLIR will let us know if anyone else shows up."

"Or anything," Gertie said.

"The killer should be bigger than a skunk and smaller than a bear, so you're forewarned either way," Ida Belle said.

"So we wait," Gertie said and plopped down on the log. "I should have brought my tablet."

"Because the lit screen wouldn't have given us away," Ida Belle said.

"Oh, right," Gertie said. "This is going to be worse than church. Nothing to read. No singing. Can't even hum quietly."

"You could meditate," Ida Belle said. "I swear to God, the mosquitoes are less annoying than you."

"Just don't sleep," I said. Gertie snored like a train.

Gertie let out a long-suffering sigh and slumped a bit. I looked over at Ida Belle and shook my head. I really hoped the killer showed up soon. Otherwise, this was going to be a very, very long night.

My body automatically positioned itself for a long wait. I'd done this so many times I didn't even have to think about it. The only difference being I was usually in the desert and had Harrison sitting next to me, or no one. Now I was resting on a rotted log in a mosquito-infested forest worrying that a skunk or a bear would show up before the killer did.

I began to mentally recite all the weapons I'd fired and then disassemble and reassemble them in my mind. It was a way to pass time and keep my pulse steady. In between weapons, I checked the FLIR but so far, I'd gotten only small heat signatures from local critters. Nothing large enough to be a bear or a random confused alligator that might have wandered into the trees. Ida Belle had told me that rarely happened, but then Gertie had managed to get one into her bathtub, so all bets were off with me as far as alligators were concerned.

I had just finished putting the scope on a particularly awesome automatic weapon when I glanced down at the FLIR and saw movement. I looked over at the house and saw that Deputy Breaux had decided it was time to take a security lap around the house or more likely, had gotten a cramp from sitting in the same position too long. He was moving around the far side of the house and as soon as I lost sight of him, he disappeared from the FLIR as well. I had a moment of sadness when I realized civilian equipment wasn't nearly as awesome as what I'd had in the CIA, but then Marge's budget wasn't nearly as awesome as the federal government's, either. For that matter, neither was mine.

I stood up to get a better view of the house.

"What is it?" Ida Belle asked and rose beside me. Gertie had nodded off an hour ago, but fortunately, since she was upright, she wasn't snoring.

"Just the deputy taking a walk," I said.

"We've been here two hours now," she said. "You still think he's coming?"

I nodded. "I think he'll wait until Deputy Breaux is more likely to be asleep."

"That would have been the past two hours," Ida Belle said. "He doesn't know the deputy is one of those early to bed, early to rise people. You think I should move in closer since the front is unguarded?"

"Nah. It won't take him a couple minutes to circle the whole house. If anyone approaches, we're in position to handle him. I'd rather Deputy Breaux not be in the mix anyway. He carries a gun and might get confused as to who to fire on."

"Good call."

I was watching the near end of the house, waiting for the deputy to appear, when I heard a thump and a low moan.

"Something's wrong," I said, and shoved the FLIR at Ida Belle. "Stay here and cover the front."

I took off through the woods parallel to the side of the

house until I had a decent view of the back. The deputy was nowhere in sight and that was troubling. The yard wasn't well kept but he would have easily towered over the marsh grass behind the structure. I wondered for a second if he'd tripped over something in the overgrown mess of a yard and taken a tumble. That would account for the thud and the moan.

I crept out of the woods and hurried over to the back of the house, inching my way down the side, scanning the ground for any sign of the deputy. I almost tripped over him before I saw him. I dropped onto my knees to check his condition. The moonlight provided decent illumination for most of the yard, but Deputy Breaux was slumped partially underneath the house, so I couldn't see if he had an injury. What I could see was that he wasn't moving.

I checked his pulse and let out a breath of relief when it was beating strong. I shook him gently and whispered his name, but he didn't respond. I scanned the area surrounding me, making sure no one was nearby, and pulled out my penlight and shone it on the deputy's face. He was definitely out. In the marsh grass near his head, I saw specks of red and gently turned his face to the side. The blow to his head was bleeding a bit but I was relieved to see it wasn't as bad as I'd feared.

I pulled out my nine and rose from the ground. Hooch's property was a mess, and there was no shortage of rubbish scattered around the yard, but the deputy hadn't tripped and hit himself on the back of the head. Someone had struck him with something. And that someone couldn't be far away. I crept to the far end of the house and as I rounded the corner, I saw someone slip around to the front of the house and climb onto the porch.

My finger twitched as I thought about Deputy Breaux, lying behind the house in the weeds, his head bleeding. I wanted to catch this guy, and if I hurt him just a little in the process, that would be the bonus plan. I crept down the side of the house to the porch and peered around the corner, spotting the intruder working on the front door.

And then Gertie started snoring.

The intruder froze, then whirled around, trying to zero in on the source of the sound. I couldn't blame him for his obvious confusion. It wasn't exactly the sort of thing one expected to hear coming from the woods. I could see something in his right hand, but with the shadows, I couldn't determine if it was a tool or a gun. If it was a gun, I didn't have good enough position to rush him before he could aim and fire. And since this one wasn't sanctioned by the federal government, I couldn't just shoot him. Technically speaking, I was already breaking the law just by being here.

He lifted his arm and this time I had little doubt. The shape was a firearm. He walked down the steps, scanning the road as he went. The only vehicle in sight was Deputy Breaux's, so he'd walked in from somewhere as we had, probably on the opposite side of the road, which is why the FLIR hadn't picked him up. I inched down the side of the porch, crouched low, hoping for an opportunity to rush him from behind.

And that's when Ida Belle jumped him.

She must have been hiding on the side of the steps because as soon as the intruder stepped off the last one, she launched up and tackled him. I had to give her credit for the move. He was taller and bigger than her but she managed to send him sprawling onto the ground. Unfortunately, he popped right up and took off running. I set out after him at a sprint, but I could tell he was pulling away. Whoever he was, he could move. If he reached his vehicle or knew the woods well enough to navigate them at night, he was going to get away.

The first bottle rocket hit him right in the chest and he stumbled, almost falling. The second one caught him in the side of the head and he yelled. His left hand flew up and started shaking his hair, as if attempting to rid it of something, most likely burning paper. I turned on the afterburners, gave one huge leap, and grabbed him around the waist, sending us both hurtling onto the dirt road.

He dropped his gun when I hit him, but he scrambled to get up and I had trouble holding on to him. He kicked me in the face and it caused me to loosen my grip enough for him to get upright. I grabbed his foot and twisted it, bringing him back down to the ground next to me, then sent my elbow straight into his face.

"Stop or I'll shoot." Ida Belle's voice sounded above us.

"Me too," Gertie said.

We both froze, and I looked up to see Ida Belle standing over us with a .45 trained at the back of the intruder's head and Gertie holding a bottle rocket in one hand and a lighter in the other. I jumped on the intruder's back.

"Hands behind your back," I said. I hadn't identified myself as police, but I figured that's probably who he thought we were, and facedown, he couldn't see that it was two senior citizens. Granted, one could kill him from way farther than she stood now, and the other would probably try to launch that firework into his face and get his crotch instead, but he couldn't tell any of that from where he was sitting.

"Zip ties," I said.

Ida Belle reached in her fanny pack and handed me some zip ties, and I secured his arms with several of them. They weren't impossible to get out of but once I flipped him over, there would be two women holding a gun on him and one with very scary pyrotechnics.

I hopped up and grabbed his shoulder, flipping him over.

Gertie relinquished her fireworks and pulled a huge flashlight out of her bag and lit him up like the state penitentiary. He closed his eyes and cringed, involuntarily trying to move his arms in front of his face, but they weren't going anywhere. I pushed Gertie's arm to the side so that the light was more indirect and took a good look at the man I'd tackled.

"Ricky Marks?" I asked. He fit the description that Ida Belle had given me but I'd never seen him myself so I needed confirmation.

Ida Belle nodded.

"You're in big trouble, Ricky," I said. "Breaking and entering, assault of a police officer."

"I didn't do none of that," he said. "Who the hell are you?"

"I'm the person holding a gun on you. What are you doing here?"

"Hunting," he said, clearly not about to give up the ghost easily.

"With a pistol?" Ida Belle asked. "And not only on private property but at a crime scene? What kind of animal exactly were you tracking into Hooch's house?"

"I want a lawyer," he said.

I laughed. "That's awesome. And I want a hot shower and a cold beer, but since we're not cops, we don't care."

He squinted, trying to get a better look at us. "Then who are you? What do you want from me?"

"Nothing directly," I said. "We're just helping a friend. We did the hard part, now the sheriff's department can do the rest."

"Wait!" he said. "I have money. It's not a lot, but I can get more."

"Is that what you were looking for at Hooch's place?" I asked. "That's why you killed him, isn't it?"

His jaw set in a hard line. "I didn't kill nobody."

"Well, you sound really broken up that he's dead," Ida Belle said. "It might be easy to get the wrong impression given the circumstances."

"Hooch was a piece of shit," he said. "I'm not gonna pretend I'm sorry he's dead."

Ida Belle raised her eyebrows. "That's a strong sentiment coming from someone who barely knew the man. You've been here what...six months? I mean, Hooch was no prize but he usually didn't get people to wanting him dead until he'd known them for a couple years."

He scowled and looked down at the ground. "I ain't saying nothing else."

At that's when it hit me. The scowl, the set of his jaw, the shape of his eyes.

"Hooch was your father," I said.

CHAPTER TWENTY-FOUR

"Wнат?"

"Seriously?"

Ida Belle and Gertie both yelled at once. Ricky didn't say a word.

"You're sure?" Ida Belle asked.

I nodded. "Recognizing underlying bone structure is something I kinda had to be good at. You know, for my last job."

"Might as well fess up," Gertie said. "A simple DNA test will tell everything the cops need to know."

"That piece of shit was not my father," Ricky said. "He lied to my mom, promising her all sorts of things, and then as soon as she got pregnant, he split. Back to Sinful, to his *real* wife and son. He owed her. He owed me. When I confronted him at the Swamp Bar, he told me he didn't know my mother. I had pictures of them together and he still refused to admit it."

"That must have made you mad," Ida Belle said.

"Damn right it did. He's up there bragging about all this money he's about to come into. He didn't deserve anything good. Not after what he did. But I deserve something from him, and I don't care that he died."

"You know," I said, "Hooch didn't take care of his real wife and son either. He abused her and she left with her son when he was still a young boy. You might not think so, but you were better off without him."

"It figures. At least he was consistent, right?" His shoulders slumped and he dropped his gaze back down to the ground. "Whatever. Doesn't matter anymore."

"So what were you looking for, anyway?" I asked.

Ricky shrugged. "Probably nothing. Probably just more lies."

I heard a vehicle approaching and looked over to see Carter's truck. No way he'd gotten here that fast from Sinful. I figured he must have been on his way out to check on Deputy Breaux.

"Oh my God!" I said. "We forgot Deputy Breaux. Ricky conked him on the head. He was unconscious behind Hooch's house."

Carter walked up and looked at the three of us, then Ricky on the ground with zip ties around his wrists, and he sighed. "I suppose you were hunting again tonight?" he asked.

"Yes," I said. "Just not anything with four legs. We caught this one trying to break into Hooch's house.

Carter looked down. "Ricky Marks?"

I nodded. "More importantly, Hooch's son."

Carter's eyes widened. "Seriously?"

"Fortune spotted the resemblance and got the confession out of him," Ida Belle said.

"He has a gun," I said, "and I'm guessing that's what he used to whack Deputy Breaux over the head."

"It was definitely something hard." Deputy Breaux's voice sounded behind us and I turned to see him shuffling up, clutching the side of his head with one hand.

Ida Belle hurried over to inspect his head. "You're going to have a good knot," she said. "But it only bled a little."

"How do you feel?" Carter asked.

"Kinda dizzy," Deputy Breaux said. "And things are a little blurry. My head really hurts."

"Can you drive?" Carter asked.

Ida Belle shook her head. "No way he should drive. He doesn't need his vehicle that badly. Just take him back with you. He can get his vehicle tomorrow."

"I need him to take back the perp's vehicle," Carter said. "It's parked in the bushes just up the road. I have to process it for evidence."

"I can drive it," I said.

Carter gave me an "absolutely no way" look.

"Deputy Breaux can ride with me," I said. "Hell, you don't even have to document that I drove the vehicle. Just put down that he did."

Carter frowned and I could tell he wasn't crazy about the idea but couldn't find anything horribly wrong with it, either.

"It's either that or wait for the state police," Ida Belle said.

That kicked him into gear. "Okay, but you drive straight to the sheriff's department and park right in front. Don't touch anything except the controls you need to drive. Deputy Breaux will ride with you and supervise."

He looked at Ida Belle and Gertie. "I assume you have a vehicle stashed near Young Huck's house?"

Ida Belle nodded.

"Then I'll give you two a lift," he said.

We all started for Carter's truck and I reached out to steady Deputy Breaux, who was walking a little like a drunk. Ricky trudged ahead of me next to Carter, his shoulders slumped and looking down at his feet. I know he'd killed a man and plotted to steal from his legitimate heir, but I still felt a little sorry for the guy. He'd probably taken a position near Sinful to check out his father, and that introduction hadn't gone down anything close to the way he'd hoped. I understood Ricky's feeling that Hooch owed him something. I agreed. But this wasn't the way to get it.

Carter gave Deputy Breaux and me a lift to Ricky's truck. The keys were in the ignition, so no hassle there. Ricky had clammed up as soon as Carter arrived and sat slumped in the back seat sporting a pair of real handcuffs. After an admonition to drive directly to the sheriff's department and acquiring yet another promise from me that I wouldn't touch anything besides the gearshift and steering wheel, Carter finally let us leave.

He followed us until the turnoff for Young Huck's place, then flashed his lights and turned off the highway. Deputy Breaux and I continued on toward Sinful.

We were probably ten minutes from town when the deputy turned in his seat to look at me. "Hey. What were you guys doing out there anyway?"

"Hunting," I said, figuring I might as well keep it simple. I had no idea what Carter was planning on putting in his report, so the less I said to the deputy the better.

Deputy Breaux nodded. "Lucky for me you decided to hunt tonight or Ricky would have gotten away. I don't suppose you bagged anything before you came upon my troubles?"

"I'm afraid not," I said. "Except for your troubles, things were pretty quiet out there."

"That's good. I heard a bear got into Young Huck's house the other night. Everybody's got something to worry about when bears start opening the front door and strolling inside."

"Yeah, that sounds bad."

I pulled into Sinful and directed Ricky's truck to Main Street. I parked it right in front of the sheriff's department and then went around to help Deputy Breaux out of the truck and into the building. Carter must have called ahead and informed Myrtle of what had happened because she met us at the door with an ice pack and aspirin for Deputy Breaux. We got him inside and onto the couch in the entry and took a better look at the lump.

"I think you should go to the hospital," Myrtle said.

"No way," Deputy Breaux said. "People die in hospitals."

"People die at home, too," Myrtle said. "You plan on going home, don't you?"

"It's not the same," he argued.

Myrtle shook her head. "Then you wait right here on this couch and don't move."

"What if I have to...you know?" he asked.

"Pee?" Myrtle asked. "Then you let me know and I'll assist you to the restroom. I mean it. Lie down and don't move or I'm calling 911 and your mother."

He only looked mildly concerned at 911 but the mother part put a slightly panicked look on his face, and he lay down and lifted the ice pack to the side of his head. Myrtle glanced at me, and I could tell she was dying to ask me what had happened, but I shook my head and inclined it toward Deputy Breaux.

She nodded. "You want some coffee? I don't know if Carter plans on keeping you guys around or not."

"I don't know either," I said.

"Nope," Carter said as he walked inside, guiding Ricky in front of him and followed by Ida Belle and Gertie. "I'm going to lock Ricky up and take Deputy Breaux to the hospital." He pointed a finger at the deputy before he could protest. "No argument. You got a head injury on the job. There are rules I have to follow."

Myrtle nodded her approval and took hold of Ricky's arm. "I'll take this one back."

"Once the hospital business is taken care of," Carter said, "I need to get a statement from Deputy Breaux, process Ricky, and search his vehicle. Then I'll get a warrant for his home. I'll get your statements tomorrow. I trust you won't forget the order of events by then."

"We're not those kinds of old ladies," Gertie said. "Our memories are just fine."

"I'm sure," Carter said. "It's not your recollection I question. It's your recounting of events that usually leaves something to be desired."

"Oh, well, that," Gertie said.

"Come on." Carter reached over and helped Deputy Breaux off the couch as Myrtle hurried back to the front desk.

"All secure," she said, and took her seat.

We headed out and waved to Carter as he drove away with Deputy Breaux. We stepped over to Ida Belle's SUV, but I stopped short in front of the vehicle. I turned and looked at both of them, a million things running through my head but none of them coming together to make a complete picture.

"What's wrong?" Ida Belle asked. "For someone who caught the bad guy, you don't look very satisfied."

"Something about it bothers me," I said.

"Nothing about it bothers me," Gertie said. "Well, except Deputy Breaux getting hit in the head, but I'm sure he'll be fine. Given what we've dealt with in the past, this one was easy."

"Exactly," I said. "It's too easy."

Ida Belle frowned. "You think we missed something?"

"I do, but I have no idea what," I said. "It's just all a little too perfect. I mean, don't get me wrong, it works. Ricky comes to Sinful looking for a father-son reunion, then he hears Hooch bragging about coming into money at the Swamp Bar."

Ida Belle nodded. "He tells Hooch he's his father and Hooch blows him off."

"So he kills him and tries to steal whatever it was that Hooch was planning on selling," Gertie said. "Makes sense to me. I mean, in a crazy killer sort of way."

"But that's just it," I said. "He had one fight with Hooch and that was enough to set him off? Doesn't that seem kinda premature?"

"Unless the fight at the bar wasn't the first," Ida Belle said. "He might have approached Hooch at his house before. Maybe the bar fight was just one of a string of them."

"And his mother died recently," Gertie said. "That might have been enough to put him over the edge when it came to the circumstances of his birth."

I sighed. "Yeah. I know. It all works."

"And yet?" Ida Belle asked.

"I just don't know," I said. "Maybe I need to sleep on it. Not like Ricky is going anywhere."

"Let's get home and get a shower and some rest," Ida Belle said. "Things will probably be clearer tomorrow."

I nodded and headed for my door. As I passed Ricky's truck I saw a folded sheet of paper hanging out from the door. I pulled it out, figuring I needed to turn it in to Myrtle before it blew away, then I saw a typed name in the corner on the back.

Boone Carre.

I froze.

"What's wrong?" Gertie asked.

"This has Hooch's name typed on it," I said. I opened the letter as Ida Belle hurried over to look.

MR. CARRE,

I hope this letter finds you well. I know you said at our meeting that you weren't ready to part with the items I inspected, but I wanted to inform you that I have a customer who will pay top dollar. I estimate the value of the sale would be $800,000-1,000,000. I take a commission of 10% for handling the transaction for you.

Please let me know if you're interested.

RUBEN GLASSIER
Glassier Coins and Collectibles

"COINS?" Ida Belle said. "If he had valuable coins, they weren't in his house. We searched the entire place."

"They could be buried somewhere," Gertie said. "Or stuffed in a wall or a hiding place in the floor. They'll probably have to tear the whole place down to find them."

I smiled. "No. They won't. Remember Gertie, you said there was a plastic container of quarters in Hooch's nightstand. Why would a man who stores his dirty underwear in his bed go to the trouble of putting quarters in a plastic container?"

Ida Belle's eyes widened. "We were searching with flashlights and your vision isn't what it used to be."

"My vision is just fine," Gertie said. "What's lacking is my knowledge of collector coins."

"Fair enough," Ida Belle said. "Well, I guess the mystery of what valuables Hooch was hiding is solved."

"Yeah," Gertie said, "but how did Ricky get this letter?"

I stared at the letter and frowned. Sure, one question was

answered, but this letter created several others. The last three days of activity and conversations rushed through my mind, all of it jumbled together. Until suddenly it wasn't.

I grabbed Ida Belle's arm. "We have to go back to Hooch's place. Now."

CHAPTER TWENTY-FIVE

I HAVE to give Ida Belle and Gertie credit. They were both clearly confused, but my urgency must have convinced them that I was serious. Everyone hurried into the SUV and Ida Belle took off.

"Why do we need to go to Hooch's place again?" Gertie asked. "Ricky's locked up and Carter called the state police when we left Hooch's place. They said they'd send someone out there as soon as they could."

"If I'm right," I said, "it might not be soon enough."

"Tell us what you're thinking," Ida Belle said.

"I'm not sure Ricky killed Hooch," I said.

"Why not?" Gertie said. "I know he said he didn't do it but the guilty always say that."

"This letter, old habits, unpaid debts, and lies about dating, to name a few," I said. "And when Ricky said he didn't kill Hooch, I sorta believed him."

"I'm so confused," Gertie said.

"And I'm not completely convinced either," I said. "But there's too many things that don't fit for me and only one way

I can put them together. How do you think Ricky got this letter?"

"From Hooch's place?" Gertie said.

"But it wasn't there when we searched the house," I said.

"Maybe Ricky was there before us," Gertie said, "and took the letter."

"But didn't take the coins?" Ida Belle said. "They were right there in the nightstand. I suppose he could have taken it off of Hooch at the Swamp Bar, or from his vehicle, if Hooch had it in there."

"*Or* he could have stolen it from the motel this morning," I said.

Gertie's eyes widened. "From Margarita and Junior? You think Ricky broke into the motel? But there was stuff missing from a bunch of rooms."

"Minor stuff," I said. "If you want to make the burglary of one place or item look like something else, what do you do?"

Ida Belle nodded. "You steal things from other rooms. But why would Margarita and Junior have the letter?"

"I'm not sure about that part," I said. "Not completely. But if I'm right, and they know about the coins—"

"Then they have to take them before the appraiser finds them tomorrow," Gertie interrupted.

"And you think Margarita and Junior killed Hooch?" Ida Belle asked.

I shook my head. "Maybe not. Maybe they just got hold of the letter somehow and wanted to collect the coins before they're confiscated to settle Hooch's debts. But this letter is dated a month ago. If Ricky took it from their motel room then they probably knew about the money before Hooch died."

"The hotshot driver," Gertie said. "The one who used to date Margarita. My plumber said his route came through here some. He probably stopped in at the Swamp Bar. If he overheard Hooch talking, he might have felt obligated to get word to her about the potential windfall, especially if he knew about the back child support Hooch owed her."

I nodded. "Maybe, but it still doesn't explain how they got the letter. That's the thing I can't work out."

Ida Belle nodded. "Because if they were in Hooch's house, they would have taken the coins along with it, same as Ricky."

"Exactly," I said.

"Where do you want me to go?" Ida Belle said. "Young Huck's place and we hike?"

"No. Head toward Hooch's," I said. "You can park in the same place Ricky did, just pull farther in. I don't think anyone will be able to see the SUV but it will still be fairly close."

Ida Belle nodded and continued past the road to Young Huck's place, then turned on the road to Hooch's.

"They were expecting to get access to the house right away," Gertie said. "Then Carter made it a crime scene, and the DA ordered the appraisal. Do you think they knew about the coins before they came here?"

"I think so," I said. "I don't have any evidence, though. It's just a hunch. For that matter, all of this conjecture is."

Gertie frowned. "We should probably call Carter, right? Get him back over to Hooch's place?"

I shook my head. "Because I have a hunch? He's taking Deputy Breaux to the hospital. I could be completely wrong about all of this. If he detours back to Hooch's and nothing happens, I'll never hear the end of it."

"Pride is both a wonderful and a dangerous thing," Ida Belle said.

"It is," I said. "And if you two don't want to be involved, I wouldn't blame you. I don't have anything concrete to offer you."

"A hunch is good enough for me," Gertie said.

"A vivid dream would be good enough for you," Ida Belle said. "But I'm with Gertie on this one. If you think there's smoke, then I'm ready to fight fires."

She pulled the SUV into the spot where Ricky's truck was parked before and inched it forward and around a set of dense bushes.

"Perfect," I said as I climbed out. "No one will see it if they're driving by."

"There's enough moonlight to forgo flashlights," Gertie said.

I nodded. "We should walk along the edge of the road. That way, if we hear anyone coming, we can hide." I stopped walking and looked at them. "I'm apologizing ahead of time, in case I'm wrong about everything and wasting your time."

Gertie waved a hand in dismissal. "What the hell else did we have to do? Sleep's overrated."

Ida Belle grinned. "Let's go put out a fire."

We headed toward Hooch's place, and I wondered with every step if I was completely off on everything and this was a huge waste of time that would only result in more mosquito bites, but there was no way I could go home and pretend I was okay with the way everything was.

When we reached the end of the road, we stopped and peered around a set of dense shrubs. We hadn't seen another vehicle along the way, and there were none in front of Hooch's place. I didn't see any signs of life. No lights. No sounds that indicated people were present.

"Looks clear," Ida Belle whispered.

I nodded. Maybe I'd been wrong. Maybe all this planning for my future as a PI had caused me to make inaccurate leaps. Maybe I needed more sleep. Or maybe I was better at a career that allowed me to confront the bad guys after others identified and vetted them.

"Might as well wait a bit," Gertie said. "At least until the state police show up."

"I agree," Ida Belle said. "Carter specifically asked for two cops. Even if Margarita and Junior want to collect the coins, they won't take on two cops. I don't mean to disparage the boy, but Deputy Breaux was a much easier target."

"Then we wait," I said, not sure whether to be pleased that my friends wanted to stay or worried that they were humoring me. I finally settled on pleased. Either option meant they cared about me enough to endure sleeplessness and the world's largest mosquitoes. You couldn't say that about just anybody.

Every second felt like a minute. Every minute felt like an hour. And as the minutes ticked by, I became more convinced that I'd been wrong. That Ricky had gotten the letter from Hooch's truck or boat and killed him after Hooch had denied being his father. And I'd created some elaborate plot in my mind just because of a few things that didn't make sense. Okay, maybe more than a few. But at the base of it, it was entirely plausible that Ricky had done it. All of it.

And then I heard the sound of an engine approaching. A marine engine.

I grabbed Ida Belle's arm and she nodded. We listened, waiting to see if the boat passed or stopped. I knew that some people fished at night because different kinds of fish were active, and some ran their crab pots at night because it was cooler, so this might be nothing more than locals doing their thing. I'm pretty sure I was holding my breath as the engine quietly ran toward us. When it cut out behind Hooch's house, I wanted to shout.

The state police wouldn't arrive by boat and I couldn't think of any reason why someone would stop by Hooch's house in the middle of the night, so that left only one option. Now I just had to see if I had the right people. We hurried just inside the tree line around the side of the house, moving as silently as possible. I stopped when we had a view of the bayou and pointed to the bass boat tied to the dock.

I spotted two silhouettes moving up the path toward the house.

Then the clouds cleared and Margarita and Junior came into view.

Gertie grabbed my arm and squeezed and Ida Belle took a quick snapshot with her phone. I'll admit to feeling a rush over my hunch being right, but now we had a problem.

"What do we do?" Gertie whispered.

"We wait," Ida Belle said. "At least until after they break into the house and get the coins. Maybe we'll luck out and the state police will show up and nab them."

"How's that lucky?" Gertie asked. "I want credit for this takedown."

"You have been watching too many cop shows," Ida Belle said.

Margarita and Junior walked up the porch and Junior made quick work of the lock. They slipped inside and I saw the occasional beam of a flashlight through the side window.

"We should disable their boat," Gertie said.

I frowned. In theory, it wasn't a bad idea. It left them stranded in the middle of the marsh, and if anyone was capable of disabling a boat it was Gertie. But if they looked out a back window and saw her, it was also risky.

"A five-year-old could make a shot from the house to the dock," Ida Belle said.

"But it would definitely be to our advantage to leave them on foot."

"Then we'll cover her," I said. "We'll move as close to the

dock as we can get without exposing ourselves, then Gertie will make a run for it as soon as the next cloud cover happens."

"You want Gertie running on the dock with no light?" Ida Belle asked.

"Worse case, she falls in and is out of the line of fire," I said.

"I'm not going to fall in," Gertie said. "I can walk a straight line and once I'm in the boat, I'll be low enough that they can't see me from the house."

"Let's go," I said, and we hurried along the tree line, then crept in the brush until we were a couple feet from the dock. We waited a few minutes and finally, the moon began to slip behind a thick set of storm clouds.

"Now," I said, and Gertie took off down the dock. Ida Belle and I had our pistols out, ready to draw fire off of Gertie if necessary. About ten seconds later, the moon began to peek out again. I glanced over at the dock and breathed a sigh of relief as Gertie slipped down into the boat. Halfway there.

Then I saw Margarita and Junior coming around the corner of the house.

I grabbed Ida Belle's arm and pointed. Gertie was trapped. And I could clearly see a pistol in Margarita's hand. We couldn't let them get to the dock, but we couldn't exactly shoot them, either. This civilian crime-fighting business was a lot harder than my CIA missions. So many restrictions. Mainly, not being able to shoot the bad guys.

But were they the bad guys? I still didn't know for sure if they'd killed Hooch. What if they were just trying to collect the coins before the appraiser confiscated them?

Ida Belle lifted her pistol and for a second, I thought she was going to forgo all the rules and just take them out right there, but instead, she fired a round into the giant rainwater reservoir behind Hooch's house. The sound of the bullet tearing through the metal had both of them ducking and then the water began to pour out of the hole, dousing them.

"State police," Ida Belle yelled, forcing her voice lower than usual. "Drop your weapons and put your hands over your head."

Without even a moment of hesitation, Margarita lifted her arm and fired. The bullet whizzed right over our heads and into the bayou. I knew she couldn't see us, but she had taken a shot in the general direction of Ida Belle's voice and it had been dangerously close. Any doubts I had about Margarita and Junior being killers fled completely from my mind. She'd just fired on who she believed was the state police.

As she fired a second shot, Junior whirled around and took off running for the front of the house. Margarita followed right behind him. Ida Belle and I sprang up and took off after them. I knew they couldn't outrun me on the road, but if they got into the woods, it gave them an opportunity to get away or ambush us. I preferred not to engage in a game of cat and mouse in terrain that I was unfamiliar with.

I heard Gertie's footsteps on the dock and knew she was moving in behind us. Then I heard a giant splash and mentally ticked one off the backup list. We rounded the corner of the house and I spotted them headed directly for the woods on the far side of the house. If they made it to the tree line, everything was going to be so much harder.

And that's when the bear arrived.

CHAPTER TWENTY-SIX

HE MUST HAVE BEEN LURKING JUST inside the tree line, and when he heard the commotion, decided to come out and take a look. He took two steps out of the woods, spotted Margarita and Junior barreling toward him, then rose up on his hind legs and roared. Margarita slid to a stop, almost falling. Junior changed direction and took off down the road, leaving Margarita behind. So much for family loyalty.

Margarita scrambled to get her balance, then took off after Junior. Ida Belle fired a warning shot at the bear, who retreated back to the woods, then we set out after them. I could see them ahead of us, rounding a bend in the road, when I heard the unmistakable sound of pursuit. It wasn't Gertie. It was something much larger and on four legs.

I glanced back and saw the bear running behind us at a scary pace, his mouth open and about a million teeth glistening in the moonlight. We turned on the afterburners and rounded the corner just a couple feet behind Margarita, but with the bear right behind us, we couldn't afford to take her down. Instead, I ran right up to her and wrenched the pistol from her hand before sprinting after Junior.

He wasn't that far ahead—maybe twenty yards—and I was closing fast. He was quick but he lacked endurance. His pace was slowing. He rounded a corner and I prepared to tackle him as soon as I had him in my sights, then I heard a loud thump. I slid around the bend in the road and saw Junior slumped over the hood of a truck. I heard a roar and turned to see the bear rounding the corner behind me.

I raised my pistol to fire, knowing I had one chance to shoot the charging animal between the eyes. But before I could get off the shot, there was an enormous boom behind me and the bear dropped. I spun around and saw Young Huck standing next to the truck holding a rifle and grinning like he'd just won the lottery.

"Whoot!" he shouted. "I'm gonna have me some good eating for a long time."

I ran over to Junior and grabbed his arms, twisting them up behind his back. "You got any rope?" I asked.

"Of course I've got rope," Young Huck said. "What kind of man do you think I am?"

"The kind who killed a bear and saved the day." Ida Belle's voice sounded behind me, and I turned around to see her walking just behind Margarita, her pistol trained on the back of the woman's head. Gertie was following close behind, completely soaked but looking entirely too pleased.

"You were right!" she said.

"Maybe," I said, and looked at Margarita. "Why did you do it?"

Margarita glared at me. "You have to ask?"

"No. I guess I don't."

"Hooch didn't deserve that money. He owed everybody he'd ever met, but he owed me the most. Those coins would have given me the life I should have had. Instead of one scrimping and barely getting by raising his son by myself."

"Hooch was a loser," I agreed. "Everyone knew that. But what I really want to know is how you convinced your boy toy to go along with this harebrained plan."

"Boy toy?" Gertie and Ida Belle both stared at me.

I pointed a finger at the man I'd just tied to Young Huck's bumper. "I don't know who this is, but it's not Hooch's son."

"You're sure?" Gertie asked.

I nodded. "The facial features aren't right and he's no artist. When I met him in the café, I noticed his socks didn't match. One had a red stripe. One had green."

"He's color-blind," Ida Belle said. "Then who is he?"

I shrugged. "Probably one of the biker guys that Margarita likes to hang with. Remember Carter said their hotel room was broken into. *One* room. At first, I thought he was shy and slightly embarrassed about his lousy father, but that wasn't it at all."

"He was scared they were going to get caught," Ida Belle said. "And embarrassed that he was dating a woman old enough to be his mother."

"He was not embarrassed," Margarita argued.

"Look at that," I said. "Accuse her of murder and she doesn't care. Accuse her of robbing the cradle and she gets defensive."

"So what do we do now?" Gertie asked.

The sound of an approaching vehicle had us all throwing our hands up to block the headlights. The vehicle stopped behind Young Huck's pickup and when the headlights went off, I saw it was Carter's truck.

He walked up to us and took it all in—Margarita and Junior tied up, the dead bear in the middle of the road, Gertie soaking wet—and he did the one thing I never expected.

He started to laugh.

Gertie looked over at me, her eyes wide. "He's gone stark raving mad. We've finally pushed him over the edge."

He looked at her and shook his head. "If I were going to lose my mind over the stunts you guys pull, it would have happened a long time ago. Maybe I'm so exhausted I've given up. Or maybe I'm so relieved to have these two in custody that I'm not thinking straight."

"You don't look surprised," I said.

"That's because I'm not," he said. "While I was at the hospital with Deputy Breaux, the New Orleans police were executing a search warrant on Margarita's house. Guess what they found inside?"

"Cyanide?" I asked.

He nodded. "And a box of Twinkies with two of them missing."

"She injected the cyanide in the Twinkies," Ida Belle said. "That's genius. All she had to do was drop them in Hooch's boat and wait for him to die. He could never turn one down and since he was drunk half the time, he wouldn't remember whether he bought them or not."

"There were wrappers blowing out of his boat, remember?" I said.

"So who is this guy?" Gertie pointed to the man who'd posed as Junior.

"Nobody," Carter said. "But he's about to be a long-term guest of the state."

"Where is the real Junior?" I asked.

"Dead," Carter said. "Car accident two weeks ago. There's still a lot of details I have to work out, but I have more than enough for the ADA to press charges. I'm sure we'll be able to fill in the blanks as we go. Speaking of which, I need to get going now or my luck, the state police—who were supposed to be here hours ago—will show up and try to take all the credit."

"Uh," Young Huck interrupted, looking completely and utterly confused. "You don't have a problem with me keeping the bear, do you? I shot it legit. It was charging."

"That's true," I said. "He saved all of our lives."

Carter looked over at Young Huck. "Then looks like you'll be eating bear meat for a while."

"Whoohoo!" he yelled. "I'll just fire up my winch. I went ahead and secured it in the bed of my truck...just in case."

"Uh-huh," Carter said. I'm sure he knew Young Huck had been out trying to nab that bear ever since it had torn down his front door, but he wasn't about to try to prove it.

"What about us?" I asked.

"I'll deal with you three tomorrow," he said. "If I were you, I'd go home, wake up Ally, and celebrate."

Best. Plan. Ever.

CHAPTER TWENTY-SEVEN

THE CELEBRATION LASTED WELL into the night. I'd awakened Ally as soon as we got back to my house and filled her in on everything that had happened the last few days. When I was done, she hugged everyone, then cried, then hugged us all again and cried some more. We ate and drank whiskey and when Ida Belle and Gertie finally left, the sun was already starting to peek up over the bayou.

Ally had the dinner shift at the café, so she didn't have to climb out of bed early. I didn't have any work obligations at all, so there was no reason for me to be up before noon either. But I still was.

At 8:30 a.m., I was sitting out back in a lawn chair, holding a cup of coffee and watching the fishermen head out. The storm the night before had been a front moving through, so a cool north breeze had dropped the temperatures down a good fifteen degrees. It was also keeping the mosquitoes away.

"I thought I might find you here." Carter's voice sounded behind me. He slid into the chair next to me. His chair.

"Normal people would be asleep," I said.

"I never could sleep," he said. "Not right after a mission.

Too much adrenaline. Too much excitement. It took me a bit to come down, but once I did…"

I nodded. That was exactly it. Right now, my mind was still cataloging everything that had transpired. But by midafternoon, I'd be out for the count.

"How did things go with Margarita and her lover?" I asked.

"He rolled on her."

"That doesn't surprise me. When we took off after them last night, he hauled butt. Didn't even glance back once to see where Margarita was."

"He was in it for the money all right."

"Where did they get the letter?" We'd dropped the document off at the sheriff's department on our drive home the night before.

"Margarita got it at Junior's apartment."

"But why would Junior have the letter? I can't believe Hooch was going to share his fortune with the son he never cared about."

"I'm sure he wasn't," Carter said. "But I just got off the phone with that coin dealer. He said that Hooch had brought the items in and he'd done an appraisal but that he wasn't interested in selling. When he mentioned the appraisal to a longtime customer, the guy offered top dollar. Hooch hadn't left any contact information but a cell phone number, which had been disconnected."

"Probably didn't pay his bill."

He nodded. "So he did a basic search in the area."

"And he found Junior," I said, all of it making sense now. "Then sent the letter to him, thinking it was Hooch."

"Exactly. But Junior had died in a car wreck a couple days before."

"How come that didn't show up when you were trying to locate him?"

"The accident was in another state. The databases just haven't been updated yet. I figure after he died, Margarita must have been at his apartment going through his things and found the letter."

"She must have lost it when she realized Hooch had something that valuable," I said.

"I'm sure. She hates Hooch with a passion, and the thought of him skipping off with a fortune when she scraped by to raise their son was enough to put her over the edge."

"So she plotted to killed him," I said, "which would have been the easy solution if Junior had been around to claim his inheritance, but with Junior dead, she had a problem. Did she really think she was going to get away with having her boyfriend pretend to be her son?"

"If I hadn't refused her entry to Hooch's house, she probably would have. Think about it. The only people who knew about the letter were her and the coin dealer. If I'd let her in Hooch's house on Sunday when they arrived, she would have left with what she came for in a matter of minutes."

"I guess so."

He grinned. "The irony is, all she would have left with was a couple bucks."

"Why? I thought the coins were worth a lot of money."

"It wasn't the coins that Hooch took to be appraised. All that was in that plastic container was regular ol' quarters."

"Then why were they in a container at all?"

Carter shrugged. "Maybe to mislead anyone that came looking? Our friend Hooch might not have been as foolish as we thought he was. Not all the time, anyway."

"If not the coins, then what did he have appraised?"

"Stamps. In particular, one printed during the First World War called an Inverted Jenny. It's very rare and worth a lot of money."

"The letters! We found a box of letters from one of Hooch's ancestors but we figured he had them because he never threw anything away."

Carter raised an eyebrow. "I did not hear that part about you finding anything in an active crime scene."

"Oh, right."

"But I'm sure you're correct. Hooch was too lazy to throw anything away. The thing is, about a month ago there was a television special on rare stamps on the History Channel."

"Hooch saw it and recognized the stamp as one he had in his hoarder collection." I shook my head. "And Ricky? What will happen to him?"

"He'll face charges for attempted B&E at Hooch's place and for successful B&E at the motel. We found the items he'd stolen at his rental house. The biggest charge will be the assault on Deputy Breaux, but it could be worse. He could have been charged with murder."

"I feel sorry for him," I said before I could change my mind.

"You?"

"Yes, me. I can feel sorry for people. He had a crappy human being for a father and his mother was clearly not one with good judgment. But she was the only person he had and she died too young. He came to Sinful looking for a family."

"And instead, he got Hooch." Carter sighed. "Yeah, I guess I feel a little sorry for him too. But if it makes you feel any better, once the courts sell those stamps and settle Hooch's debts, Ricky will inherit everything that's left. He probably won't serve much time on a first offense, maybe even none if he pushes for a good deal with the ADA for his testimony about the letter."

"That's something, at least," I said. "What about Ally's window?"

He shook his head. "We might never know which one of Sinful's awesome residents pulled that stunt. But I don't think Ally has anything to worry about."

I looked over at him. "So, are we good?"

"You mean about you and the terrible twosome sticking your noses into police business?"

I nodded.

"I'm not going to say that I like it, but I understand. You had to protect Ally." He looked out over the bayou and was silent for several seconds, then he looked back at me. "I don't expect you to be someone else. I mean, I would love it if you toned things down some, but I don't think people really change. Not deep down. Not people like us, anyway."

"The leopard doesn't change its spots."

"There's a lot of truth in that."

"So you're okay with me sticking my nose in because it's against my nature not to. Is that it?"

"I won't say I'm okay with it, and I have to ensure my job is protected or this town isn't."

"Meaning if you have to arrest me, you will."

"Without prejudice."

"I would expect nothing less. I'm glad we cleared the air on this."

"Why? You planning on becoming a permanent pain in my law enforcement backside?"

He was joking when he said it. He thought my interest in this case was only because of Ally. But I knew better. Ally was the fuel, but the fire was already burning before he'd thrown her in jail.

"Maybe. But with a little more authority." I pulled out the envelope that had been tucked under my leg and handed it to him. He opened it up and pulled out the contents, then his jaw dropped.

"This is a PI license," he said.

I grinned. "Fortune Redding. Act II."

WANT to know more about Swamp Team III and Jana? Join her Facebook reader group.

For release notification, sign up for Jana's newsletter.